Pleasure's Edge

Pleasure's Edge

EVE BERLIN

HEAT | NEW YORK

THE BERKLEY PUBLISHING GROUP
Published by the Penguin Group
Penguin Group (USA) Inc.
375 Hudson Street, New York, New York 10014, USA
Penguin Group (Canada), 90 Eglinton Avenue East, Suite 700, Toronto, Ontario M4P 2Y3, Canada
(a division of Pearson Penguin Canada Inc.)
Penguin Books Ltd., 80 Strand, London WC2R 0RL, England
Penguin Group Ireland, 25 St. Stephen's Green, Dublin 2, Ireland (a division of Penguin Books Ltd.)
Penguin Group (Australia), 250 Camberwell Road, Camberwell, Victoria 3124, Australia
(a division of Pearson Australia Group Pty. Ltd.)
Penguin Books India Pvt. Ltd., 11 Community Centre, Panchsheel Park, New Delhi—110 017, India
Penguin Group (NZ), 67 Apollo Drive, Rosedale, North Shore 0632, New Zealand
(a division of Pearson New Zealand Ltd.)
Penguin Books (South Africa) (Pty.) Ltd., 24 Sturdee Avenue, Rosebank, Johannesburg 2196,
South Africa

Penguin Books Ltd., Registered Offices: 80 Strand, London WC2R 0RL, England

This book is an original publication of The Berkley Publishing Group.

This is a work of fiction. Names, characters, places, and incidents either are the product of the author's imagination or are used fictitiously, and any resemblance to actual persons, living or dead, business establishments, events, or locales is entirely coincidental. The publisher does not have any control over and does not assume any responsibility for author or third-party websites or their content.

PRINTING HISTORY
Heat trade paperback edition / November 2010

Library of Congress Cataloging-in-Publication Data

Berlin, Eve.
    Pleasure's edge / Eve Berlin.—Heat Trade paperback ed.
        p. cm.
    ISBN 978-0-425-23687-1
    1. Authors—Fiction. I. Title.
    PS3602.E7577P54 2010
    813'.6—dc22

                                                        2010017219

PRINTED IN THE UNITED STATES OF AMERICA

10 9 8 7 6 5 4 3 2 1

acknowledgments

A huge thank-you to my critique partner and dear friend, R. G. Alexander, for holding me together through some difficult times, and for reading everything I write. And thanks to the fabulous Lauren Murphy, for beta reading this manuscript in only a few days, for loving my hero as much as I do, and for the combination of squeeing fan-girl and soft-edged honesty that helped to make this a better book.

I must also thank my editor, Kate Seaver, for wanting me to write for her, and for inspiring me to write this story.

one

Dylan Ivory knew the moment she saw the hulking figure pull into the parking lot in front of the Asian Art Museum on a classic Ducati, the motorcycle in flawless black and chrome, that it was *him*. Alec Walker, the man she was there to interview. A man famous for his talents and knowledge as a sexual dominant in the Seattle BDSM scene.

It wasn't the black leather jacket that gave him away. It wasn't his massive size. It was an attitude of fearlessness and utter confidence as he brought the bike to a stop, revving the engine once before shutting it off. The way he swung his leg over the gleaming tank and pulled his helmet off like a cowboy dismounting a stallion. It was an aura of pure power she could feel even from several yards away, like a soft blow to her body.

Alec Walker without his helmet was even better. Dark hair—nearly black—that curled just a little and brushed the collar of his jacket. A strong profile that could have been carved from marble.

Dylan stood next to her car, door still open, keys forgotten in her hand. Why was her heart racing? But she couldn't tear her gaze away from the graceful movements of his large hands as he pulled his leather gloves off and buckled his helmet to the motorcycle's seat.

She was still watching when he lifted his gaze and found hers. Piercing, brilliant blue eyes that *knew* her. And knew she'd been watching him. For the first time in her adult life, Dylan felt completely flustered.

If only her pulse would calm down, damn it!

This is a professional meeting.

Yes, but that didn't seem to inhibit her response to this man one bit. She would have to pull herself together before she talked to him. She was here to learn from him. To do research. Jennifer, the submissive woman she'd connected with via the Internet who she'd met with the week before, had told her she should talk with Alec Walker; but she hadn't warned her how overwhelmingly gorgeous he was.

Alec Walker was a man who should come with a warning.

He smiled, a stunning flash of brilliant white teeth, his mouth a lush slash in an otherwise completely masculine face, surrounded by a trim black goatee that made him look a little evil. She liked it, that evil look. Heat spread out from her belly like liquid fire.

He was moving toward her now. Her knees shook.

Closer and closer, until he was standing on the other side of her white Audi sedan.

"I have a feeling you're the woman I'm here to meet."

Deep voice, rich and surprisingly soft. Sexy.

She could only nod her head.

His lips quirked at the continued silence. "Dylan Ivory? Erotica author?"

"Yes . . . "

What was wrong with her? Why couldn't she put a sensible sentence together?

"I'm Alec. Shall we go inside?"

"What? Yes, of course."

She shut her car door, clicked the lock button. And tried to ignore the heat creeping all over her skin. Suddenly her wool coat felt too heavy, even in the usual Seattle autumn damp. She was far too aware of the man walking beside her as they approached the imposing Art Deco entrance of the museum, flanked by its pair of stone camels. She'd always loved this building, as well as the exhibits. When Alec had suggested they meet at the café inside, she was pleasantly surprised. She had a fondness for art, and for Asian art in particular, and she'd been to this museum a number of times.

They mounted the wide stone stairs and Alec put a gentlemanly hand at the small of her back. A shiver went through her. She glanced at him, found him smiling at her. But they were both quiet as they moved through the entrance, their footsteps echoing on the marble floors, then up the small flight of stairs leading to Taste Café, which was in the center courtyard of the museum.

They moved through the café, and Alec gestured to one of the small tables beneath the vaulted atrium ceiling. Surrounding the courtyard were statues: Buddha, Vishnu, Kali. Dylan swore she could smell the ancient stone beneath the scents of coffee and tea in the still air. Diffused light filtered in through the frosted glass of the atrium windows, accented by amber wall sconces that gave off a subtle golden glow. It was a peaceful place, where Dylan had often come to have a quiet cup of tea, but today she was all nerves inside.

Why was she so worked up? He was just a man. Just another interview.

He helped her off with her coat, held her chair for her. Nice, old-world manners. All too rare in this cosmopolitan city.

He took his leather jacket off and laid it across the back of his chair, sat down, his pose relaxed, assured. He wore a charcoal gray sweater that outlined his broad shoulders. The man really was massive, built like a pro football player. His features were pure male, from his square jaw to his chiseled chin and cheek-bones. Only his mouth was soft, and such a contrast to the rest of his face. Sexy as hell.

Dylan shifted in her seat, grabbed the menu from the table and perused the tea selection.

"What are you having?" Alec asked.

"I usually like the jasmine and green tea blend."

Alec signaled the waiter, and before she could say anything more, he ordered for them both.

"I hope you like biscotti," he said, smiling at her. "They're almost as good here as they are in Rome. There's this little café there, right by the Spanish Steps. You wouldn't expect anything spectacular in a tourist area. But that place makes the best biscotti in Italy."

"I haven't been to Rome in years. But I do remember the biscotti there."

"I was there last year, on my way home from a backpacking trip in Spain."

"Do you travel often?"

"As often as I can. I don't like to stay in one place for too long, although my writing deadlines keep me home a lot these days. It makes me restless. There's so much to do in the world."

Dylan leaned in, her fingertips sliding over the spoon that rested on the paper napkin on the small table. "Like what?"

God, was she flirting with him?

"Everything." He grinned. "Anything. I've been rock climbing in Brazil, shark diving off the coast of Fiji. Backpacking in Nepal."

"So, you're a thrill junkie."

"Yes, I suppose I am. I don't mean to be a braggart, though. These are simply the things I love. Challenging the odds." He shrugged, one corner of his mouth quirking into a small grin. "Going fast. I love my motorcycles. Love to ride fast, see how hard I can take a turn."

She shivered. "I could never get on a motorcycle. Not in a million years."

"You might like it."

"No. I don't think so." She sipped her tea. "So . . . your travels are about finding thrills?"

"To some extent. But a lot of these trips have been spiritual journeys for me, as well."

"And you write horror fiction, Jennifer told me. She mentioned the fact that you're a writer as well as a . . . dominant . . . might be helpful in the research I'm doing for my book."

He nodded. "Yes, I think so, too. You seem a bit uncomfortable with the term 'dominant.'"

"Do I? Perhaps I am. I may be an erotica author, but this is still not the sort of conversation I'm used to having."

"Fair enough."

The waiter delivered their tea, and Dylan took great care in pouring from the small, beautifully glazed Japanese pot into her cup, avoiding his blue gaze. Jasmine-scented steam immediately rose around her, accented by the earthier touch of green tea. The fragrance was familiar, grounding.

Alec pushed one of the biscotti into her hand. "Here. You must have one."

It was a command, not a suggestion. She surprised herself by taking it.

"I actually write psychological thrillers," Alec went on. "Perhaps you've read some of my work?"

"No. I'm sorry."

"Perhaps you should."

Dylan was getting annoyed. The line between confidence and cockiness was getting blurred. "Perhaps you should read something of mine."

"I have. As soon as Jennifer told me about you, I picked up your last book."

"And?" she challenged him.

"And I think you're very good. Intelligent. Thoughtful. Excellent character development. The romantic aspect doesn't overshadow the story, as it does with so many other writers. And you know how to write sex in a very real way. There's a rawness to it I admire."

"Oh." Not what she'd expected him to say. She was momentarily flustered. Again. "Thank you."

"So, tell me about this latest project, why you needed to talk to me."

Those blue, blue eyes on her. It struck her suddenly how very like Quinn's eyes they were, although Quinn's had been innocent in a way she thought Alec's maybe never had been, even when he was young. But they were that same shade of turquoise that made her think of the Caribbean.

There was sincerity in his eyes, despite his cockiness. She had to glance away, to where his fingers caressed his teacup. It looked so tiny in his hand. Fragile. As though he could break it with the barest squeeze. And those fingers gliding gently over the smooth surface . . .

She forced herself to look away from his hands, back at his face.

Not helping . . .

"I'm writing about a couple exploring BDSM. The power exchange, some bondage, which I've written about before. But this time I'd like to delve deeper into it. Possibly explore the pain play. And I want it to have some authenticity. I don't want to do it otherwise. I knew I'd have to do some very thorough research, talk to people who have experienced these things. I found Jennifer on a local BDSM community website recently, e-mailed her and asked if we could talk. I interviewed her, and she was very nice, very open with me. But as a submissive she didn't feel she was qualified to give me the whole picture. That's why she referred me to you."

He nodded. "It's difficult to get a good idea of what the BDSM scene is about, what the dynamic and the psychology is about, from talking to one person. Everyone's experiences are varied and personal. And if she's purely submissive she wouldn't have too much insight into the way a dominant's mind works, our process."

"Yes, that's the idea she gave me. And it makes sense."

"You've never written BDSM before?"

"No. I've written about some minor fetishes, a little bedroom play bondage, but not anything really serious."

"You feel BDSM is serious?"

"Isn't it?"

He didn't answer. "You've never experienced these things for yourself?"

"I . . . no."

"Ah, you'd like to keep this discussion professional. Purely for research purposes."

"Yes. Of course."

He leaned forward, resting his elbows on the table, moved a little closer, until she could smell the scent of his cologne, something clean and dark at the same time. Like the ocean and the woods.

He lowered his voice, suddenly making the conversation seem more intimate. Maybe more intimate than she was entirely comfortable with. "I'm going to tell you something, Dylan, and this is simply the truth. There is no way you can portray the lifestyle in any accurate manner by dipping your toes in. You have to experience it, really dive in. There are too many components—physical, psychological, emotional—all overlapping. It's complex, which is what those of us who practice these things love about it. The complexity. The intensity." He reached for her hand, grazed his fingertips over the back of it. His skin was hot. Hers went hotter. "It's about sensation. And what goes on in your head. It can be sensual, or it can be sexual. Or both. You cannot begin to describe the dynamics involved without having been there."

Her throat went dry. The idea wasn't shocking to her. Not nearly as much as his touch was. She picked up her cup, sipped her tea, cleared her throat. "I suppose you're right. And this is an interesting subject. But, I don't know . . . "

"Don't pretend it's nothing more than an interesting subject to you, Dylan." He slid his fingertips down the inside of her wrist, beneath the sleeve of her cashmere sweater. "I can feel your pulse racing."

"Alec—"

"Come on, Dylan. You don't need to do this with me. That's part of what BDSM is all about. That basic honesty about who we are."

"I was going to say that . . . you're right."

Had she really admitted that to him? But maybe he *was* right about it all—that she had to be honest with him in order to learn anything. Would have to dive in, as he'd said.

It had nothing to do with her ridiculous attraction to him. Did it?

She pulled her hand away, tucked it safely in her lap. "You and Jennifer must know some submissive men. Are there any you trust, that you can refer me to? And would they consider playing with a woman who has no experience as a dominant?"

Alec laughed, sitting back in his chair. "You're talking about topping, dominating these men?"

"Yes."

"Ah, Dylan. Don't you realize you're a bottom?"

"What?"

"I saw it the moment I met you. I could sense it out there in the parking lot, even before we spoke."

"I don't know what you mean."

Why were her cheeks heating up? Why was she thrown so off balance? She hated that he had such an effect on her.

"I think you understand enough about this subject to know exactly what I mean."

She blew out a breath. "Of course I have some idea of what a bottom is. A submissive. But that's not me. Being a top, a dominant, simply makes sense for me. I'm not afraid to admit that I'm someone with control issues."

"Which is exactly why you need to bottom. You need to let go. You need the safety in handing the control over to someone else in order to do that."

She was getting angry now, but trying to keep her temper in check. "You're very arrogant."

"Yes, I am. I'm also right. I am always right about this. You do have control issues; I can see it in the way you hold yourself. I can see it in the anger in your eyes. In the tight set of your jaw. And you could probably manage to successfully 'switch' now and then, top a man. Or a woman. But it wouldn't reach inside you as deeply as bottoming would. It wouldn't give you what you truly need."

She shook her head, her teeth clenched.

He leaned forward again, reaching across the table and taking her hand in his once more. It was large, enveloping hers in heat and strength.

"Dylan, let me make a proposal to you. Bottom for me."

She tried to yank her hand from his, but he held on tight.

His gaze was hard on hers, his eyes that impossibly compelling, brilliant blue. "Try it," he went on. "See how you respond. If it turns out I was right, you'll have learned something about yourself and you'll have some very personal and unique research for your book. And if I'm wrong, well, you'll still have done your research."

"I can do that research as a top."

"No, you can't. It's extremely difficult for a bottom to teach an inexperienced top. Once the endorphins begin to pump through a bottom's body, once they're down in subspace, that head space where everything goes quiet and all they can feel and see is that interaction between top and bottom, the sensations and scents, they aren't present enough to act as teachers for you. You can't possibly learn as much that way. But you can learn from me. I'm very good at what I do." He waved his free hand. "I know, I'm being arrogant again. But it doesn't matter. What matters is that this is the truth."

"Maybe."

Maybe it was true that this was the best possible way for her to learn. Maybe it had nothing to do with the fact that Alec sitting so close to her, holding on to her hand still, was making her hot all over. Was making her wet, for God's sake. But this was nothing more than intense chemistry. It didn't mean anything, didn't lend any credence to his argument. She was sure she could prove to him just how wrong he was.

She bit her lip.

He was definitely wrong about her.

"How long would we try this for?" she asked.

He shrugged. "For as long as it takes. For as long as you need to discover what you should know. For your book. For yourself."

"So we would sort of play it by ear? See how things go?"

"Oh, I know how things will go."

"Really? And how is that?"

She was angry again. And he was still holding her hand. His thumb caressed her knuckles, sending a spark of lust deep into her system. But she wouldn't give him the satisfaction of trying to pull away again.

"You'll fight it at first. I'll have to really work with you. Gain your trust." His voice was low, a gravelly murmur. She had to lean closer to hear him. "But bit by bit, you'll turn yourself over to me. Into my hands. I'll be hard on you. And gentle."

He lifted her hand and brushed his lips across it, the heat scalding her, shocking her. She couldn't say a word. Her mind was in a small state of chaos.

Alec laid her hand down on the cool tabletop, his gaze locking with hers. "That's how it will go, Dylan."

She hated that she felt dizzy, confused. She didn't understand it. And she refused to give in to it. Or to Alec Walker.

She picked up her teacup and sipped, swallowed. Drawing in a deep breath, she forced herself to calm, and put the cup down on the table with a steady hand.

"You can think whatever you like, Alec. But you obviously don't know me yet."

He picked up his own cup, took a long swallow, taking his

time. His piercing gaze never left hers. "Not as well as I will, certainly. If you agree to my proposal, that is."

"Oh, I'm agreeing."

"You like a challenge."

"Yes."

"So do I."

That steady blue gaze bore into hers, but she wouldn't look away, wouldn't back down. He was right about one thing: She'd fight it. Because it wasn't in her nature to give in. Not even to Alec Walker and his amazing eyes. His warm hands, his soft, lush mouth . . .

She had to keep things under control, as she always did. And ignore the way he looked. The way he spoke. The way he touched her.

He was going to *really* touch her soon.

She silently commanded herself to calm once more, took a long, quiet breath. Control was the key here, and she was nothing if not the queen of control. Her life had dictated that she be exactly that, ever since she was a child. She'd had to be, with her mess of a mother. Someone had had to be, and she was the oldest. She'd had to take care of Quinn.

You did a lousy job of it.

Why was she thinking about all of that now? She pushed her past to the back of her mind, where it belonged. And focused on the man sitting across from her, watching her so carefully.

Yes, she could handle Alec Walker, whether he thought so or not.

"Alec."

"Yes?"

"I have a proposition of my own."

"Oh?" One dark brow raised.

"If it turns out you can't break me, as you seem to think you can—"

"Oh, I will. Although I prefer to think of it as taming."

"So you keep saying. But if it doesn't work, you'll let me play you. Top you."

He surprised her by grinning. "Fair enough."

An image flashed in her mind, of Alec naked, on his knees. But even in that brief fantasy, he didn't appear to be submitting. No, he was strong, defiant, as confident as ever. She didn't think he could appear to her any other way. There was nothing soft or easy about this man.

Except for that mouth . . .

"We have a deal, then?"

He nodded once. "Absolutely. We have a deal."

He took her hand once more, his large fingers curling over hers. And before she knew what was happening, he was pulling her into him, leaning across the small café table, whispering against her mouth, "The best deals are sealed with a kiss."

His mouth was so close to hers, that lush, delectable mouth. Her body went weak, and she found herself leaning into him, pulling in his sweet, tea-scented breath. Waiting for his kiss.

He backed away, sank into his chair.

"But we'll have to wait until you're ready for me, Dylan. Until you're begging for it."

Jesus. She was nearly ready to beg for it now!

She shook her head. She wanted to press her cool hands to her heated skin. To push the dark red ringlet of hair that had fallen into her face from her cheek. But she refused to let him see how unsettled she was. How full of need. Need that made her ache. For him.

She needed to get out of there, needed to get outside, into the cool, damp air. Needed to breathe.

"I have to go," she lied. "I have another appointment."

"Of course. I'll walk you out." He stood.

"There's no need."

He bowed his head to her, all old-world manners once more. "If you insist."

She stood, gathered her coat, her purse. "I . . . we didn't really begin the interview."

"I think we did."

"Oh. Well, yes. I suppose we'll talk more when . . . after . . . "

"Yes, we will. Although I believe if you experience these things, you won't find a formal interview necessary. I'll e-mail you about when we'll meet next."

It wasn't a question. But she didn't know how to phrase any sort of protest.

Damn it.

"Yes, we'll talk." She went to pull her coat on, and he was right there, slipping it over her shoulders. She could smell him again, that ocean and deep woods scent. "Thank you for meeting with me today."

"It was my pleasure."

He was looking down at her, smiling. She drew in one last surreptitious breath, breathing him in.

God, she really had to get a handle on things. Get back to her usual self. But everything felt different with him. He was a dangerous man. But she'd never backed down from a challenge before, and she wasn't about to now. Even if this particular challenge already had her doubting herself, had her wondering which one of them would really end up on top.

It had to be her.

Had to be.

two

Alec locked the side door to the garage behind him and stomped up the front stairs of his gray Craftsman-style house on Beacon Hill. He shoved his key into the lock on the heavy wooden door, pushing it open with his booted foot and slamming it a little too hard behind him. Yanking his leather jacket off, he slung it over the coat tree, knocking it over and catching it with a muttered curse.

Why the hell was he so on edge?

It wasn't as if there was any chance he'd lose in this deal with Dylan Ivory. He could spot submissive tendencies in a woman from fifty paces, and he'd been sitting right next to her. Close enough to smell the vanilla scent coming off all that wild red hair, mixed with something else. Something spicy and pure sex.

His boots scuffed across the wood floors until he reached the thick Persian rug, where his footsteps were muffled until he hit the wood again on the other side of the room. He grabbed a glass from the heavy Spanish sideboard and poured himself two fingers of scotch, straight up.

Dylan would be a challenge; he'd realized that right away. But he enjoyed a challenge. That wasn't what had him so off balance. No, it was the fact that he *had* to have her. Had to have this woman in a way that made his skin itch to touch more than her hand. No question about it.

Had to have his hands on her bare skin. Had to bind her, feel her muscles go loose as she gave herself over to him . . . *Had* to . . .

He didn't like that. Didn't like that he felt so commanded by his desire for her.

When was the last time that had happened to him? Had it ever?

He was not the kind of man who *needed* anyone. Anything. He'd learned from his father well. Independence was the key. Knowledge, experiences: These were the important things. And one reason why he'd spent most of his adult life looking for answers: reading, traveling the world. Not that he'd come up with anything conclusive yet.

But he didn't need to think of his father now. That was an ache that never seemed to go away. Dull now, after all these years, but still present. Like a scar that wouldn't heal.

He threw back most of the scotch, reveled in the burn as it slid down his throat. But it did nothing to soothe him. He topped off the glass and took it to stand by the bay window overlooking the sprawling city.

Seattle was its usual gray, but there were clear patches in the darkening afternoon sky, and he could see the distant silhouette of Bainbridge Island off Puget Sound. He sipped at his scotch, brooding over the view.

Brooding over Dylan, damn it.

Something about the way she held herself, so tightly controlled. He knew what happened when a woman like that let go. Was forced to let go.

Oh, he'd never really force a woman. He lived by the safe, sane and consensual credo, as did most of the people who traveled in his circle of BDSM clubs and groups. Still, that wouldn't change the fact that if he was able to bring Dylan down into subspace, if he could get her to open up, to let go, she would go down hard. She would unravel like a beautifully made sweater.

Not if. When.

Where the hell was his confidence today?

Maybe because he wanted her so badly. Too badly.

He was half hard just thinking about her, remembering the pale freckles scattered across her cheeks, her skin like the finest porcelain. Those gray eyes, like two pieces of smoky quartz. All brilliant, sharp edges, intense, her intelligence shining through. And that plush red mouth, like sex itself.

Her body was lean, athletic, not overly curved. He liked that. Appreciated the delicacy of her collarbones, her wrists, her hands. Small breasts, but firm and tight beneath the soft sweater. He didn't need large breasts on a woman. That never really mattered to him. But her tight, fine ass was something to look at.

Something to touch . . . to spank . . .

He gulped down the rest of the scotch, left his glass on a side table by the wide windows and slumped onto the overstuffed brown leather sofa.

She was too damned smart for her own good. And maybe for his. Not that they'd talked for long. But long enough for him to know he was in very big trouble if he didn't keep it together with this woman.

His phone rang and he picked it up without thinking about it, his mind still on Dylan.

"Hello?"

"Hey, it's Dante."

"Hey."

He and Dante De Matteo had met at a lecture on the psychology of BDSM and fetish cultures at the Pleasure Dome, the local fetish club, three years ago. After discovering their mutual love of motorcycles, they'd become close friends, often taking long rides through Washington's national forests.

They'd gone back to the club many times, each of them exploring their dominant tendencies with any number of willing submissive females there. They'd even traveled together, taking their bikes through Arizona and New Mexico the previous spring. Even though Dante was an attorney and Alec an author, they had plenty in common. They understood each other.

"So, are we on for that ride on Saturday?" Dante asked.

"What? Yeah, Saturday." Alec ran his fingers around the rim of his empty glass. Maybe he needed another drink.

"What's up with you, Alec?"

"What do you mean?"

"You sound distracted."

"Yeah, I'm distracted, all right," he muttered, more to himself than to Dante.

"So?" Dante pushed.

"So . . . I met this woman . . . "

Dante laughed. "It's always a woman. Or a motorcycle."

"I'm full up on motorcycles at the moment."

"But not on women?"

"Not that that's ever a problem, but this woman . . . "

"Alec, you aren't finishing your sentences. In case you haven't noticed."

"Shit."

"That bad, huh? Or that good?"

"I don't know. I mean, yeah, it's good." He got up, went to pour himself another drink, knowing Dante would wait patiently for him to pull his thoughts together. "This woman, Dylan Ivory. I mentioned I was going to meet with her today. She wasn't what I expected. There's no photograph of her on her website, and I guess I thought . . . well, I never expected her to be gorgeous. Really beautiful."

"And?"

"I made a deal with her."

"A deal?"

"She's never explored BDSM before; not at our level certainly. And she's never bottomed before. But I can see it in her. I can *smell* it. And I am never wrong about this."

"So, what's this deal?"

"She thinks she's a top."

"I'm sure you'll show her the error of her ways soon enough." He could hear the amusement in Dante's voice.

"If I don't, I agreed to bottom for her."

Dante chuckled. "That's not likely to happen."

"No. No, it's not."

"So what's the problem?"

Alec found himself sighing, and stopped. "I'm not sure yet. Maybe I'll know more once I get my hands on her, play her." He paused, sipped at his drink. "Yeah. I don't know what the hell the problem is. She's just . . . under my skin."

"So, the great Alec Walker falls," Dante said softly.

"I never said anyone was falling, Dante." He gripped the glass in his hand, the cut-glass edges biting into his palm.

"No, you didn't."

"I'm fine. Fine."

"Okay." He could hear Dante mentally shrugging. "So, we're on for Saturday?"

"Yeah."

"And are you taking her to the club Saturday night?"

"Jesus, Dante." He rubbed at his goatee. Sighed. "I thought I'd wait a week or two."

How had he ever thought he could wait that long to see her again?

Oh yes, he was in big trouble.

"Alec, not that I'd presume to tell you what to do, especially with a woman you're introducing into the lifestyle, but it sounds to me like you'd better see her sooner than that."

"Why?"

"Because I think you're going to have a stroke if you don't."

"Come on, Dante. It's not that bad."

"Isn't it?"

He rubbed his beard some more. Wanted to sigh again, but didn't. "I'll see you on Saturday."

"Okay, okay. See you then."

Christ, was it that obvious? Was he in such bad shape over a woman?

Keep it together, buddy.

He would. He always did, didn't he?

Well, didn't he?

Dylan downshifted as she came off the 5 and headed west, toward the Sound. The sky grew heavier with fog as she neared the water and her neighborhood. She didn't mind. She loved the fog, the ethereal moodiness of it. Moisture gathered on her windshield and she hit the wipers, glad for the seat warmers in her Audi. Even if she loved the fog, she still hated being cold.

She pulled onto Western Avenue and into the garage she rented next to her building. Belltown was an older area of Seattle. The architecture was beautiful, but the old converted warehouse she lived in had no parking of its own.

The area was a little rough around the edges, although that was beginning to change. Still, since the sun was setting she was watchful of her surroundings as she walked to the front of her building. It was an enormous brick structure with soaring windows, opening up to the view of Puget Sound, only a few blocks away.

She'd been lucky to get the place, and hadn't paid nearly as much for it as these flats went for even a few months later, as a younger crowd moved into the neighborhood and renovated. There were trendy cafés and restaurants popping up all over the place, some boutiques and galleries, nicer bars than the old-school dive bars that had populated this area for years. Even a few newer amenities, like the small gourmet grocery store that had opened across the street last month.

She took the elevator up to the fourth floor and let herself into her loft apartment. It was an open space, with floors she'd white-washed herself when she'd bought the place two years earlier. Most of the outer walls were still the old exposed brick. The few walls she'd had built to divide the rooms were painted in the rich colors she found most soothing: amber, dark terra-cotta, gold, mossy greens. They were decorated with her collection of black-and-white prints, mostly architectural photographs.

She was still looking for furniture for the place. She was most often drawn to the spare lines of contemporary pieces, like her L-shaped sofa done in peridot green suede. The place was warmed by the ornate light fixtures she had in each area, the piles of pil-lows in the same brilliant shades as the walls, and by the potted plants in every corner.

Moving into the kitchen area at one end of the loft, the heels of her high black boots clicking softly on the wood, she shed her wool coat and laid it over the back of a stool at the tall granite counter.

She needed a cup of tea to chase the damp from her bones. To clear her head, maybe.

She'd done a good job of pretending to ignore her response to Alec Walker all the way home by means of blasting her favorite opera on the stereo. But now that she was home, in the quiet, there was nothing to distract her.

She filled the chrome kettle with water and set it on the stove to heat, pulled a tea bag, her favorite imported jasmine, from the box she always left on the counter and set it in a ceramic mug.

She was restless waiting for the water to boil. Loo[king out] the windows, watching the water bead on the glass, [...] view into a darkening watercolor smear, she rubbed her arms, trying to warm up. Trying not to think about Alec.

But of course, he was all she could think about.

He was a most amazing man. There was something about the sheer size of him that was astounding in some way. And something more . . . there was something in her that responded to him in a way she wasn't used to. Something that made it possible to consider that she might actually be able to submit to him, as bizarre as the idea had seemed in those first moments.

She wasn't certain she could do it, even though images had raced through her mind since he'd first suggested it: his hands on her, holding her. Nothing more than that, nothing more explicit, nothing clearer. Except for that almost-touch of his lips on hers.

She shivered, desire a small, hot spark she tried to mentally tamp down.

But desire didn't mean taking a sexual fantasy into the realm of reality was going to work. It was more likely that it wouldn't. Some things were better left as fantasy, after all.

Not Alec Walker.

But she'd agreed to this little experiment. And her attraction to him could probably carry her a little way, even if she wasn't able to truly submit.

Her thoughts were invaded by the singing of the tea kettle. She poured, the steam wafting around her face, along with the soft fragrance of the tea. She moved back into the living room, idly sifted through a pile of mail on a high table by the front door, waiting for her tea to cool. It was several moments later that she realized she had no idea what she was looking at. Instead, Alec's face filled her mind, those brilliant blue eyes, the way the dark, glossy curl of his hair fell just over his collar, against the skin of his neck. His goatee was even darker than his hair, framing his mouth. Lips that were too lush on such a masculine face.

He was all contrasts. The way he looked, his behavior. The way he talked about the whole BDSM thing—bondage and pain play—in that soft tone, as though it were a perfectly natural conversation.

She didn't want to admit to herself how exciting it was. Her nature fought the idea. She was too much a control freak, something she could readily admit to. But her body knew, burned with the idea of it. And especially with the idea of Alec being the one in control.

She closed her eyes, the teacup warm between her hands, and imagined him standing over her. Just that simple picture and her sex clenched with need.

Alec . . .

"Damn it."

She stalked into the bedroom area, sat down on the sleek, dark wood four-post bed covered in a white down comforter and piles of white pillows, and pulled her boots off. Standing, she unzipped her skirt, slipped her cashmere sweater over her head, her tea forgotten on the night table.

She caught sight of herself in the big, wood-framed mirror across the room. She was pale in her black lingerie. Too thin, probably, but she loved to work out. Loved the release it gave her. But now she needed a different kind of release.

Just a fantasy. Harmless.

Still watching herself in the mirror, she pulled off her bra, cupped her small breasts in her hands. Her nipples were already rising, two dark red points, hard, needy. She gently pinched the tips, and groaned.

What would his hands feel like on her body?

Slipping her hand beneath the edge of her bikini panties, she reached lower, until her fingers brushed her mound. Pleasure shot through her, making her breath catch.

Alec . . .

Yes, his hands on her, touching her. Spreading the lips of her sex wide to slide into her wet heat. And she was soaking wet for him, aching . . .

She spread her legs a little wider and watched her own hand working between her thighs. But soon it was too much. Frustrated, she slid the bit of black fabric down her legs, kicked her way out of them. The sight of her own sex, the lips plump, her pink clitoris peeking out from between them, made her tremble.

Alec . . .

She spread more, letting her fingers skim through her juices, then slipped one inside. She gasped, bit her lip. She was so hot inside, her inner walls clenching at her finger immediately. She added a second, then a third, needing to be filled.

Would his cock be as large as the rest of him?

"Oh . . . "

She moaned, using the heel of her hand to press against her clit. She rubbed in a small circle, pumped her fingers inside herself. Imagined Alec's piercing blue gaze staring at her through the mirror, watching her.

With her other hand, she reached up to pinch her nipple once more. Pleasure, hot and sharp, shot through her.

"Alec . . . "

Oh yes, his big hands on her, inside her. Rubbing, pinching. Pleasure like molten liquid in her veins, moving through her like silk.

She thrust her fingers in and out, the motion moving her palm hard against her clit. And her body clenched, shook as she came, as she called out his name to the empty room.

"Alec!"

Her legs weak, she nearly fell, but she caught herself with one hand on the edge of the dresser. She was panting, gasping for breath. Her image in the mirror was flushed: her breasts, her cheeks. Her eyes were enormous, the gray irises almost obscured by her glittering pupils.

Her body still buzzed with need, despite her orgasm.

Alec . . .

She glanced at the rattan basket next to the bed, thought of the collection of vibrators she kept there.

Yes, need to come again. And again.

How had this man gotten to her? And how was she going to work him out of her system?

She moved across the room, sat on the bed and pulled one of her favorite toys from the basket, a heavy, turbo massager that made her scream when she came. Maybe that would be enough.

But even as she laid back on the pillows and switched it on, lowering the powerful instrument between her spread thighs, she knew no toy would ever be enough.

What the hell had Alec Walker done to her?

The alarm went off and Alec slapped at it blindly, turning onto his back. He'd slept on his stomach and come awake with a painful erection pressing into the mattress. And Dylan's face in his mind.

In his body.

He'd gone to sleep hard and woken harder.

He willed himself to calm, but his cock throbbed with need.

In his mind's eye he saw long curls shining auburn and amber in the sunlight, falling around her narrow shoulders. A pair of cool, gray eyes that seemed to hold some mystery, something she kept secret from him, something he wanted—*needed*—to know. Pale, pale skin like polished ivory. The delicate line of collarbone at the edge of her sweater, and beneath it, the curve of her breasts, perfectly formed. He'd been up late last night imagining what they would look like, feel like in his hands. The taste of her beneath his tongue. What it would be like to have her long legs wrapped around his waist as he pumped into her, her pussy hot and welcoming . . .

He groaned.

"Fuck."

Throwing back the blankets, the sheet, he reached down and

stroked himself, his fingers gliding over his hard shaft, curling around it.

What would her lush, red lips feel like wrapped around him, her tongue snaking over the head of his cock?

He moaned, stroked harder, his hips pumping into his fist.

Her mouth would be wet, warm, but not as wet as her pussy. He would part her lean thighs, thrust into her, hard, over and over.

Dylan . . .

Her eyes would glaze over, her lips parting, her body shaking as she came, her pussy clenching him, so damn tight.

He arched into his palm, stroking, feathering his fingertips over the swollen head. He could feel the come rising in his body, his cock pulsing.

Dylan . . .

Yeah, just need to spank her gorgeous ass, then get inside her. To make her come. To fuck her.

Dylan!

He came, hard, pleasure racing hot in his veins, making him shudder. He kept stroking, milking his cock of every last bit of come. Every last moment of pleasure. Trying to work his need for her out of his system.

It didn't work. He'd known it wouldn't.

Nothing would work but seeing her, touching her. Commanding her. And commanding this woman wouldn't be an easy task. But maybe then he could command himself, get some control back.

He looked down at the sticky mess on his stomach, shaking his head. He needed to do it again. He was still trying to catch his breath, knew it would be a little while before he could even get hard again. But if he had her here he'd be on top of her, ravaging her skin, making her come with his hands, his mouth . . .

His cock gave a twitch and he was surprised to feel a rush of blood there as it swelled once more.

He sat up, walked across the cool wood floors of his bedroom. The day was just beginning outside, the dusky gray light filtering through the windows. The air was cold on his skin, but inside he was burning hot. Needy. Aching once more.

In the bathroom he reached into the big shower, tiled in shades of copper, brown and bronze, blasting the hot water. Stepping under the spray, he rinsed the come from his belly. But the sharp heat of the water on his skin only made him harder.

He grabbed the handheld shower massager from its hook and aimed it at his stiffening cock, leaning his back into the cool tiles behind him and closing his eyes.

There she was again, her hair a wet tangle down her back, her lush mouth a lovely O as he knelt between her thighs, his tongue licking at her wet slit, her hands in his hair, holding him against her as she moaned.

His breath hitched in his lungs. He was going to fucking come again. Just from the water pounding on his cock and the image of Dylan Ivory's spread thighs in his head.

"Jesus."

He angled his hips into the water, reached down and cupped his balls; they were tight with need. And that was all it took. His body shook, his hips jerking as he came.

Dylan . . . God damn it!

He sagged against the wall behind him, his legs weak.

Pleasure shimmered through him, a small electric buzz all over his skin, deep inside his belly, his still-throbbing cock.

He pulled in a breath, then another, as he let the water rinse the come away.

It was bad enough that he'd had to jerk off twice in a row, like some teenager. *Had* to. But this was one of the first times in years he'd gotten off to just . . . sex. No power play. No bondage. No paddles, no leather or ropes or chains. Just Dylan, in his head.

What the hell did that mean, anyway? Did he even want to know?

Sex was the one thing over which he'd always felt completely in control. But something about this woman had gotten to him. And he had a feeling all bets were off.

Not that he'd end up submitting to her. But even when he got her on her knees—and he would, there was no doubt about that—he had a feeling it would be as much of a mind-fuck for him as it would be for her. That something in him would be giving himself over to . . . Dylan.

His gut clenched, partly with annoyance, partly in a panic he didn't want to admit to and partly in the ever-present desire simmering in his veins.

Things were different with Dylan Ivory. And as much as he didn't want to admit to the way she affected him, he was going to find out what the hell that was all about. What *she* was all about.

And meanwhile he would keep things under control, damn it, just as he always did.

God damn it.

three

Dylan sat on her sofa, a pile of books spread out before her on the coffee table, her notepad in her lap. She'd been researching bondage, pain play, power exchange, the reasons *why* these things turned people on. The things she'd read about had turned her on, no doubt about it. And she'd imagined herself in the various scenarios: being tied up, spanked, even flogged. She could blame the low throbbing between her thighs on that. If she wanted to lie to herself.

The truth was, it wasn't some faceless partner doing these things to her. Alec had been in every single scenario with her, his hands on her, commanding her.

She sighed, picked up her tea and sipped. She'd sweetened it again. The hot, fragrant liquid soothed her throat, but the rest of her body was as taut as a wire.

It had been three days since she'd spoken with him, and she

hadn't heard from him yet. She had to wonder if this was part of him showing her that he was in control, or if he was simply busy. Either way, she didn't like it. Didn't like that she was feeding into the dominant behavior.

She knew she was spending too much time dissecting it. But she couldn't help it. She wasn't some passive submissive girl who was going to melt at his feet and do anything he asked of her. Who would sit by the phone like a good little puppy, waiting for his call.

Then why was she doing exactly that?

She'd dated plenty, and she'd never been one of those girls. She didn't have to wait around for anyone. Sex was plentiful for a woman who was open-minded about it, and she always had been. She let a man know that about her as soon as she was interested. They didn't seem to feel any need to play those games with her they played with other women. She kept herself at enough of a distance that they never felt they really *had* her. And in fact, none of them ever did. She didn't play that game, either.

But Alec had a strange grasp on her she didn't understand . . .

Setting her tea mug down, she picked up one of the books and paged through, trying to refocus on her task. She was looking for a deeper explanation of the psychology and chemistry of subspace: that trancelike state many submissives reached during BDSM play. She understood the chemical process, how endorphins were released in the body in response to pain or sexual stimulation, but she wasn't as clear on the mental and emotional part of the process.

Why did people respond to certain things and not others? She'd read a number of times that some submissives could begin their descent into subspace simply by being bound, by being commanded. Even by nothing more than hearing a dominant voice.

The soft, rich tone of Alec's voice drifted through her mind, humming over her skin like a faint electric current. As though she could *feel* the subtle vibration from the sound. She squeezed her thighs together at the sudden ache there.

Okay. Maybe she could get that part.

She flipped through the book again, her gaze landing on a photograph of a woman bound in ropes, a complicated harness. But it wasn't the ropes that caught her attention, or the woman's smooth flesh as she knelt, naked but for the rope. It was the hand of a man standing somewhere off camera, the way it—he—caressed her face. The gesture seemed tender, somehow. She loved the contrast, the implication that this man's hand belonged to whoever had bound her, and now had complete control over her.

Her body surged with desire.

Some small part of her wanted to be that woman. If the man were Alec Walker.

She slammed the book shut and jumped up from the sofa.

Ridiculous! She was a strong woman. Independent. Even if she did have some desire to bottom for Alec, it was only about being at the receiving end of stimulation. Being made to just sit there and let him *do* things to her.

She moaned. That train of thought wasn't helping.

The telephone rang and she grabbed it, relieved to have some reason to redirect her thoughts.

"Hello?"

"Hey, it's Mischa."

"Mischa, hi."

Mischa Kennon, a tattoo artist who also wrote short erotic fiction, was one of her best friends. They'd met several years earlier when Dylan had gone to San Francisco for a writers' conference. When Dylan returned to San Francisco several months later to have Mischa tattoo her, they'd spent some time together and had become fast friends. Now, despite the miles between them, they talked every week and saw each other whenever they could.

"What are you up to, Dylan?"

"Oh, brooding, mostly."

Mischa laughed. "Why?"

Dylan moved to the wall of windows overlooking the waterfront. The late-morning sky was obscured by clouds, a heavy gray curtain promising rain.

"I wish I could figure that out."

"Do you need to brainstorm a book?"

"I'm actually still in the research stage for my next novel. It's an erotic story with a BDSM theme. Which brings me to why I'm brooding. Sort of."

"Okay . . . are you going to actually tell me what you're talking about, or what?"

"Sorry, I don't mean to be so vague." She stopped, pulled in a breath, blew it out. "I met this man."

"That sounds promising."

"Maybe. No. God, Mischa, I don't know . . . this man, Alec, he's . . . different than anyone I've ever met."

"In what way?"

"In every way." She stopped once more, placed the flat of her hand against the window, feeling the cold on her skin. "Alec is part of my research. Well, at this point he's all of it. I was referred to him by this submissive woman, Jennifer, to talk about the whole BDSM thing. I just didn't feel I knew enough to write that sort of intense power play accurately."

"I don't see why not. You've written about almost everything else. And it's not like you're some prude. You're the one the rest of us look to for answers to almost everything about sex. You're our queen, Dylan," Mischa teased.

"Hah—I'm hardly the queen of erotica. Having some experience with sex isn't the same thing. This is pretty specific stuff. And this time I understand I am out of my league. But the more I found out about the dynamics involved, the more I realized I needed real information. That I had to base it on something more than reading a few books."

"So you decided to talk to someone involved in these things?"

"Yes."

"And? Because I can tell from your voice and the way you're beating around the bush that there's an 'and.'"

Dylan lifted her palm from the glass, trailed her fingertips down, pulled away.

"The 'and' is pretty big, Mischa."

"Hey, it's me. I'm hardly shockable. Neither are you. Which is why I'm so curious to know how any man has managed to unsettle you like this."

"Alec is a sexual dominant."

"So I assumed."

"And he's asked me to—he's challenged me—to submit to him. I can't believe I did it, but I agreed. I'm sure it won't even work. The idea is ludicrous. He's just so . . . charismatic. No, it's more than that. Incredibly good looking, but he'd be powerful even without that." She saw his face in her mind. His wicked black goatee, that dazzling smile. His eyes, piercing her with blue fire . . .

"Dylan?"

"What? Sorry. I was just thinking . . . of him. I can't seem to stop. I don't know the last time something like this happened to me. When I felt so out of control."

"Maybe that's the whole point here."

"So you think it's just some sort of mind fuck he uses on the women he interacts with?"

"No. Well, maybe he does. But I meant maybe that's the point for *you*. On some universal level. Maybe this is what you need, Dylan."

"What do you mean?"

"You're always so in control. And there's nothing wrong with wanting to be in control of your life, especially after what you went through growing up with your mom. But it could be good for you to hand that over to someone else for once, even if it's only for a little while."

"I doubt the universe put Alec Walker in my path so he could tie me up."

"I think that may be it exactly."

"Mischa!"

"Dylan, you know I love you, and I love you enough to tell you that you could use a little loosening up."

"I've been with plenty of men, done plenty of experimenting when it comes to sex."

"Yes. But that's not the same thing, is it? You just said so yourself. If what I think I know about this BDSM stuff is correct, it's about the roles each person takes. The play of power. Right?"

"Yes, that's the basics, anyway, as far as I understand it."

"So, it seems to me that you have to let that power go for once."

"That's the part I don't like."

"Which is probably why you need to try it."

"I don't know. Maybe." She twisted a ringlet around her finger, pulling tight. "You're probably right. And I guess some part of me knows that, which is why I agreed to it. Well, some of why I agreed to it, anyway."

"You'll have to report the rest back to me when you're done. You are going to do it, aren't you? See him, be with him?"

Was she?

Had she ever actually thought for one moment that she'd back out?

She sighed. "Yes. But it's going to be hard for me."

"Sometimes the hard stuff is how we learn about ourselves."

"I know you're right. I'm just . . . fighting it."

"Just do it, Dylan. Take that leap. As long as this man is safe, but you did mention someone you knew referred you to him. I really think you should do this."

"I do, too." And the fact that Alec's blue eyes, his voice, the scent of him, made her melt all over, would make it a little easier. It was making it—making him—irresistible. "I don't know what will happen, exactly, and I'm not entirely comfortable with that. Hell, I'm not comfortable with that at all. But to be honest, there's just as much excitement there, this . . . exquisite sense of anticipation, maybe simply because I don't know."

"Wow. I've never heard you like this, Dylan. Unsure."

"That's because this is not the usual me. But this man . . . "

Her mind whirled with the possibilities. What would Alec do to her, demand of her?

Her stomach knotted up, and a melting heat began between her thighs. She was about to find out. The one thing she was certain of, though, was that Alec Walker was going to change her. Irrevocably.

It was several hours later when the phone rang again. Dylan put her book and her notepad down and glanced at the caller ID.

Alec.

Her heart raced, a jangling rattle in her chest.

"He's just a man," she said to the empty room, then shook her head. She knew already he was going to be a lot more than that.

"Hello."

"Hello, Dylan."

God, his voice was like an electric current running hot in her veins, pooling between her thighs.

"Alec, hi."

"How are you this evening?"

"I'm fine. Fine."

Had he called to make small talk? She didn't think she could take it. Pulling an embroidered throw pillow into her lap, she gripped the rolled edge between her fingers.

"Don't you want to know how I am?" he asked, humor in his voice.

"Yes, of course. I'm sorry. I was . . . very involved in doing research when you called. My mind was wandering."

"I'll have to work harder to gain your full attention."

"Oh, I don't think—"

"Don't worry. I know just how to go about it."

She paused, stuttering, but he went on.

"That's why I'm calling. We should begin to prepare for our first time together."

"Oh . . ."

When had she ever been rendered speechless by a man? But all she could think of was his big hands on her, tying her down. Touching her. She couldn't even think beyond that, although she knew there would be more. And she was fighting her response to him every inch of the way.

Pull yourself together.

"I thought you said you'd e-mail me."

"So I did."

She waited, but he didn't seem inclined to explain himself, which unsettled her even more.

"Wh . . . what do I need to know?" she asked him.

"We both need to know what our limits are. Our desires. A lot of people use written questionnaires, but I prefer to talk. I can gauge more if I hear your response to my questions."

"So you're a psychologist now?"

She heard his sigh. "Dylan, if we are going to do this, being sarcastic with me is only going to get in the way."

"You're right. I'm sorry. This just isn't natural for me." She settled back into the sofa cushions, taking the small pillow with her.

"We're just talking now, okay?" His tone had changed; it was more soothing than commanding now, as though he could read her mood, her needs, through the phone.

"Yes. Okay."

She would do this. But her heart was a small hammer in her chest.

"First I need to know that you have some understanding of what BDSM means. I know you've been doing a lot of reading, gathering information. But tell me your definition. What it's all amounted to in your mind."

She thought for a moment about all she'd read on the subject, her brief discussions with Jennifer, the research she'd done online. "Well, I know that BDSM stands for bondage and discipline, domination and submission, sadism and masochism."

"Now tell me your interpretation of it, not what you've found in books or on the Internet."

"I think . . . the definition seems to cover a broad range of sexual and sensual behaviors. Desires. Fetishes. Everyone seems to have a different personal definition of what it's about for them. And not everyone practices everything. Some people may be into the milder aspects, like spanking or simple bondage. But it's still BDSM, even if they don't choose to call it that themselves. And at the root is the exchange of energy between the participants."

"Yes. But there's more to it than a textbook definition. How do you feel about it? What do you want from it, besides information for your novel?"

"I want the experience, to try it, before I reject it out of hand. I still think I'm more naturally a top, not a bottom, so perhaps part of this is proving that to myself, despite your 'expert' opinion."

"And to me?"

"Yes. Maybe. Yes."

"What else?"

"I don't know what else yet. I think I have to get there before I know exactly what appeals to me and what doesn't."

"You're right. Some of that we'll discover as we go. But why don't I ask you a few questions? I want you to try to answer instinctively. Don't think about it too much," he told her. "And don't be self-conscious. If you hold something back from me, this won't be nearly as effective. All right?"

It was as much a command as it was a question. Her first response was to argue with him. But he was right; it would only delay the process.

"Yes. Sure, go ahead."

"Have you ever thought about experimenting with bondage before?"

"Yes."

"Have you ever done it?"

"I . . . tied up an old boyfriend with silk scarves once."

"And did that do anything for you?"

"It was fun. Different."

"What about it didn't work?"

"I'm not sure. It was fine. But the reality wasn't as exciting as the idea."

"Could it have been that the scarves were too mild a symbol for you?"

"Yes. Maybe. It did feel fairly tame. Silly, almost. As though I couldn't quite take it seriously."

"And could it also have been that you wanted to be the one to be bound? To be rendered helpless?"

She shivered, her mind going blank. "I . . . I don't know. I don't think I consciously thought of that at the time, and I've never really analyzed it since. In my mind, if I was going to ex-periment with any of this stuff, I was going to be the one on top."

"And now?"

A small catch in her breath, a tightening in her chest. She was angry, suddenly. Defensive.

"I've agreed to try bottoming, haven't I?"

Alec was quiet for a moment. She could hear him exhaling slowly on the other end of the phone. She didn't know why that made her hold her own breath.

"Dylan. We're not going to get anywhere until you admit that at least some part of you wants this."

Her cheeks were going hot, her hands fisting around the pil-low in her lap. "Okay, I can admit that. I suppose it's natural for anyone to consider it, at one time or another, as part of being a sexually open person. Which I am. Or I wouldn't be an erotica author."

Stop babbling, Dylan.

"Good. That's a start."

"That's enough of an answer for you?"

"For now, yes. I want you to consider these things. You don't have to leave this conversation entirely convinced. It's a process."

"Okay."

She loosened her grip on the pillow a bit.

"Where were we? Oh yes. Have you ever wanted to be spanked?"

"I . . . yes."

Had she really said that out loud?

"Ah. Very good." He lowered his voice, until she had to strain to hear him. "And are you, at this very moment, a little flushed with pleasure, knowing I'm pleased with your answer?"

Her breath stuttered in her lungs. God, was she? She lifted her hand to her face, felt the small smile on her lips with her fingertips.

"Are you still there, Dylan?" he asked quietly, his voice that soft, smoky tone that went through her like silk against her skin.

"I'm still here."

"Are you going to answer me?"

She shook her head, bit her lip. "I . . . would rather not."

"But?"

She had a feeling he would wait all day to hear her answer, if necessary.

"But . . . yes, it gives me pleasure."

He was quiet again for several moments. "That's lovely, Dylan. Really. I can hear it in your voice. I can also hear how difficult it was for you to tell me."

"Yes."

"I want you to spend some time thinking about these things. We'll talk again before we see each other. Be ready to meet me at the Pleasure Dome on Saturday night. Nine o'clock. I'll e-mail you the address. You'll take a cab. I don't want you driving that night."

Her head was spinning. She was angry. Inarguably stimulated. Damn him. Shouldn't she be debating some point? But all that came out of her mouth was, "Okay."

"I want you to be home tomorrow evening at eight. We'll talk more then."

"I . . . all right. I can be here tomorrow night."

"That wasn't a request, Dylan."

"I didn't think it was."

"You sound mad."

"Maybe I am."

She ground her teeth, her jaw clenching tight. What was all of this ordering her about? They weren't at the Pleasure Dome yet, hadn't assumed the roles of dominant and submissive. Had they?

"It's all right to be angry," he said. "That's often a part of the mental process. It's hard to let it all go, to hand over your power to another person. Just remember there is power in doing that. In making that choice. Do you understand?"

"I . . . maybe. I need to think about it."

"Do that. I'll call tomorrow night. Sleep well."

He hung up, and she pressed the OFF button on her phone with a shaking hand.

Right now she wasn't sure she'd ever sleep again.

How had he known these things about her she barely knew herself? And how had she, considering herself to be fairly sexually sophisticated, failed to see this side of herself?

She didn't know. All she knew was that anger and desire warred in her body until she couldn't sit still any longer. Getting up from the sofa, she paced the length of her loft, her gaze on the fog-obscured view outside.

Below her, Western Avenue was lit up: the bars and cafés and passing headlights. It wasn't raining for once, the evening a sort of crisp black beneath the fog layer. In the amber glow of a streetlamp, a couple were making out, arms twined around each other. She watched them kiss, watched them grope each other, and burned even hotter.

Groaning, she turned away, thinking to go into the kitchen and pour herself a glass of wine. But it wasn't wine she wanted.

Instead, she moved across the living room and into the bedroom end of the apartment. The snowy white of her bed gleamed faintly in the lamplight shining from the living area, a stark contrast against the shadow of the moss-green wall behind it. But it wasn't the relaxed comfort of her bed she wanted, either.

Quickly, she stripped her clothes off, the cool evening air a gentle bite on her bare skin. She loved this, to be naked. But tonight she felt it even more.

She climbed onto the bed and pulled out the wicker basket that rested on the floor next to it, opening the lid. Inside was her collection of vibrators and other toys. She touched the turbo vibrator she'd used every night since she'd met Alec, but put it aside. She wanted something gentler, wanted to come more slowly, more luxuriously. Instead, she chose a flesh-colored vibrating dildo that looked like the real thing, the head of it plump and sleek. She held it a moment, the pseudo–skin texture tempting in her hand, then, biting her lip, pulled out a small chrome egg, as well. Laying back against the pillows, she spread her thighs, the cool air caressing her naked sex.

Turning the fleshy phallus on, she lowered it between her legs, touched the tip to her clitoris and moaned softly. Pleasure shivered through her system, a small trembling wave. She closed her eyes, saw Alec's face, and pressed it to her again, sliding it over her hard clitoris.

"Ah . . . "

She teased herself with it, letting sensation build a little at a time, until she was squirming on the bed. Her sex was soaked. She spread wider, pushing the phallus inside.

"Oh, God . . . Alec . . . "

What would it be like to have him fuck her? To fuck her while he held her hands high over her head, imprisoning her. He was so big. She would be powerless against him, beneath his hulking body. His muscles would be hard and powerful. And she could imagine his cock, pushing into her . . .

Yes . . .

She angled the vibrator, hitting her G-spot.

"Oh . . . oh, yes."

Her legs were shaking now, pleasure a quiet roar in her body, building, building. She slid the vibe in deeper, then slid it out, her hips arching into the motion, over and over.

Would he fuck her slowly? Or would it be all hard, fast, animal sex?

Alec.

She needed more.

With her hand she spread her juices over that tight hole between her cheeks, using it as lubrication, then slid the small egg into her ass. Pulling in a breath, she forced herself to relax, turned the egg on before pushing it past the tight ring of muscle. She was so turned on there was no burn, no difficulty. Her body opened willingly, her sex clenching, her hips bucking.

Oh yes, going to come . . .

Alec.

His strong hands would hold her down, his cock pushing into her, ramming into her.

She thrust the big vibrator hard, burying it in her sex, the vibration sending pleasure deep into her body. That and the egg quivering in her ass, the sensations joining together.

"God, Alec, fuck me . . . "

One more hard thrust and her entire body clenched as she came, pleasure a rumbling thunder in her body: her pussy, her ass, her belly and breasts. She rode the wave, surged with it, her hips pumping.

Alec!

"God . . . "

She kept pumping, kept coming, her climax an endless spiral of pleasure.

Finally, spent, she lay shivering on the bed. In her mind was Alec's face, his big hands. The thought of his naked flesh against hers. And him holding her down. Her wanting him to.

Oh yes, the mind fuck had begun already. How much worse was it going to be? And how much better?

four

Alec sat at his wide oak desk, staring at the computer screen. He'd been trying to write since the early hours of the morning, trying to organize his current work-in-progress into some cohesive form, but his mind kept wandering. He leaned in and tried to read the page he'd just typed, but the words blurred together.

He'd hardly slept, waking at five, bleary eyed. Hell, he'd hardly slept for days. He'd tried to get back to sleep this morning, but after lying in bed, thinking of Dylan for over an hour, he'd gotten up, gotten into the shower, and brought himself to orgasm again beneath the spray of hot water.

His cock pulsed, hardened.

This was getting ridiculous. He'd masturbated every day, several times a day, since he'd met her. And it was even worse since his telephone conversation with her the night before. Too hot, talking with her about her desires. And every bit as hot hearing the anger in her voice, imagining working that small rage out of her. He'd had an almost constant hard-on all night, like some twisted Viagra ad.

God, the woman was like some sort of demon, invading his dreams, too damn many of his waking moments. He couldn't wait to get his hands on her. To take all that fight and fury out of her.

To bind her.

Spank her.

Oh, yeah.

His cock surged with need at the thought.

He really had to get himself under control.

He had to get *her* under his control.

He groaned.

Need to see her.

Why was he fighting it? When he wanted something, he simply made it happen. Why should this be any different?

Probably because seeing her before the appointed time went against his usual protocol. It disturbed the pattern of a dominant/submissive relationship, no matter how casual the connection.

This didn't feel casual.

Fuck it. He was calling her. It wouldn't hurt to take her by surprise, anyway. To shake her up.

Feeling more in control of the situation, he picked up his cell phone and dialed, heard her intake of breath on the other end when she picked up.

"Alec?"

Oh, yes. Lovely, breathy voice.

"Dylan. How are you this morning?"

"It's eight A.M."

"So it is."

"Do you always call people so early?"

"Were you asleep?"

"No, but . . . never mind."

"I want to see you, Dylan." He didn't care about the sullen tone in her voice. He picked up a pen, tapped it against the edge of his desk, realized what he was doing and stopped.

"You want to see me now?"

Yes.

"Tonight."

He clicked the top of the pen, letting the small bit of metal bite into his thumb, waiting for her to answer.

"Why tonight?"

The pen dropped, and he lurched to catch it, but it hit the floor with a clatter.

Fuck.

"Do you need to question it, Dylan?"

Did he? He didn't want to think too carefully about whatever the hell was going on with him. He just wanted to see her, damn it.

"I . . . no, I suppose not."

"Meet me at seven at Wild Ginger on Third. Do you know the place?"

"Yes, I know it."

"Don't be late."

"I'm never late."

A hint of stubbornness in her voice, but she wasn't really fighting him at this point. He sat back in his desk chair, his muscles loosening.

"And, Dylan, you are to wear all black. Do you have a black dress?"

"What woman doesn't?"

"Black stockings? Boots?"

"Of course."

He couldn't tell from her tone how she was taking being given orders. But he would deal with that later. It didn't matter to him right now as much as it should.

"I'll see you tonight, then."

She blew out a breath. "All right. Fine."

Oh yes, a little fire in her, but he expected that. Enjoyed that.

"Until tonight, then."

He hung up without giving her a chance to respond. He felt the annoyance coming, the fight. He'd let her stew on that today. Let her work some of it out of her system. Or let it build into real anger by the time he saw her. Either way it would work. Part of his job as a dominant was to elicit some sort of response from her. And if she was going to fight this process—and that was a given, with Dylan—it would be better if those issues were dealt with as soon as possible.

He'd enjoy this fight. Seeing her struggle. And even more, that moment when she finally gave in. Too much, maybe. But he would deal with that, too. Work this weird *need* out of his system. With Dylan. Or another girl. It didn't matter, did it?

Did it?

It never had before. And he wasn't about to start now, getting hung up on a woman. His insane attraction to Dylan Ivory was just that, and nothing more.

Just work her out of your system. Just work her.

Tonight would be about getting to know her, because the more he could get inside her head, the easier it would be to get her to truly submit. She was complicated. The power-play dynamic would be more effective once he had a better idea of how her mind worked. It was as simple and clear as that.

He shook his head, turned back to his computer screen. And knew deep down that he was lying to himself.

Dylan got out of the cab in front of Wild Ginger, slamming the door shut behind her. She'd been fuming all day.

She smoothed her hands over her dark brown slacks, straightened her caramel-colored leather jacket.

There was no way in hell she would have worn the damn black dress.

She yanked open the door to the restaurant a little harder than was necessary. Inside it was all spare Asian elegance, the dark red walls making a dramatic backdrop to the black lacquer tables, the fragile sprays of white orchids in tall vases.

She spotted him immediately. He was lounging against the bar, a drink in his hand. Huge and handsome—no, handsome was not a powerful enough word for him—in his dark slacks and a dark shirt that fit his muscled body like it was custom-made for him. It probably was. There was no other way a shirt could fall perfectly over those enormously broad shoulders, and lie smooth and close around his narrow waist. But no matter how gorgeous he might be, his looks were not going to make her give up the simmering irritation she'd arrived with.

He smiled when he saw her. There was something smug about

it, making her blood heat with fury. And her body heat with desire. She swallowed the desire down, nodded her head and made
her way toward him.

"Hello, Alec."

"So you showed up but had to be sure to let me know you're
not to be pushed around, is that it?"

She lifted her chin. "Yes. That's it exactly."

He grinned at her. "You look beautiful, Dylan."

She hadn't expected that. But she wasn't going to be a push-
over and she wanted to be clear about that.

"Maybe it's part of your ritual with the girls you play with at
the club, but I'm no slave girl. And my foray into this branch of
kink does not mean that has changed. That's not what I'm interested in."

He kept smiling, which she found a little disturbing.

"That's what we're doing here tonight. Getting a better picture of what you *are* interested in. Shall we get our table?"

"I . . . yes."

She didn't know what else to say, and felt foolish for what she'd
already said. Why couldn't she calm down?

Alec gave an imperial nod of his chin and the hostess appeared out of nowhere, a slim, attractive girl with shining black
hair. She smiled at Alec, batting her long lashes at him. Dylan
wasn't surprised, nor could she blame the girl. Alec was probably
the best-looking man in the place, his smile charming, rakish.

Good Lord, had the word *rakish* actually just passed through
her mind?

She shook her head to herself as she followed the hostess to the table, Alec a step behind her. She swore she could feel the heat of his big body.

He leaned in and whispered to her, "I didn't actually expect you to wear the black dress, Dylan. Not you."

She turned to stare at him, blinking, but he just smiled as he helped her out of her coat and draped it over the back of her chair before pulling it out for her, then took the opposite seat.

"We'll have a pot of jasmine and green tea," he told the hostess, his gaze steady on Dylan's. His eyes glowed a deep, dark blue in the dim lighting.

"You surprise me," she found herself saying.

"Do I? In what way?"

"All of these nice manners. Holding my chair. Remembering the kind of tea I prefer."

"Being a dominant doesn't mean being an asshole, contrary to popular belief. And I never conform to popular belief."

"No, I'm sure you don't."

"Neither do you."

"What do you mean?" She fingered the edge of her cream-colored angora sweater.

He shrugged. "You're an erotica author. There are those who might have some preconceived notions about what sort of person that makes you."

"Probably. What do *you* think that makes me?"

He leaned in, looking at her. *Through* her. She shifted in her chair. She wanted to hear his answer a little too badly.

"I think it makes you a woman who is more open-minded when it comes to sex than the average woman might be. More

open-minded in general, perhaps. Although I don't think you apply that to yourself."

"I don't know what you mean."

"It means that I believe you judge yourself more harshly than
you do others."

"I'm sure I do. Doesn't everyone?"

"Yes. You're right about that."

"Even you?"

He grinned at her, his teeth a dazzling white, his goatee wicked-looking even as he smiled. And she was, as always,
charmed by him.

Damn it.

"Even me," he said. "Ah, here's the tea."

To her surprise—once more—he picked up the pot and
poured, handing her the small red and white ceramic cup. She
took it, warming her fingers around it.

"Thank you."

"You're welcome."

She could not figure this man out. And he was right: She did
have preconceived notions about what a sexual dominant was
about. Notions she was apparently going to have to toss out and
start all over again.

If only he didn't have to be so absolutely in control all the
time. Or maybe if *she* didn't . . .

She laughed softly.

"What is it?" he asked.

"Oh, just coming to terms with a few things," she admitted.
"Readjusting my thinking. Not that I like it."

He leaned back in his chair, sipped his tea. "Ah, exactly what I hoped to achieve."

She sighed. "And there you go again," she muttered.

He was silent a moment, studying her, and she felt her cheeks begin to heat under his scrutiny.

He lifted his steaming teacup, blew on it for a moment, sipped, then set it down. Every tiny motion seemed measured. Or perhaps it was simply that she was waiting for him to say something, his study of her making her anxious.

"You intend to be a great challenge for me, don't you, Dylan?"

"I don't 'intend' anything."

"Don't you?"

"I just am who I am."

"And who is that, Dylan?"

"Are you being condescending?"

"Absolutely not. I want to get to know you. It's part of my job, as it were. But I also just *want* to know you. Is that all right?"

He leaned in once more, covered her hand with his. His was large, warm, the heat seeping into her skin in much the same way the heat from the teacup had. Her body went loose all over.

"Yes. Of course. I don't know why I'm being so combative. Or maybe I do. But it's rude of me. I'm sorry."

"It's fine. Let's start again. Just relax, talk. Why don't you tell me something about yourself?"

"What would you like to know?"

"Start at the beginning."

"Well . . . "

She realized his hand still covered hers, making it hard to

think. She glanced down at their hands, up at his face, and he smiled briefly and withdrew his hand as though he understood.

"Start with your writing, Dylan. I'd love to know about your work."

She settled her hands in her lap, her fingers clenching, feeling the heat he'd left there. "I've been writing full-time for the last four years."

"And have you always written erotica?"

"Yes, always. I started to write in my early twenties, but I didn't think about getting published until four years ago. Things happened pretty quickly, then. I got an agent, sold my first book, then three more, and several novellas. I've been very lucky. Before that I was in banking. I did quite well."

"Banking? I can't see you in banking. I imagine your real talents were wasted there, in some stiff corporate environment. You're too . . . exotic."

She shifted in her seat, her fingers twining tightly. She'd never thought of herself that way.

This man could unbalance her like no one else ever had.

She sighed to herself and went on. "I hated it. But the money I made there gave me the opportunity to stop working and just write, so I'm grateful for it. Luckily, I got my first contracts before my savings ran out. What about you? What did you do before writing professionally?"

"I taught English at the university here."

"But you gave it up to write?"

"Not immediately. I stopped working three years ago. Too many book deadlines to keep it up. I didn't feel I could do both and put enough energy into each. I didn't want to rip off my students. I loved teaching, actually. Some people think of it as a banal existence. But I enjoyed it."

"I'm sure you did. And I'm sure you found your thrills elsewhere."

He grinned. "Of course. I don't bother denying who I am." He sipped his tea again. "Unlike some people."

"Oh, a barb. Should I be injured?"

He grinned, a wicked glint in his eyes. "Not yet. We'll get to that later."

Her cheeks heated once more, her sex going warm. It hit her all at once that this man was really going to touch her soon. Spank her. And what else?

She crossed her legs under the table, fighting the ache between them.

Focus. Just keep talking.

The talking made this almost seem like a normal date. She could handle that.

"Alec, tell me more about this thrill-junkie stuff you mentioned the other day. The extreme activities."

Alec smiled. "I like anything that gives me an adrenaline rush. I snowboard. I've been skydiving. The shark-diving I believe I mentioned. And my motorcycles. I've raced, but not professionally."

She shuddered. She hated to think of that. She had most of her life.

"Dylan? What is it?"

She waved her hand. But she could feel herself going pale. And Quinn was a big part of what had made her who she was.

Just tell him. Get it over with.

"I . . . I lost my younger brother, Quinn, in a motorcycle accident. The idea of anyone driving a motorcycle makes me . . . uncomfortable."

"I'm sorry. Was it recent?"

"No. No. Can we change the subject? It sounds as if you've traveled a lot."

"I have. I particularly love Southeast Asia, the entire eastern hemisphere. Thailand is beautiful. Bali. And Tibet was an adventure, although not a comfortable one. I was tattooed there by an old man, using the ancient methods. They take a long spoke of sharpened bamboo and tap it over and over to push the ink into the skin. It takes two people to hold you down, to hold the skin tight. It takes hours. But you get into this sort of trance space after a while. It's on the back of my shoulder, a bony area and it hurt like hell, but it's my favorite tattoo. These tattoos are custom-made, and have a spiritual meaning the artist discovers for each individual. A unique message. It was an amazing experience."

"I've seen it done in documentaries. It looks painful, but the designs are beautiful."

"I'll show you mine eventually. Do you like tattoos?"

"Yes. There's something so personal and interesting, so much a statement about a person. I have one myself."

"Do you?"

"You look surprised."

"Maybe not. What is it?"

"A branch of plum blossoms sort of arching over my right hip."

"Ah. Plum blossoms are a sign of perseverance."

"Yes. The blossoms can survive a winter frost."

"Perhaps you'll tell me sometime what that means for you."

She smiled. "Perhaps. You have other tattoos besides the one you had done in Tibet?"

He nodded. "A pair of dragons on my forearms. I had them both done in Hong Kong. I'd roll up my sleeves to show you but a partial view wouldn't really do the work justice. I'd have to take the shirt off."

God, what would this man look like with his shirt off? She shivered.

"And what do they mean for you?"

"The dragons are a symbol of power. Strength. And protection."

"What do you need to be protected from, Alec?"

A shadow crossed his face, but disappeared so quickly she wasn't certain she'd seen it.

"Everyone has their vulnerabilities. We wouldn't be human otherwise, would we?"

"I don't suppose you're going to tell me what your vulnerabilities are?" she asked.

"Not now. But I should know something about yours. That's part of my job, as well."

"Is this necessary?"

He said simply, "Yes."

"Why?"

"With power comes responsibility. I need to have some insight into how you'll respond when we play, and why. So that I can properly care for you."

"Oh . . . "

That small reminder of what they planned to do together made her body ache with need, and her mind reel. Were they really having this conversation with these small, utterly erotic references in the middle of a crowded restaurant?

"Why don't you tell me about your family, Dylan?"

"My family?"

"That's often a good place to start."

"Okay. Okay." She paused, thought a moment. What to tell him? "I'm originally from Portland." She paused. She really didn't want to give him details. It was too hard. She did better when she pushed most of her family from her mind. Especially her mother. How did one explain that sort of thing?

She uncrossed her legs, picked up her teacup, but found it empty. Alec reached for it, refilled it, handed it back to her.

"Go on," he prompted. "Is your family still there?"

"No. They're mostly in Ashland, Oregon, now. My aunt Deirdre and my mother. And my grandmother Delilah, who I'm very close with."

"But you're not close with your aunt and your mother?"

"Things with my mother are . . . difficult."

"Tell me about her."

"No."

She locked gazes with him. He didn't flinch.

"Another time, then."

She nodded, looked away.

"Do you want to tell me about your brother?" he asked quietly.

"Not particularly."

"Will you do it anyway?"

He was being so gentle with her. It made her *want* to tell him. To let him know her. A little, anyway.

"Quinn was . . . he was three years younger than me. A good

kid, basically. A good student. He had a sense of humor, which I seem to have missed out on. He could always make me laugh. We were close. We didn't fight like most siblings do. We needed each other I guess . . . "

She trailed off.

Really do not want to go there.

"Losing him must have been difficult."

"It was."

The waiter came then, interrupting them, and she was grateful.

Alec ordered for them without consulting Dylan or the menu. When the waiter left, Dylan asked him, "Do you always do that?"

"Take charge? Yes." He leaned toward her, humor in his eyes. "Did you really expect anything else from me?"

That made her smile. "I suppose not." She picked up her tea again. "Your turn. Tell me about your family."

"We're not close. My mother and her husband live in Scottsdale. My stepbrother and -sister, Gavin and Marianne, are there, too. But we were all adults when our parents married and don't know each other well."

"No other siblings?"

"No."

"And your father?"

"My father . . . "

Alec paused, sipped his cooling tea, shifted in the wooden chair.

It was hard talking about his father and he usually skirted the subject. But he was comfortable with Dylan, despite the sexual tension, the pure, aching need for her that he couldn't fail to recognize for a moment. He forced himself to focus.

"My father was a physicist. A professor. A brilliant guy. He really was. That's not just hero worship. He taught me a lot. He had a lot to do with who I am."

"You said 'was.' What happened to him?"

"He died when I was twenty-two."

"I'm sorry, Alec."

True sympathy in her tone, in her face. Her crystal-gray eyes. Not pity. Just sympathy.

"He was walking across the street and was hit by a car. It was so random. But, being a physicist, he'd always believed in the randomness of the universe. I did, too, for a long time. I still do, to some extent, although I've spent a long time looking for a better answer. That's partly what all my traveling has been about, I guess."

He paused, ran a hand through his hair. He'd said too much, damn it.

"That must have been terrible for you. It sounds as though he was the one family member you were close with."

"Yes."

He felt himself shutting down, shutting her out. He didn't want to do that. But he couldn't talk about this anymore.

Their food arrived. Perfect timing.

He shifted the conversation and they spoke about less personal subjects through the meal: films they liked, local politics, art, music. He was surprised to find how much they had in common. Maybe he shouldn't have been. Chemistry this powerful was bound to be something other than the fact that she smelled better than any woman he'd ever met.

When they were done the waiter cleared their plates, and he ordered more tea. He'd been watching her. He was fascinated. By the way her gorgeous mouth moved when she spoke, when she slipped a morsel of food between her lips. Her alabaster skin was absolutely flawless, just a pale pink blush to her cheeks and that faint, sweet scattering of freckles. Beautiful.

He couldn't wait to bring that pink to the surface. All over her slender body. The flush of desire. The blush of a well-spanked bottom.

His cock went hard at the thought.

Control.

"Did you enjoy your dinner, Dylan?"

"Yes, very much. Thank you."

"I won't keep you out late. I want you well rested this week. Let's discuss what will happen at the Pleasure Dome on Saturday night."

"Oh."

That pale pink went darker, her pupils widening. She glanced around them, probably wondering if anyone could hear what he was saying. He didn't mind if someone did, but he kept his voice low.

"Do you understand what safe words mean, Dylan?"

"I think so."

"Your safe word is *yellow* if you want me to slow down, if something truly gets to be too much for you. If you need a break. If you need water. If you're panicking. If anything is happening in your body that goes beyond discomfort. I will be checking you for circulation if I bind you. I probably will."

She was going a little pale now. That was all right. He didn't mind her being shocked by the reality of what they were going to do. It pleased him, in fact. His cock gave a small twitch.

He went on. "*Red* means you want to stop. The scene will end. If you are bound I will release you immediately. I'll cut you out of your bonds if I have to. I will never argue that with you. In this way, you have the ultimate power, and you are always perfectly safe with me. Do you understand?"

He saw her swallow, her slim throat working.

"Yes."

"You should also know that I don't play without some sexual contact. You don't have to sleep with me, of course. But if you are opposed to me touching you, to being naked, tell me now and we will stop here. Sexual stimulation can help you to take more. It helps you to let go. Some people can play without it. I don't."

He watched her carefully, saw her eyes gleaming, the acceleration of her breath. Even her lips were a darker shade of red, as though someone had bitten them. Desire there. But would she balk at this?

He didn't know what the hell he would do if she backed out now. He wanted her too badly.

But she simply nodded, said, "All right."

One simple phrase and he was as hard as he'd ever been in his life.

Control.

"Do you have any questions for me?" he asked her.

"I . . . I don't know."

"You can e-mail me between now and Saturday if you do."

She nodded once more, trying to look brave, but she was still going back and forth between paling and flushing.

He leaned toward her, took her wrist in his hand, pushed his fingertips beneath the hem of her sleeve. Her pulse was racing, hot. Her skin was like satin.

"Dylan, listen to me now. If at any time you change your mind, it's up to you. That's how this works. There will be no anger on my part. No resentment. No judgment."

He hated how desperately he didn't want that to happen.

"Okay. Yes. I understand."

"Are you still in?"

She paused, and his heartbeat ratcheted up a few notches.

"Yes. I'm in. I want to do this. You're right. This is the only way I'll really know. And . . . I *need* to know. Not only for the book. I need to know this about myself."

He nodded, trying to look calm. But inside, he was pure chaos, his heart hammering, his cock pulsing with need for her.

Dylan Ivory was *not* just another woman. What she would turn out to be for him he didn't know. And for the first time in his life since his father had died, he felt fear.

five

❧❧❧❧❧❧

Dylan had done exactly as Alec had instructed in his e-mail to her. She was in a cab on her way to the Pleasure Dome, dressed as he'd asked, in a short black skirt, black patent high-heeled leather pumps, a black sleeveless top with a low scooped back. Beneath it she wore a black bra and panties in a sheer mesh. Not that he'd asked for it to be sheer. But she wanted him to want her. Wanted him to be as affected as she was.

She wasn't about to try to deny it. What was the point? It wasn't lust she fought against. That had never been an issue for her. She loved sex and had always been open to exploring her desires. It was the idea of giving up all control to another person. She simply wasn't sure she was capable of doing it.

There was a small rush of panic even now, doing nothing more than imagining it.

It was raining, as it so often did in this city. The tires of the cab splashed in the puddled streets as they moved through the night. Streetlights reflected off the water in pale, shimmering silver. Storefronts were lit, casting colored light into the dark.

Her heart was a small thumping hammer in her chest.

She could not believe she was really going to do this.

The ride was over quickly, and she pulled some bills from her small black clutch and handed them to the driver. The Pleasure Dome was housed in an old warehouse, very much like her own building: four stories of brick painted charcoal gray, the tall windows darkened. Imposing, as she peered through the window of the cab, her eyes rising to the top of the structure, where the moon was trying to gleam through the clouds.

When she stepped from the car Alec was waiting beneath an umbrella, dressed all in black, his hand out to help her.

"You look beautiful, as always," he told her, smiling.

She tried to smile back, but it didn't work.

He pulled her in close to his side as he walked her to the large red-painted door to the club. It felt . . . territorial. Protective. And she liked it.

"It's all right. Don't be nervous, Dylan. I'll take care of everything."

"That's the part that makes me nervous."

A small, wicked laugh from him that did nothing to comfort her.

A doorman opened the door wide for them and they stepped through, into a dark entryway. Alec paused long enough to rid himself of his coat and his umbrella, handing them to a coat check girl behind a narrow counter. She hadn't thought to wear a coat, despite the weather. She'd worn only what he'd told her to.

Odd to think about it now. She pushed the idea, and everything it might mean, into the back of her mind.

As her eyes adjusted to the dim lighting she noticed that the sleeves of his shirt were rolled up, revealing the Chinese dragons tattooed on the inside of his forearms: black and red on his right arm, black and gold on the left. The work was exquisite, detailed, the long tails twining around his arms, the heads, with their snaking red tongues, at the inside of each wrist. She wanted to look more closely. She wanted to touch them. But being in this place was too new, too distracting.

She could hear the faint bass pulse of music coming from somewhere. She could feel it reverberating in her belly.

"Are you ready, Dylan?" Alec asked her.

She nodded. "I'm ready."

She wasn't entirely sure that was true. But Alec had his hand on the small of her back and was guiding her through another door.

The room was large. The walls were painted some dark color, and all around the room were lights in deep amber, purple, red. The corners were full of shadows, and there were people there, but she couldn't quite see what they were doing. All she could make out were pairs and small groups. Looking more carefully, she saw black leather pants and vests, body harnesses, corsets in red, black, white. Collars encircling the necks of men and women: some made of leather, some of shining metal. And naked flesh.

Here and there, against the walls, were pieces of equipment. She recognized the leather-covered spanking benches, made so that the person being spanked could bend over it, resting their knees on the lower padded rails. There was a pair of large standing wooden racks people used for rope bondage, a seven-foot-tall wooden X she knew was called a St. Andrew's Cross. And even as she took in the scene before her she was acutely aware of Alec next to her, the heat of his big body, dwarfing her even though she wore her highest heels. The scent of him, that divine mixture of the forest and the sea. Alec and the scents of leather, a faint whiff of perfume, of sensuality in the room.

She was trembling all over. With nervous anticipation. With desire. And something else . . .

"You all right, Dylan?" he asked her.

"Yes. I'm fine."

He stopped, put a hand under her chin, forcing her face to him. "Are you?"

She swallowed. "Yes. I am. I promise. This is all just . . . new to me. I'm trying to take it all in. It's different from any place I've ever been."

"Yes, it is." He smiled at her, dropping his hand.

"Where are we going?"

"Shh, just come with me."

She did it, simply closed her mouth against all the questions whirling through her mind suddenly and followed him through the room. She couldn't believe she was doing this. Letting someone else handle everything, make the decisions. Except the one to be here at all, she reminded herself. That was still up to her.

They reached the other side of the room and stopped in front of a low sofa upholstered in red leather.

"Sit down, Dylan," Alec said, his voice low, but full of authority.

She did it, trying not to question herself. This was why she was here: to let go, for once. To explore this.

Alec sat next to her, slipping an arm across the back of the sofa. She could feel it brushing the back of her hair. He smelled too damn good tonight, his scent alone making her body heat, making her dizzy.

"We're just going to watch for a while," he told her, his face close to hers. "I want you to relax, to take it all in, as you said. And while you watch, you are to track your breathing, keep it slow and even. Do you understand, Dylan?"

She nodded her head, her gaze on the room, the figures writhing. She could see more now that her eyes were adjusting.

"Dylan."

"What?"

"Look at me."

The absolute command in his voice startled her and she turned her head. Her pulse was racing, a low thrum in her veins. She wanted to argue, but his expression told her not to.

She'd never been cowed by anything or anyone in her life. But that wasn't what this was. Something was happening to her, gears beginning to shift in her head. She didn't understand it.

"I know this is difficult for you," he said. "But you have to make an effort to give yourself over to it. To me."

"Yes," she whispered, her throat tight. She couldn't seem to take in enough breath to speak normally.

"There are going to be rules here. Once we get started you are not to speak unless I ask you a question, or unless there is something you absolutely must tell me. And I mean *absolutely*: only if your physical or mental well-being is compromised. If you feel you are in real danger. Simply being a bit scared is not reason enough. I expect you to have some fear. Frankly, I wouldn't be doing my job if you don't, at some point."

She looked at him, her mind emptying out at an alarming speed. She didn't like this distinct melting sensation in her arms and legs. The sensation of weakness.

"Do you hear me, Dylan?"

"Yes. I hear you."

"But?"

"But . . . I don't know if I can do this."

"You can. I can feel it in you, Dylan. I have since the moment we met. And I am not being arrogant. I've spent a number of years learning to see these things."

"I know. It's not your abilities I'm doubting."

He put a hand on her thigh, and she felt it down to her bones, that electric tingle.

"Why do you doubt yourself?" he asked her.

His gaze was hard on hers. Solid. The blue was dark, deep, his pupils wide in the dim light.

"I've always considered myself to be sexually sophisticated. I've had plenty of experience. I'm not . . . bragging. But . . . I thought I could handle this. That it would be easy. But now that I'm here . . . God, I can barely admit this to you. To myself. I feel like an idiot. And I don't like that."

She was really shaking now.

"There's no reason to feel you can't admit to being scared or uncertain."

"But I do. Even if this is a normal response for other people who come here for the first time. This is . . . *me*. And I don't know if . . . I don't think I can stay." As she said it her heartbeat thundered, and she wanted to flee. *Needed* to. "I really have to leave, Alec. I can't do this."

She got up, her knees so liquid she could barely stand.

Alec got to his feet beside her. His arm went around her and he pressed his cheek close to hers. She tried to pull away, but he held her tight.

"Dylan, calm down. You can do this. You're fine."

"I'm not."

She felt like crying. But she wouldn't do it. She would *not* cry.

"You are. You're with me. I'll take care of everything."

When had any other man said that to her? When would she ever have trusted it if they had? But she trusted Alec, despite the fact that she hardly knew him. Despite herself. Despite her need to be in control. She couldn't figure it out.

Maybe she didn't need to.

"Come on, Dylan. You're okay," he said, his voice a low murmur.

She let him help her back onto the sofa. This time he kept his arm around her waist, holding her close to his side. And after a few moments, the scent of him, the feel of him, went to work on her. Her senses filled with him, and the rest of it—her fears, her need to be in charge of everything—began to fade, and desire began to take over.

"Look at what the others are doing," he said in her ear, his breath a warm whisper on her skin. "See how beautiful they are, all of them. It doesn't matter here what anyone looks like. What matters are the gifts of trust and energy they exchange. That's the beautiful part. That's what it's all about, Dylan."

She looked directly across the room, to where a naked woman was bent over one of the spanking benches. Her blonde hair hung down around her cheeks, and the man standing next to her brushed a lock from her face, leaned in to kiss her before moving behind her and running his hands over the curve of her ass. There was tenderness in the way he touched her, even as he began to spank her.

Desire quivered between Dylan's thighs.

Was this what she wanted?

She turned to look at Alec. His eyes were glittering. There was hunger there. But there was also absolute control.

Yes, she could trust him.

She still wasn't sure she could trust herself. But she was going to do this.

She swallowed the hard lump in her throat.

"Okay. Okay. Can we . . . just get started?"

Alec's face was perfectly serious. "You can always decide to stop, Dylan. That's the beauty in this. The ultimate safety in it. It's up to you."

She nodded.

He smiled.

"Then we'll begin."

Alec took her hand and felt her trembling. He didn't want her to be afraid, not really. But a little fear, some nervous anticipation, was a challenge he always enjoyed. And she was so damn gorgeous like this, with her hair a wild mass of curls around her pale cheeks, her eyes enormous, glossy.

He led her to a shadowy corner of the room, to a large red leather chair with a wide seat and no arms. He set his black bag, filled with the implements of BDSM play—paddles, canes, floggers, cuffs—down next to it.

"What is this?" Dylan asked, looking at the chair.

"Did you want something more extreme for your first experience?" he asked her, taunting her a bit. He already knew the answer.

"I don't know."

Her face was absolutely serious. He could see the muscle working in her jaw. She was trying so hard to intellectualize her way through this. She would have to learn that didn't work in this arena. He had to take her past the wheels churning in her mind. Had to disarm her.

"Don't worry. I do. Now take your clothes off."

"What?"

She actually took a step back from him, which made him grin. He couldn't help it.

"Come on, Dylan. Surely you didn't think to play fully dressed?"

There was no real surprise on her face. Only a little shock that it was happening to *her*. She was silent a moment, then, without saying a word, began to pull her shirt over her head. She kept her eyes on his, but they were no longer the usual cool gray. A storm was raging in there, despite the firm line of her mouth, the stubborn set of her shoulders, her silence. But that was part of her process. He'd expected it from a woman who held herself so strictly in control. And it made her even more attractive to him: the battle he knew was going on inside her. Her willingness to do this, anyway.

He crossed his arms and waited while she unzipped her skirt and stepped out of it, and didn't say a word when she handed her garments to him. He was too busy looking at her in her sheer black bra and panties, the long line of her legs in her high black heels. The graceful branch of the plum blossoms tattooed over her right hip. The design was delicate, sinuous, like her. The blossoms were white, edged in a deep pink. So innocent-looking on a body he wanted to do very dirty things to.

Fucking gorgeous.

She lifted her chin, a small show of defiance, and his fingers tightened around the fabric of her clothes. They smelled like her, pure female. Still watching her, he lifted her top to his face, inhaled deeply. Grinned when she blushed.

This woman had absolutely no idea how keenly responsive she was. But he saw it. And knew it was going to be good.

"Dylan," he said softly, "stay right there. Just hold still."

He hung her clothes on one of a row of hooks set into the wall and bent to open his bag of toys. Not that he planned to use any of them just yet. This was her first time at the club, and anyone new to BDSM had to be introduced at a slow pace. How slow depended on the individual, and things were going fast enough with Dylan. But he didn't mind seeing her squirm as he withdrew each item, placing them on the low wooden table next to the chair: a wide leather slapper made of two flat lengths of thick leather, a wooden paddle, a short riding crop, a coiled three-foot-long single-tail whip in black and white woven leather, a vampire glove, a clear Lucite cane. Some of his most wicked-looking pieces.

Her eyes were wide, the pupils enormous, but she remained

stubbornly quiet. He let his gaze lower to her breasts. They were small and firm, the rounded flesh just spilling over the top of her bra. And through the mesh he could see her nipples. They were going hard as he watched.

Perfect breasts.

He had to ignore the erection growing between his thighs.

Concentrate.

He brought his gaze back to hers. "Come here, Dylan."

She took one wavering step forward, and paused. He wrapped a hand around her slim waist and pulled her in. She let out a startled gasp.

"Dylan, if we are to work together you must learn to follow instructions. If you fight it there is no point."

Her breathing was fast and ragged. "I know. I can't help it."

"You will get through this initial panic. Just do as I say. Trust me."

She nodded.

"Say it."

"I . . . I'll do as you say. I trust you, Alec."

A hint of resistance in her voice still. But that was fine. He'd get her past that soon enough.

Meanwhile, the heat of her body was making him a little crazy, distracting him.

Focus.

He drew her in tighter, settled into the chair and held her in his lap, his hand around her waist. Skin like fucking satin, pale and smooth. He could feel the heat of her sex through his slacks.

He brushed his fingertips over her cheek, then pushed his fingers into her hair, drew them through the curls. So soft . . .

"Just breathe, Dylan, Try to relax. Listen to my voice."

She nodded her head.

"Close your eyes."

She did, without argument.

"I want you to focus inward. To think about each breath. Just your breath. My voice. My hand in your hair. Nothing else."

Her sex was going hotter and he knew he had her already, whether she understood that or not. And his cock was growing harder, pulsing with desire.

"Breathe in and hold it for a moment," he told her. "Good. Now push the air out slowly. Again. And as you breathe, feel it everywhere in your body. Your lungs, your stomach, your arms and legs. And feel my hands on you."

He stroked her bare back, up, then down again, feeling the delicate bones of her spine, her shoulder blades, the narrow column of her long, slender neck. She was built like a dancer, her body lithe and slim and toned.

Perfect.

"Very good, Dylan. Just breathe. Focus."

He moved his hand lower until it brushed the edge of her mesh panties. She held perfectly still as he slipped his fingers beneath the fabric at the rise of her buttocks to caress the skin there.

He kept her there for some time, simply having her breathe, stroking her flesh, which grew hotter by the second. But she was finally relaxing. He could feel her muscles loosening, her breath evening out.

Her cheeks were still pale, but her nipples were hard and swollen, growing darker beneath the mesh fabric of her bra.

Need to touch them. Taste them. Need to taste her.

He pulled her in closer, lowered his mouth to hers.

Her lips were soft, loose. And as he ran his tongue over her plush lower lip, they parted, opened for him. He slid inside.

Her tongue was like a shock, so hot and sweet. He didn't expect it, this jolt of pure need that cut into him like a knife. He'd meant to keep the kiss light, just to feel her lips for a moment. But desire took over and he crushed his mouth to hers.

She moaned, her warm breath going into him. He breathed her in, exhaled into her, and her arms slipped around his neck. So damn sweet. He kissed her harder, and she was kissing him back, until they were both breathless.

His cock was hard as steel between his thighs.

Torture.

He buried his hands in her hair, held her face to his, hard between his palms. He couldn't do it any other way with her.

Her tongue pushed into his mouth. Her body pushed into his, her breasts crushed to his chest. And desire burned, scorching him. Making his mind go blank of everything but her name.

Dylan.

She shifted in his lap, her hip pressing against his cock. He was going to explode, just come like some teenager.

Damn it.

He pulled away.

"Alec?"

Her cheeks were flushed now, her eyes blazing.

He had to take a moment to draw air into his lungs. Had to think.

He was hard as hell, with her body warm in his lap, her need written all over her beautiful face. It was his job to serve that need. His own need was like a hammering beat in his groin, one he could barely control. He wasn't used to that. To how extreme it was: heat, desire, pure animal lust.

But he could handle it, he reminded himself. He always had. He simply had to keep a reign on it, bank it for now. And give her what she desired. It was his job, one he did well.

Keeping one hand behind her neck, he squeezed a little. Confusion crossed her features.

"Quiet, Dylan."

She looked as if she was going to speak, then closed her mouth.

"Good girl."

A small shiver ran through her at his words.

Ah, she would be the perfect bottom, this woman. That compelling combination of strength and fire and a natural submissive response.

He squeezed harder, simply holding her, a means to control her. Physically, but this was something that always seemed to have a psychological effect on anyone with submissive tendencies, as well. And it was working with her beautifully.

He kept his gaze on her face as he slipped his other hand between her thighs, used it to spread them apart.

Her mouth went into a small O, but she didn't say a word.

He moved his hands in between that lush flesh, found the heat of her mound through her black panties.

"Tell me you want this, Dylan," he commanded.

"I . . . yes. I want this."

He found the edge of the fabric, slipped his fingers under it.

A small moan from her. But she kept her eyes open, her gaze on his, as his fingers skimmed the swollen folds between her thighs.

Christ, she was wet. Soaked. And it was going to kill him to touch her like this and do nothing about the hammering pulse of his cock. But he would do it.

He slipped his fingers over her pussy, parted the full flesh, his fingers resting there for a moment. So damn hot. Then he found her clit and pinched it lightly.

"Oh!"

Still her gaze didn't waver.

He pulled on the swollen nub of flesh, massaged it. Her breath came faster, until she was panting, her red lips parted. When he pushed two fingers into her, she gasped.

His cock twitched.

Like heated velvet inside, hot and wet and his cock wanted *in*. *Control*.

He took a deep breath, thrust his fingers inside her. She squirmed on his lap, making him ache. But he was intent on her, his hand inside her, pushing deeper, until he knew by her mewling cries that he'd found her G-spot.

"Come for me, Dylan."

And she did; it was that simple. Her sex clenched around his pumping fingers, her body arching. His cock thrummed with need, his pulse racing.

"Ah, God . . . Alec . . . "

She bit her lip and it was too good to resist. Leaning in, he took that plump flesh between his teeth and bit down, just hard enough, then opened her lips with his tongue. She was coming, panting into his mouth. And he took it all in: her pleasure, her sighs, the sharp scent of her desire in the air.

She was still shivering when he pulled back and moved her, laying her facedown on his lap.

"Alec?"

Her body went tense all over.

"Shh. It's time, Dylan. This is why we're here. You're ready."

"Alec . . . No. I can't . . . "

She was struggling to sit up, but he held her more firmly.

"Are you telling me *red*? Are you safe-wording out of the scene? If you are, I will let you up and we'll get you dressed and leave here. Is that what you want?"

"I . . . no."

He could barely stand to do it, to hold her down. Spank her. It would only make his straining cock harder, make it more difficult to keep himself under control. No woman had challenged his self-control the way Dylan did. But he could deal with it. He simply *would*. He wanted to touch her more than anything in the world at this moment.

"Are we staying, Dylan?"

"Yes."

He could feel the slightest give in her body. It was enough. He pulled the sheer mesh of her panties into the sweet line between her cheeks, baring them to his hands. He smoothed his palms over the silken flesh, just stroking her skin. Eventually, she went loose in his lap. Perfect. As perfect as the tight curve of her bare ass.

He began to tap with his fingertips, just hard enough that he knew she could feel it. He listened to her breathing for any sign of panic, but she was fine so far. He slapped a little harder, the flat of his palm making a small smacking sound. Her breathing didn't change, but her flesh grew warm and showed the slightest tinge of pink.

"Are you all right, Dylan?"

"Yes."

She was still loose and warm, and he knew she was slipping into the edge of subspace, had perhaps already reached it when he was working her with his fingers, before she even came.

His cock twitched, swelled.

Don't think about that now. Concentrate.

He smacked her harder, his other hand still holding the back of her neck firmly. He knew she was feeling some pain. He also knew the desire in her body could convert it to pleasure if he handled her correctly.

He intended to.

Pausing to stroke her pinking skin, he smiled to himself at the lovely blush there. Drawing his fingertips over her buttocks, he pinched at the undersides. She squirmed, but her breath was still even. There wasn't an ounce of tension in her muscles. He knew if he could see her face her pupils would be dilated, her cheeks flushed.

"Dylan, are you with me?"

"Yes."

"I'm going to really spank you now."

A soft moan, then she said, "Yes . . ."

"Good girl."

He raised his hand, brought it down on one tight buttock. She gasped, but held still.

"Excellent, Dylan. Just breathe in, then out, as I showed you earlier."

He waited until she took a good, long breath, then brought his hand down again on her flesh.

"Oh!"

"Good, Dylan. You can take it."

He smacked her ass again, which was pinking gorgeously. And she *was* taking it.

Beautiful girl.

Driving him fucking wild.

He began a rhythm then, his hand coming down over and over, keeping time with the music playing in the background. Nothing else existed. Just the music, the perfect curve of her ass, and the stabbing desire he could barely contain, but did, somehow.

For her.

"Alec . . . " Her voice was low, breathy.

He stopped. "What is it?"

"I need . . . to come again."

Ah, Christ. This girl was flawless. Fucking flawless. There was a bravery to her, an honesty about the sex, that really got to him.

She really got to him.

This had never happened to him in his life. He'd never allowed it to happen. But Dylan . . .

She was perfect. And he knew she could very well be the end of the control he'd spent his entire life perfecting.

six

Dylan floated in that warm, ethereal place Alec had taken her to. A very small, distant part of her couldn't believe she was doing these things: letting him spank her, making her come. That she had asked him to make her come again. How badly she wanted to beg him to do it *now*. But mostly, she was too far gone to really think about it.

All she could think of was the lovely touch of his hands, the heat of them on her flesh. The pleasure swarming over her in wave after wave. The spanking, the desire burning in her body, it was all the same. Pain and pleasure, and she wanted more of both.

Her breasts were crushed against his thighs, the weight of her body pressing her down onto his lap. His cock was a hard ridge against her side. She wanted to feel it inside her. Wanted him to spank her again, harder, faster. Wanted to straddle his body and ride him. And all of it going at a thousand miles an hour through her head, making her dizzy with need.

"Alec, please."

A small chuckle from him before he slid his hand under her and between her thighs, seeking out and finding her clitoris.

"Oh, yes . . . "

She arched into his hand as he began to press there. And at the same time, his other hand came down on her ass, the slap stinging, burning, then turning into pure pleasure. The sensation joined with the pulse beat of desire in her sex, multiplied.

He started to really spank her then, smack after smack, hard and fast. His fingers working her clitoris were just as fast, rubbing hard. And pleasure rose in her body, her climax quickly approaching.

"Alec . . . God . . . "

He pushed a thumb inside her, drove it deep.

"Oh . . . "

One more rough slap on her ass and she was coming, pleasure a dazzling flash of brilliance, blinding her.

"Alec!"

Her hips pumped into his hand, and she was coming, coming. He kept working her, spanking her.

Finally her body went limp. She was buzzing all over, tiny tremors of pleasure still shivering through her. She was exhausted. Unable to move.

Then Alec pulled her upright, into his arms. He kissed her face, lifted her hand to his lips and brushed his mouth over the inside of her wrist before tucking her hand back into her lap and turning his face into her cheek. His breath was warm in her hair, and he was saying something to her but she couldn't figure it out. She wanted to sleep, yet her body was more alive than it had ever been before.

"Dylan, look at me."

It was hard to do as he asked, but she wanted to. Wanted to see his beautiful blue eyes.

Wanted to obey him.

She opened her eyes.

He was even more beautiful than he'd looked before. His eyes were alight with adrenaline or need. Maybe both. She couldn't think. Couldn't figure anything out. Except that she wanted him to kiss her.

She raised her chin and he bent to her, brushed her lips gently with his. And desire was like a spark in her system once more, lighting her up. But she was too languid to move.

He pulled back. "That was very good, Dylan. Excellent."

His voice was rough, low. He kept touching her, stroking her hair. And she watched as a dozen different emotions seemed to cross his face. Or was it her imagination, a product of two powerful orgasms and her own confused need?

She began to shiver, then, a strange sort of trembling deep inside her body. Desire was replaced by a vague fear, a sort of shallow panic. She didn't understand it.

"Alec?"

"You're shaking." He pulled her closer into his big body. "Are you cold?"

"Yes. A little."

She fought tears she didn't understand as he pulled a soft blanket from the back of the chair that she hadn't noticed before and draped it over her shoulders.

"You'll be fine in a while."

"Is this . . . what does this mean? What's happening to me?"

"It's called 'bottoming out.' Even an experienced submissive can go through this. It's an overload of endorphins, and sometimes adrenaline. Sometimes it's simply emotion that's released as it often is during a deep tissue massage."

"I don't like this part."

"No, I don't expect you would. It'll pass. I'll stay right here with you."

But that didn't comfort her. She felt, suddenly and acutely, that being with Alec was part of the problem. He made her feel so vulnerable. Too wide open.

She squirmed, trying to get out of his lap.

"Hey," he said softly. "What are you doing?"

"I need to go."

"Dylan, hold still now. Listen to me. You're panicking. It happens. But you're fine, I promise. I'll take care of you. Just sit with me. We'll do some breathing."

"No."

"Dylan—"

"I can't do this! Help me up."

His arms went around her, a cage of pure muscle. Her heart tripped, hammered. She pushed against his hold, her fingernails biting into his flesh, but he didn't budge. The tears pooled in her eyes.

What the hell was happening to her? She had to get out.

"Dylan, calm down, it's okay. But I am not letting you up. You need to stay here with me for now. Come on. Do the breathing."

"Alec . . ."

His grip on her body tightened. "Just do it."

She realized he really was not going to let her go. And even while a part of her rebelled at the idea, another part of her was oddly soothed by it. She bit her lip, let her fingers uncurl from around his wrist.

If only she could stop the damn tears.

"Okay. Okay."

"Good. Just breathe as you did earlier. Take a deep breath through your nose. Yes, that's it. Hold it in your lungs. Now let it out through your mouth. Like yogic breathing. Have you done yoga before?"

"Yes."

"It's exactly like that. Let the air fill your body, relax your limbs. Very good."

He sat with her, took her through the breathing. She lost track of how long they were there. It didn't matter. She concentrated on his voice, her breath, the protective heat of his hold on her. And finally, her body began to relax.

"Alec, I'm so tired."

"Yes. It does that. This is why I didn't want you to drive tonight. It's difficult to understand what this is like until you've been through it."

"You're right. I wouldn't have gotten it. I didn't expect to . . . feel like this. I can't figure it out."

"Don't try too hard to dissect it tonight."

She sighed. "No. I can't. I can hardly think at all."

"This experience isn't about thinking, Dylan. It's about disconnecting that analytical part of your mind and simply feeling."

"Is that what you do?"

"My role in this is different. I have to be responsible for everything that happens here. For you."

He paused, stroking her hair from her face, making her pulse flutter. She didn't want to think about why.

"Dylan, are you better now?"

"Yes. I think so."

"I'm going to take you home. With me."

"No, I should go back to my place."

"We are not going to argue about this."

She felt too weak to argue. And she didn't like it, the feeling of weakness. But she really was not up to it.

She let him help her to her feet and into her clothes, then he led her by the hand through the club. She was only vaguely aware of the things going on around them: the sound of hands and leather on flesh, the cries and sighs, the scent of desire in the air.

In the entry area Alec draped his leather jacket over her shoulders, and despite the rebellion rising in her, she breathed in the fragrant smell of leather and man.

Don't get too silly over him.

Hard not to after what they'd just done. And perhaps that was the danger in all of this—that it rendered her helpless in some way. But Alec was walking her outside and the damp air was like a small shock to her system. When he pulled her in closer to his side she didn't complain.

The doorman hailed a cab and Alec helped her in, then slid in next to her, his arm around her instantly.

"You don't have to do that," she told him.

"Do what?"

The cab moved through the night. It had stopped raining but

the streets were wet, and she heard the soft splash of the tires on the pavement.

"You don't have to . . . hold me."

"Of course I do."

He sounded truly surprised.

"Because it's part of your job?"

He was silent for a long moment. "No."

"Then why?"

Another long silence. Then he said, "Because I want to."

She didn't know what to say to that. She wanted to make some argument. It sounded all wrong, somehow. But her still-dazzled brain couldn't come up with anything.

They rode through the city in silence, just the quiet hum of the heater, the low murmur of whatever radio station the driver was listening to. And Alec's presence, strong and warm beside her.

The cab pulled up in front of a large, two-story Craftsman-style house, painted a light gray with the classic stone pillars on either side of the wide front porch. She hadn't been paying attention, but recognized the Beacon Hill neighborhood. She was surprised to see him living there, rather than in some trendy downtown apartment.

He paid the driver and helped her from the cab, then up the stairs. Unlocking the heavy, glass-paned door, he pulled her inside and flipped on the light in the entryway.

It was warm. The temperature, the furnishings, all in soothing neutral shades of brown, gray, navy. Comfortable, overstuffed furniture, heavy antique wood. Art on the walls: wood carvings and paintings and masks from all over the world. And books everywhere, on built-in bookcases, on tables, in neat stacks on the floor. And everything large and masculine, like Alec himself.

"I'm putting you to bed," he told her, slipping his coat from her shoulders.

"Bed?"

It occurred to her then that they would be sleeping together. She rarely spent the night with a man. With most of her sexual partners, she'd go to their place, have sex, then go home to her own bed. But she was so damn tired. She couldn't remember feeling this exhausted in her life.

"Come on."

He guided her upstairs and through a door, into what she assumed was his bedroom.

All the furniture was on a large scale there, too. An enormous bed with a high headboard upholstered in chocolate brown suede. The bed was covered by a white down comforter, like the one on her own bed. A high dresser, dark wooden shutters at the windows. Persian rugs on the old oak floors.

It was too dark, with only the dim light flooding in from the hallway, for her to see more detail. But she was so tired, all she wanted to know was that there was a bed for her to sleep in. Nothing more seemed to matter, except that Alec was there with her.

She didn't want that to be important. Didn't want *him* to be important.

Damn it.

The tears threatened again, but she bit them back.

She must really be exhausted. That and the bottoming out thing Alec had explained to her at the club.

He was right behind her, stepping in close, his hands on her shoulders.

"The bathroom is through that door. Do you want a shower?"

A shower sounded lovely. But she couldn't muster the energy to do it.

"Not now. I just have to sleep."

He undressed her, his hands unexpectedly gentle. And she stood there, simply letting him do everything. She could barely lift her arms so he could pull her top over her head. But he was patient with her, undressing her like she was some kind of doll.

Finally she was left in her bra and panties. He drew her toward the bed, let her go long enough to pull the covers back, then helped her in.

The bed was soft and she sank into the layer of down ticking beneath her. Lovely. The white sheets were cool on her skin, and she shivered. Then Alec was beside her, his skin bare, warming her, as he pulled her in close, laying her head on his shoulder. His skin was soft, smooth, lovely beneath her cheek.

A strange surge in her chest as he held her close, closer than any man had in a long time. Closer than she would have allowed any man to. She would have started to cry once more, but she was so tired. She couldn't think, couldn't feel any longer. She closed her eyes and let sleep claim her.

Alec lay for a long time in the dark, listening to Dylan breathe, wondering what the hell he was doing.

He couldn't remember the last time he'd brought a woman to

his home. He preferred to scene at the club, or wherever his play partner lived. After a play session he'd make sure they had come down from their subspace high, then he'd come home alone, have a drink sometimes, or read before he went to sleep. And he always slept soundly after a play session. Even if the play hadn't gone well, if there was some issue. He'd make sure to resolve it before the night was over, to make sure everyone was calm, that every-one was okay. It was his job as a dominant.

He didn't like to do anything—or fail to do anything—that didn't leave him feeling good. Positive.

In control of the random universe, or at least his small part of it.

So why was he here, in his own bed, wide awake, with a woman in his arms? A woman he hadn't even had sex with?

And why didn't it bother him any more than it did? Just this small chunk of his brain that was kept awake wondering what was different about this situation. About her. But the rest of him felt a strange sort of peace. Satisfaction.

Was that what he found so disturbing?

He looked down at her and saw her long, dark lashes, tipped in the pale blue moonlight pouring in through the window, through a break in the fog. She had the highest cheekbones he'd ever seen, her lashes resting there. Her mouth was parted the slightest bit, her lips full, lush. And sleeping like this, she looked peaceful, in-nocent, in a way she never did while awake.

He didn't know what to call the dull ache in his chest.

Ignore it. It'll go away.

He knew immediately that was a lie. As much a lie as the one he'd been telling himself about how Dylan Ivory was just another girl. Another challenge. He'd been lying to himself since the moment he'd met her.

Fuck.

He could not have this, this getting attached. He was not the kind of man who did this. Ever. He was his father's son. He didn't need a woman in his life any more than his dad had. He was fine on his own. This strange pull he felt for Dylan would be a temporary thing. She was just so damn beautiful, so incredibly responsive . . .

She shifted in her sleep, and he glanced at the clock on the nightstand. The glowing red numbers read four-thirty A.M. She moved against him, her leg slipping over his. His cock stirred.

He held perfectly still, trying to calm his breathing.

He could wake her, touch her, make her hot and needy, as he had earlier. And because of earlier, she would be open to it.

She would let him fuck her.

But he knew if he did, it would be all over for him. He pulled in a breath, then another, filling himself up with the cool night air.

Gently, he moved her leg away. Her skin was satin beneath his hand.

Calm down, buddy.

He kept breathing, focusing on the draw and push of air in and out of his lungs. Over and over, until his eyes finally began to droop, to sting with the need for sleep.

Even as he drifted off, he was aware of the warm body beside him, the delicate weight of her in his arms. The scent of her hair: that dark vanilla. But he was too tired to fight it, finally. Closing his eyes, he slept.

*   *   *

The sun was just coming up when Dylan woke. The room was hazy with muted golden light filtering through the open slats of the shutters at the windows. Beside her, Alec's breath was a soft whisper on her cheek.

Her skin was hot where it touched his and she rolled away, feeling the cool, empty space suddenly like a small shock. It hit her then that she had really spent the night with him. Not only *with* him, but tangled in his arms as if they were a pair of lovers.

Scattered images from their evening at the Pleasure Dome filled her mind. Lying across his lap. The dim lighting. The erotic, throbbing pulse-beat of the music. His hand coming down on her tender flesh. The stinging. The exquisite pleasure. His hand between her thighs. Her thundering climax, then another.

God.

Her body was thrumming with need once more.

She turned to look at his sleeping profile. His face was all pure masculine lines and planes. And that impossibly lush mouth surrounded by the dark, evil-looking goatee. The blankets were gathered around his torso, his chest and arms bared. His tattoos stood out in stark contrast to his smooth skin, and she wanted to touch them, to trace the intricate, sinuous lines with her finger-tips. To put her mouth there and taste him. But she didn't dare.

She wanted him. Badly enough that she had submitted to him easy as silk the night before. Wanted to do it again.

How was that possible? She'd been able to admit she'd had the idea of trying some power play, some sensation play, in the back of her mind for a long time. But she had never expected herself to give into it so easily.

She didn't like to question herself. It was something she hadn't done since not long after she'd lost Quinn. She'd never stopped blaming herself, but she'd spent her entire life since then trying to be a better person, to hold herself and her life together in such a way that nothing like that could ever happen again. And now, it was as if her perception of her own strength had been diminished, and that scared the hell out of her.

Some of it had to do with Alec, with the sheer power of his size, the way he carried himself, the way he spoke to her. Who he *was*.

He was every bit as commanding now as he was when he was awake. And her body was responding exactly as it had last night: heat and a melting desire that made her want to do anything he asked of her.

Anything.

Fear throbbed as harshly as the need piercing her body.

She had to get out of there. Had to leave before he woke up. Before . . . what?

Before she gave any more of herself to this man.

She slid from the bed, found her clothes draped over the arm of a dark suede chair by the window and stepped as quietly as she could into the hall. She crept down the stairs and got dressed quickly in the entryway. It felt odd to put on her sexy outfit from her night at the Pleasure Dome in the early-morning cold, in the silent, dark house. It felt totally out of step with how she was feeling.

Just go.

She slipped her shoes on. Her heart was hammering as she opened the front door and slipped outside.

It was foggy, too cold and damp to be without a coat, but she hadn't worn one the night before. She'd been too anxious to get to the club. Alec had lent her his for the cab ride last night, she remembered. She shivered, as much from the memory of the scent of leather and Alec surrounding her as from the early morning chill.

She started to walk down the hill, stopping several blocks away in front of a small neighborhood grocery store that had a narrow wooden bench in front. Sitting down, she pulled her cell phone from her purse and called a cab.

The street was quiet, and she finally thought to check the time on her cell phone. It was nearly six in the morning.

It occurred to her that Alec might be mad that she'd left the way she had. *Would* be. But she'd had to get out of there. She didn't know how to face him after what they'd done together. After the way she'd given herself over to him, to his command. It had felt right at the time, somehow. Natural, the way her body, her mind, had responded. But now . . . she was embarrassed. Not by the fact that he'd had his hands on her, that he'd known her body so intimately. It was the way she'd gone so easily into submitting to him.

She got up and began to pace, back and forth in front of the bench, too keyed up to sit still.

God, her head was spinning! She wasn't even making sense anymore.

Think.

But maybe, for once, thinking wasn't going to get her through this situation.

She'd always relied on her mind, on her problem-solving abilities, to get her through life. She'd had to, ever since she was a child. Ever since her mother had begun to really lose it, to sink into her illness. Dylan had been the one to take over, to handle the life of their small family. But this time, logic and organizational skills just weren't going to cut it.

It had been years since she'd felt helpless about anything. She didn't like it.

But when it came to Alec Walker, she had very little sense of control. And when it came to Alec speaking to her as a dominant, her body, her mind, automatically responded as a submissive. He'd been right about that.

How had she not seen it? How had she been so blind to this side of herself?

Maybe because you didn't want to see it.

She didn't want to see it now.

The cab pulled up and she got in, gave her address, sat back against the cool vinyl seat.

Seattle was still asleep as they drove across town, as it often was early on a Sunday morning. Stores and restaurants were closed, windows shuttered or gated. The sidewalks were empty. Even the inevitable coffeehouses were closed. Everything was too damn quiet. It was too easy to get lost inside her own head.

When she got home she turned up the heat in her apartment, changed immediately out of her club clothes and into her white cotton nightgown. She turned the television on to some morning news talk show as she made herself a cup of tea, then got into bed.

She just needed to tune the world out. The news would help. It had been her shutoff valve since she was ten years old. Whenever things got too rough at home—which they did all too often—she'd turned to news of the outside world, where things were bigger, more dramatic, than what was happening at home. She could lose herself in bombings in foreign lands, political debates, crimes committed in places she'd never been. Anything that helped to distance herself from her life, herself. An old habit that brought comfort in some odd way. And when she hadn't been able to turn on the television because her mother was too stirred up, too panicky and on edge, she'd escaped into books. There had always been some form of escape for her, in between handling her mother's rages.

She saw like a movie montage in her head scenes from her childhood: her brother, maybe five years old, cringing under the fort he'd made of sofa cushions while their mother, Darcy, had one of her fits in the kitchen. The sounds of breaking glass, of sobbing and ranting. Dylan was only eight, herself, but she'd crawled under there with Quinn, holding his hand and telling him stories: fairy tales, bits of books, anything she could remember or make up, until it was over. And after, Darcy would be exhausted, regretful. Crying and apologizing. And Dylan had comforted her, feeling angry and guilty all at the same time. Responsible for everyone's well-being: her mother's, Quinn's.

Her stomach clenched.

She took a few breaths, forced her mind to clear those old images that haunted her still, whenever she was too tired to stop them.

Instead, she watched the images flit across the screen as the day grew lighter outside, but there wasn't enough going on to distract her. From her past. From the fallout from her night with Alec.

Picking up the remote, she flipped through the channels. More news, reruns of old sitcoms that had never appealed to her. She finally settled on a movie, *Sleepless in Seattle*.

She had a secret love for romantic films, something she'd never admitted to anyone but Mischa. They were comforting, even though she felt they were completely unrealistic. Maybe that was why they were so soothing. It was easier to lose herself in something that was total fantasy.

Sipping her tea, she watched as Meg Ryan saw Tom Hanks for the first time from a distance. Saw the emotion on her face. And felt an answering twinge in her chest.

She quickly flipped the channel.

Maybe not so unrealistic after all.

She flicked the television off.

She was overtired. If she could just get some sleep she'd wake up with a clearer head. She'd know what to do.

She lay back on the pillows and pulled the blankets up to her chin. It was warm in bed, with her down quilt heavy on her body.

Not as warm as Alec's skin.

Don't think about it now. Don't think at all.

About the heat of his skin. About his surprisingly soft palms on her flesh. His clever fingers. The lush sweetness of his mouth.

She groaned, her body buzzing with desire that was still somehow unquenched. She knew with sudden, aching clarity that it would be until she saw him again. Until he touched her. Spanked her. Until she had him inside her body, the one thing that had been denied her so far.

Torture, to want something she knew she shouldn't have. Because if she allowed that to happen, there would be no turning back. She would be lost in some irrevocable way, the strength she'd built her entire life disintegrating in her ridiculous need for this man, and for what he offered her.

Alec.

What had he done to her already? And how much more could she—would she—allow?

seven

It felt as though she'd fallen asleep only a few minutes before when her cell phone rang. She reached blindly for it, grabbed it from her nightstand and flipped it open.

"Hello?"

"You left."

"What? I . . . Alec."

"Why, Dylan?"

She pushed her hair from her face, trying to get her brain to engage. Why *had* she left? She remembered the warmth of his big bed, his body beside her, the sheer comfort of his presence. She remembered her fright at how much she liked being there. *Needed* to be there. With him.

Her pulse fluttered, her heart beginning to pound.

"I just . . . had to go."

He sighed quietly on the other end of the line. Or maybe it was a huff of irritation. "Dylan, we should talk about this."

"Because it's part of your job as a dom?"

"It is part of my job. You are my responsibility after a play session. I need to know you're all right before I leave you."

"I was the one who left."

"Without checking in with me."

Anger burned in her chest. "I told you, Alec, I am not some slave girl."

"No, but there are rules for a reason, no matter the level of power play involved. To keep you safe."

"I'm perfectly safe."

He was silent a moment. Then he said quietly, anger simmering in his voice, "God damn it, Dylan. I recognize how strong you are. How capable in your everyday life. But all of that shit just does not apply here. Not when you give yourself to me. When I am the one to take you down into that place where you aren't capable of making decisions, of seeing to your own well-being. And you are too new to this to be a good judge of when you come out of it."

Did he have a point? She couldn't figure it out right now. She was still so tired.

"Dylan? Did you hear what I said?"

"I heard you. I'm . . . thinking."

"Well, think about this. I will not play with a woman who cannot respect the rules I lay down. And one of those rules is that *I* decide when you're okay to be alone."

"Why are you so angry, Alec? I'm at home, in bed. I was getting some sleep, or trying to, until you called. I am obviously fine."

"Are you?"

"Yes." The small lie tripped off her tongue far too easily.

"Your first experience with pain play, your first time at a fetish club, and you're perfectly fine? No confusion about what's happened to you, no difficulty in accepting your response, your desires. Even though this is the antithesis of who you normally are?"

"I didn't say that."

"No. You didn't have to. Look, Dylan, I've been doing this a long time. Developing some intuition, understanding the transitions people go through in entering this arena, is part of what makes a good dominant. And I am very good at what I do. So you trying to tell me that you're perfectly fine, that you're not affected by last night at all, is pure bullshit."

"I didn't say I was entirely unaffected."

"You're intellectualizing this, Dylan."

She bit her lip, rolled the edge of the down quilt between her fingers. "Maybe I am. It's a habitual response to . . . pretty much everything."

"You're going to have to go deeper than that if you truly want to experience this."

She was angry now. She knew it was her self-defense mechanisms kicking in. She didn't care.

"I never said I . . . I'm just researching for my book, Alec. How far am I supposed to go to do that?"

"As far as your desires take you. As far as you're willing to go."

"I don't know how far that is. Okay?"

"Fair enough."

"Well, I . . . What?"

"I said that's fair enough."

She'd thought he would argue. That he didn't made her feel a little ridiculous. She took a breath, blew it out, letting some of her anger filter out with the air.

"I'm sorry I left," she said, only half-grudging.

"Okay."

"Why are you being so damn reasonable about this suddenly?"

"I'm being reasonable because I *am* reasonable, and I'm done being mad. Does that throw you?"

"Yes." She hated to admit it. Hated that it made her feel weak.

"Then I'm still doing my job."

"So, you admit mind-fuck is part of what you do?"

"Mind-fuck is an inevitable part of the process. It's one of the reasons why you shouldn't be alone after a scene until I determine that you're all right. Because at least half the mind-fuck is the stuff going on in your head simply from doing these things for the first time. From having to shift your perception of yourself, your desires, your sexuality. It's not all inflicted by me. And everyone entering the BDSM scene experiences this on some level. Until I know how extreme your reaction to being played is, it's my job to care for you. To make sure you're okay. And I can't do that adequately from across town."

Her fingers uncurled from the quilt. "Okay. Okay, I get that, I guess."

"Good. Because we have to be in agreement about this or it doesn't happen again. If you want it to. Do you, Dylan? Or are you done with this? With me?"

Some small part of her mind was screaming at her to hang up

and never see him again. But there was no way she was going to do that. Impossible.

"No. I'm not done."

"Come back here tonight, then."

"To your house?"

Excitement and nerves trembled through her in equal measures.

"Yes. Tonight at eight." His voice was soft, low, but the air of command was perfectly clear. "Take a cab. I'll pay for it."

"That's not necessary."

"Yes, it is," he insisted, and she knew from his tone not to try to argue any further.

Her whole body was vibrating with need, just from that tone in his voice. Absolute control. Command. She couldn't get over that. But she couldn't deny it, either.

"All right. I'll be there."

"Good. And, Dylan?"

"Yes?"

"Be prepared not to leave again until I take you home. Is that understood?"

She paused, pushed a hand through her hair. Rebellion rose in her, but it seemed silly to her now. She swallowed it down.

"Yes. Understood."

"And come hungry. I plan to feed you. To talk."

"What?"

"Talking is part of it. I thought I'd made that clear already."

"You did, yes. But I thought that since we've . . . gotten started . . . " She trailed off, uncertain as to what she was going to say.

"You thought that since we'd begun our play there was nothing more to learn about each other? We're just beginning this journey, Dylan. I'll see you tonight. Don't be late."

He hung up and she flipped her phone shut, her body trembling with nerves. With need. With an irresistible hunger. And still, the slightest edge of anger.

Oh, she was in trouble with this man. Trouble she couldn't turn away from. It was like having a tiger by the tail, but she'd chosen this tiger. Now all she could do was hold on tight and hope it wouldn't destroy her.

Alec's house looked just as she remembered it: surprisingly homey, with the wide front porch, the golden glow of light coming through the half-closed wooden shutters.

She'd called him when she was a few minutes away, as he'd instructed her by e-mail soon after their phone conversation, and he was waiting at the curb. All she could see was his tall silhouette, backlit by the light from the house.

His shoulders were so broad. There was something about the sheer size of him that just did her in. He made her feel more female, somehow. Even more so when he offered his hand to help her from the cab.

"Evening, Dylan. I'm glad you're here."

"I . . . So am I."

It was true. There was no use questioning that anymore.

He kept her hand in his as he led her up the front stairs and into the house, letting her go only long enough to help her off with her coat.

"You look beautiful," he told her, his gaze intense, assessing, and she found her cheeks warming.

"Thank you."

There was something about the fact that he never failed to tell her she was beautiful every time he saw her. Not that she needed to hear it all the time. Still, it was nice.

He was as beautiful as ever, his dark hair just a little mussed, making her want to run her hands through it. He was dressed more casually tonight, in a pair of worn jeans and a black T-shirt that fit snugly across his shoulders, the firm muscles of his chest. He looked very much the bad boy, with his goatee and his tattoos. Except that there was absolutely nothing boyish about him.

"I'm not the best cook in the world, but I make a passable pasta. Are you hungry, Dylan?"

"A little."

She noticed then that the house was warm, the air fragrant with the scent of cooking food.

"Come with me into the kitchen. It's almost ready."

She followed him down a short hallway toward the back of the house and through a doorway. The kitchen was a large space, the old architecture preserved, but the red granite counters, maple cabinets and brushed steel appliances were all new. It was modern, but like the rest of the house, had an easy, comfortable feel to it. The pasta boiling on the stove sent steam into the air, making the place even cozier.

A bell went off, and she jumped.

"Dylan, don't be nervous. We're just going to eat dinner. For now, anyway."

"I'm not . . . I just . . . No, you're right. I hate being so full of nerves. It makes me feel as though I'm not entirely in control of myself, my own responses. But I suppose dealing with my control issues is part of what the power play is about for me. I'm just beginning to realize that in some deeper way."

"The heavier BDSM play tends to bring a few epiphanies with it. That's not uncommon. And it's not a bad thing, either."

Heavier BDSM. Was that what they were doing? Her body clenched, a small tremor of pleasure running through her as she flashed to what they'd done together the night before.

"Try to relax while we eat." Alec turned to the stove and tested the pasta with a fork. "Ah, this is done. Go ahead and pour yourself a glass of wine, if you like." He paused, looking up, and she was struck again by the brilliance of his blue eyes. "But just one. Intoxication and play aren't a good mix."

She nodded her head, said, "Thank you."

She reached for the open bottle of red wine breathing on the counter and glanced at the label. He had excellent taste in wine, not that it surprised her. She picked up one of the glasses sitting next to the bottle, filled it halfway. She didn't want her senses compromised even the slightest bit. Not tonight.

"Shall I pour you some, Alec?"

"Yes. Thanks."

She did, handed the glass to him. He eyed her over the rim as he took a sip.

"You do that well."

"I do what well?"

"Serve."

"It's nothing more than good manners."

"Perhaps."

"You're teasing me now."

He grinned before turning back to the pasta. She watched as he poured the pot into a strainer, then spooned the pasta onto a plate, added what looked like a marinara sauce from a pan on the stove.

It struck her that this was an odd situation: him cooking a meal for her, sitting down to eat and talk like perfectly civilized people, despite what they planned to do later in the evening. It was a little thrilling. Maybe more than a little, she had to admit when she pictured herself naked, under Alec's command once more. A small shiver of lust ran through her belly.

"Dinner's ready. Let's go into the dining room. There's a salad and bread already on the table."

She followed him through a doorway into the dining room. The wood floor shone in the light of a dozen candles burning all around the room: on the heavy oak table, the antique sideboard. The table was set simply with thick stoneware plates in earthy tones, pale linen napkins, the bread in a wicker basket. In the center of the table was a low bronze bowl, unexpectedly filled with floating camellias.

Alec set the plates down and it was a moment before she realized he was holding her chair for her, waiting for her to sit. She did, let him push the chair in, wondering at all this gallantry. It made the evening seem too normal, when it very obviously wasn't.

"Is this how it always goes?"

"What do you mean?"

He'd seated himself at the head of the table and was putting his napkin in his lap.

"Like a date."

"Isn't that what this is? Whether or not the night ends with me giving you a chaste kiss on your doorstep?"

"I don't know. Is it? Is that what we're doing here, Alec?"

He was quiet a moment while he picked up a piece of bread and pulled it apart. She was distracted by the motion of his hands. They were so strong-looking, like he could pull her apart, if he wanted to.

She shivered.

Finally, he said quietly, "What we are doing is getting to know each other. Do I do this with other women I play with? Yes. Sometimes. It depends on if it's a night of casual play at the club or something more serious. And I mean 'serious' in that it's over a longer period of time."

"You felt a need to clarify that."

"To clarify what?"

"That for you 'serious' does not refer to a serious relationship."

"I'm not a relationship person. Not in that sense. Is that what you wanted to know?"

"I was simply making an observation."

"Ah." He took a bite of his pasta, chewed. "How is your dinner?"

"I don't know yet, but the wine is very good."

"Try a bite."

She knew he was avoiding the conversation, but it didn't really matter. She wasn't looking for a relationship, either. She tasted the pasta, which was tender and delicious.

"You can cook."

He smiled, looking pleased with himself, and lifted his wine in a mock toast. "I can. What about you?"

"Truthfully, I'm a terrible cook. But I'm very good at ordering out. I don't like to have to stop what I'm doing to deal with inconsequential matters when I'm writing, so I have my favorite delivery places on speed dial."

"Food is never inconsequential."

"Well, it's necessary . . . "

"Necessary doesn't mean it has to be without joy. Sex is necessary."

"You have a point. Maybe I've just accepted that I can't create it. I'd rather sit back and enjoy a good meal someone else has made."

He smiled, lifted his glass once more. "Some of us are more active in our roles than others."

She couldn't help but grin at him. "You do like to emphasize that, don't you?"

"You're onto me." He paused, smiled. "And you're more comfortable with me tonight."

"Yes . . . Maybe it's the wine. But I am more relaxed. Maybe it's just that we're sitting here and simply talking."

"That was part of my evil plan."

She laughed. "Well, it's working. I like that I don't feel I have to explain myself to you. And it's not the same thing as when we're in role, you know—it's not all about the dominant/submissive thing. Am I making sense?"

"Yes, absolutely. The power play is always going to be there with me. It's too much a part of who I am for it to ever be entirely absent. But it does take things to a deeper level. The play itself is more intense, the sex, the levels of trust required."

"Yes."

She liked that he understood it wasn't simply about her responding to the power play in a way that rendered her helpless. And she didn't want to question it all too carefully right now. All she needed to know was that she felt comfortable with him, at ease. She wanted to enjoy it without picking it apart, for once.

Dangerous.

Yes, this level of comfort with him was dangerous. It would be all too easy to lose herself. *He* was dangerous. But it was a game she was willing to play. For now.

Alec took a bite of his pasta, watching her: her hands, the way her throat moved as she swallowed. He could not get over how gorgeous she looked in the candlelight. Her hair was a shining cascade of fiery curls framing the delicate bone structure of her face.

She'd probably appear fragile to most people in her day-to-day life, if she didn't radiate such an air of authority. But under his hands she was so different. That authority crumbled away. He'd watched her struggle to hang on to it, and loved that she couldn't, ultimately.

He was getting hard thinking about it. He had to shift in his chair, force his mind away from the memory of her naked skin.

Get it together. Focus.

He took a long swig of his wine. This would work much better if she was the one off balance.

"So Dylan, are you ever going to tell me about your mother?"

She looked momentarily surprised. Then she lifted her wine-glass and drank. She took her time in setting it down on the table again. "Probably not."

"It's an ongoing situation, then?"

She was looking right at him, her gray eyes clear, glossy in the candlelight. She was alert, on edge. He could see by the tension in her face how guarded she was on this subject, even if she hadn't been openly refusing to discuss it with him. "Yes."

"One that you absolutely do not want to talk about."

She sighed. "Are you going to keep pressing me until I do?"

"Not now."

"Thank you."

She was still watching him, her eyes blazing. He enjoyed that little bit of anger in her. He could admit that he got a charge out of it, an added sexual thrill. Her fighting him made bringing her to her knees, literally and figuratively, all the more satisfying.

He eased back in his chair and smiled at her. "I want you in the right frame of mind for what I have planned later."

"Oh."

Her features immediately softened; he was certain she had no idea she was doing it. That she wasn't completely accepting of how easily she went down, submitted to him, even in these small ways.

Oh yes, perfect for what he had in mind for later. But they had to digest their food first, and he was fine taking his time.

"Tell me about your past relationships, Dylan. We've never discussed that."

"Oh, well . . . there's not much to tell."

"You're not a relationship person, either?"

She paused, sipped the last of her wine, seemed to gather herself, her eyes becoming more focused. "Not really. I've been in a few. I had a boyfriend for two years when I was in college, but when school was over I realized I wasn't in love with him. It didn't seem fair to drag it out."

"So, that had to be a few years ago? I've just realized I have no idea how old you are."

"I'm thirty-three. So yes, it's been a while."

"And there's been no one since then?"

"I've dated a lot, sometimes the same person for several months. But there's been nothing more permanent."

"Why not? I have my reasons. I'm wondering what yours might be."

He watched her face shutting down. "I've never really thought about it."

He couldn't help but prod her. "You write erotica. You write about relationships, as well as sex. But you've never thought about why you avoid them?"

"I didn't say I avoid them."

"I can admit it, Dylan." He shrugged. "I avoid relationships."

"And I suppose you feel perfectly comfortable explaining why?"

"I love women. I love sex. It's simply never translated into something I wanted to make more permanent. I haven't seen any reason to do that. I'm perfectly happy with things the way they are."

"And that's gone on for how many years?"

"Well, I'm thirty-six. I've been that way my whole adult life."

"There must be some reason why."

"Maybe I don't care to look any deeper."

"Yet you seem to require that I do."

She was really glaring at him now. He loved to see that fire in her eyes. To know that he could quench it with a few carefully chosen words, by laying his hand on the back of her silken neck. He'd rather think of that, than the question she'd asked him. He needed to keep in mind that it was *Dylan* who was supposed to be off balance. And he didn't want to ask himself the questions that had begun to filter through his mind ever since he'd met her. Questions about whether or not his father's views on leading a solitary existence were entirely correct, or appropriate for him simply because they shared the same genes. Those questions were far too big to tackle right now.

"All right, Dylan. Change of subject, for both of us. I realized after our last meal together that you've never mentioned your father."

Was it really a change of subject? Well, better to talk about her father than his.

"That's probably because I haven't seen him since I was six years old."

"Ah."

"What do you mean, 'ah'?"

Oh, she was really getting worked up. She wasn't going to like what he was about to say. Not at all.

He shrugged. "Maybe that's why you avoid relationships."

She turned her head away for a moment, her jaw clenching so hard that he was immediately remorseful for pushing her so hard.

He reached for her hand. "I'm sorry, Dylan. I can see I've taken my teasing too far."

She turned back to him, her face going loose and soft again.

"It's . . . it's all right. I know I can be stubborn."

"Yes, you can."

"There are certain things in my life, in my past, that are just too personal, Alec. Things I don't talk about with anyone."

"With no one?"

"My best friend, Mischa, maybe."

"It's good to have a best friend. Someone you can confide in. Maybe someday you'll feel comfortable telling me some of these things."

"Maybe."

She smiled a little, and his chest knotted up. He didn't want to know why. Or why her telling him about her life was so damn important to him. But it was.

He'd better watch himself with this woman. Or he'd get in too deep, deeper than he ever meant to go. With anyone. He was not the kind of man who did this, who got attached. When it came to the sex, he was always in control. Anything outside that sphere was too random, too vulnerable to chance, as his father had taught him. Chance had separated his parents, hadn't it?

Or had it? He was beginning to wonder . . . But this was no time to dwell on his parents' relationship. Why was his mind wandering so much tonight? What was important was right now, this evening, with Dylan. And right now, it was safer for everyone involved if he maintained his usual distance.

He had to focus, to get back on safer ground, back on task. Luckily, the task itself was pretty damn good. Irresistible.

"Has your dinner settled, Dylan? Because it's time we got started."

"Now?"

"Yes. Now."

The look on her face was priceless. He could see emotion shifting across her features: confusion, desire, fear, that first edge of subspace. It happened all at once. And he felt it like a kick to the gut, it was so powerful.

His body filled with adrenaline. Lust. His cock rising between his thighs. Powerful enough to chase the other thoughts away. The questions. The doubts.

He'd be fine as long as he didn't think about it, if he just did what he did best.

He watched her bite her lip, that plump red flesh denting under the edge of her white teeth. Beautiful.

She was beautiful. He wanted her so damn badly he could barely stand not to touch her.

But he was about to.

He got to his feet, held her chair for her and helped her stand. She was trembling the slightest bit beneath his hands. Lovely.

He pulled her closer, taking in the vanilla scent of her skin, her hair. Leaning in, he whispered in her ear.

"I am going to take you upstairs now, Dylan. And I am going to do all of the things to you I've been dreaming of since the last time I had you in my bed. But first I'm going to play you. Are you ready?"

"Yes." Her voice was a soft whisper, so soft it made him shiver.

He didn't want to think about what he'd just told her: that he'd been dreaming of her.

But this was no dream. And he was going to have her. He would spank her. He would fuck her tonight. Over and over. And he would be in control as he always was.

In control. As always.

He repeated the words to himself one more time. And tried to ignore the fact that he didn't quite believe them.

eight

Dylan followed Alec up the stairs, his large hand surrounding hers. There was something about his hold on her, light and warm as it was, that made her feel in some subtle yet physical way that she was under his command.

She would not think about how much her body loved this. How his command made her pulse flutter, her sex heat. She would not recognize the mental struggle still going on inside her moment by moment. If she thought about it she might put a stop to it. *Would* put a stop to it.

Better to just go with it. To give herself over, as he'd said. To try, anyway. It felt too good to stop. She was in some weird state of denial, she knew. Pretending that this was just about kinky sex. That it didn't mean anything more: about her, about the way Alec made her feel.

Yes, it's just sex. A purely physical response. It doesn't have to make sense.

His bedroom was dimly lit by a lamp on the dresser; a halo of golden light pooled there, illuminating the big bed. She could remember the feel of the crisp sheets, of his bare skin next to hers.

Her sex ached with need.

Soon enough.

He turned to her, and standing so close to him she had a real sense of his size, the height and breadth of his big body. She glanced down at the tattoos on his arms. What was it about them that made him seem a little more wicked, a little more sexy?

"Dylan, pay attention."

He lifted her chin with his hand, holding it just firmly enough to let her know he was there, that he was the one in control. No doubt about it. Not that there ever was, with him.

She realized in some distant way that this was the first man she'd ever met who she felt was more in control than she was. Maybe that's what this insane attraction, as well as her ability to submit to him, was all about.

A surge of fear, of resentment, trembled through her.

Don't think.

"Dylan, I need you to focus. To be right here with me."

She looked at him, locking on his steady blue gaze. "I'm here."

He narrowed his eyes, assessing her. "Yes, you are now. Better."

He dropped his hand, stood back, and she thought he would tell her to strip, as he had the last time. Her heart was a hammer in her chest, a flurry of anticipation and nerves and the effort to keep her mind blank, to resist dissecting what was happening.

Silently, he stepped toward her, and began to undress her. Slowly, gently, while she shivered under his touch. Her mind was emptying out now; there was nothing she could do about it. She couldn't remember what she'd been trying so hard to figure out only moments earlier.

He ran his hands over her arm as he slipped her blouse from her shoulders. "Such gorgeous skin. I love the paleness of it. You have a few freckles here . . . like some small, sweet surprise."

His fingertips skimmed across her shoulder, and pleasure arced through her like an electric current, humming in her veins.

He was only touching her shoulder!

He dropped his hand to help her step out of her high black pumps, then unzipped her slacks, slid them down over her hips. She was left in nothing but her lacy white underwear and bra.

She was left with nothing but the power of her desire.

"Ah, I love this, that you'd wear such innocent things to see me. So pretty, the lace against your skin. But these will have to come off tonight, too."

She'd expected it. But she still felt shocked, somehow. Paralyzed.

"Come on, Dylan. I've felt every part of your body already. And it's an amazing body. You can't possibly be shy about me seeing it."

"I'm not."

"Then what's this lovely blush about? Not that I mind it. But I'm curious to know."

"I . . . I just feel a bit . . . breathless. As though I don't know what to expect, even though I do, to some extent."

"You have to let that go. The expectations. That's part of letting go of the control."

"Yes, I understand that. But I don't know how to do it."

"Maybe you need some distraction."

He smiled at her, a brilliant flash of strong, white teeth. He had no idea what he did to her when he smiled at her. Or maybe he did.

But he was touching her again and she couldn't think straight. His hands were running over her arms, then her hips. He slipped them around behind her and cupped her ass, lightly at first, then pulling her in close. She could feel the solid ridge of his erection against her stomach through the dense denim of his jeans.

Nice.

His breath was hot in her hair, right next to her ear, as he whispered, "Just do it, Dylan. Let it go. Give yourself over to me. I will take care of you. I promise."

She knew he would. And something about the rough, low tone of his voice, his hands on her body, made her go loose all over, her limbs melting in the heat, the pure aching need.

She held perfectly still as his hands came up behind her and unhooked her bra. She felt the soft cotton of his T-shirt as the bra dropped to the floor and he crushed her against his chest. Her nipples hardened immediately.

She moaned softly.

"Ah, that's it. Good girl."

She trembled as he said the words that always got to her. Like some sort of aphrodisiac. And when he pushed her lace panties down over her hips, the trembling turned into a hard shiver.

"Come on, step out of them. Yes, that's it."

She did as he asked, kicking the scrap of white lace aside. He still held her so close, his hands on her back, she could feel every inch of his body, and it was all hard-packed muscle.

Something strange about being entirely naked with him still clothed. It made her feel vulnerable. It made her go quiet inside, her head spinning.

His hand slid up to cup the back of her neck, and that one small motion put her right over the edge. Her mind blanked of all thought, except for the one word she wanted to say to him, over and over.

Yes.

"I can feel it, you know," he murmured to her. "I can feel you giving yourself over. It's as though your body is lighter, isn't it? Your mind quiet. This is exactly how I want you, Dylan, in this space. And you went into it so easily this time. It's going to be very good tonight."

He stood with her, stroking her hair with one hand while the other tightened on the back of her neck until his grasp was almost uncomfortable. But she was sinking further into that quiet place, where everything was a strange silence and calm mixed with this exquisite desire. She was shivering all over with it.

"Please, Alec," she whispered.

"Please what?"

"Please touch me."

A small chuckle from him. "Oh, I will."

He wrapped his hand in her hair then, coiling it around his fist, and pulled her head back. She didn't try to fight it, even though it hurt a little. Just enough to let her know she was truly in his hands. Even though a part of her was panicking a bit.

Some tiny voice in the back of her head was telling her to stop this, to run. But the pleasure, the need to please him, overrode it.

Time to give up control.

As he bent to kiss her neck, she let her head fall back, into his hands. Her sex was heating up, going warm and wet. And as though he knew exactly what she needed, he slid his hand between her thighs.

"Spread for me, Dylan."

She parted her thighs, and his fingers slipped into the damp folds.

"Oh . . . "

"You're ready, my girl."

He removed his hand and disappointment surged through her. But she didn't say a word as he led her to the foot of his bed. He placed her on the edge and she sat, waiting, watching as he pulled his shirt over his head. Her sex clenched at the sight of the rippling muscles in his stomach, his chest, his arms. His flat nipples were dark against his skin. She wanted to touch them, to put her mouth there. But her hands remained quiet at her sides.

"You're very good," he told her, standing back to look at her with an appraising gaze. "You sit there, waiting for me, without even being told. Perfect. Like a doll. You're a natural, Dylan. I knew you would be."

She could barely take in what he was saying. She didn't want to think about what was happening to her. She simply wanted to *do* it.

He knelt on the floor in front of her and parted her thighs, settling his body in between them. She could feel the hard scratch of his jeans against her calf.

"Lean back a bit, but hold yourself up on your elbows."

She did as he demanded.

"Good. Stay just like that. I want you to watch me. Don't close your eyes, is that understood?"

"Yes."

Desire was molten heat in her body, seeping like liquid through her limbs, her veins. And when he used both hands to spread the lips of her sex apart, she went soaking wet.

"Spread wider for me, yes, that's it."

He pushed her legs apart, until she was wide open to him. She felt wanton. Beautiful.

"This is my favorite part of a woman's body," he told her quietly, using his fingers to massage the swollen folds. "Some say it looks like a flower, an orchid. I agree. Just as sweet. Just as precious. And so damn soft."

As she watched, he lifted one hand, pressed two fingers between his lips and sucked.

She moaned. She could barely hold still.

"Ah, you like that?"

"Yes," she whispered, barely able to speak.

He smiled, used those same fingers to push between the lips of her sex. He rubbed at her opening, and she thought she would lose her mind if he didn't thrust into her soon. Pleasure was a hard ache in her sex, her clitoris burning with need.

"Please, Alec . . . "

"Do you need to come already, my girl?"

"Yes!"

He pushed his fingers in, and she arched against him. With his thumb, he pressed against her clitoris.

"Oh!"

He began to move his hand, his fingers and thumb, in small circles. Pleasure rose, burned through her.

"Are you going to come?"

"Yes, yes . . . "

"Hold it back."

"No . . . "

"Yes. Hold on, Dylan."

She bit her lip, trying to bear down against the tide of pleasure threatening to take her under. And as she did, his other hand went under her buttock and pinched, hard.

"Oh . . . "

"Is that good?"

"It . . . it hurts."

"But is it good?" he demanded.

"Yes. It's good. Ah . . . "

He pinched again, harder this time, and the pain bit into her system, mixing with the pleasure.

"Alec. I'm going to come. Please . . . "

"Not yet. Does the pain make it better?"

"It makes it . . . better. Yes. Need to come now!"

"Hold it back. Do it. Tell me you will."

"I . . . God . . . "

Another hard pinch, this one punishing, going beyond the level at which the pain converted to pleasure.

"I'll do it," she gasped. "I'll hold it back."

Her body was writhing. She didn't care. His hands kept working her, his fingers inside her, his thumb rubbing, pressing, on her hard clit. And his other hand pinching her buttock, her thigh. It hurt. It felt indescribably good. She was lost in sensation.

"You are so good, Dylan. So damn beautiful. I want to see you come now. For me."

He thrust his fingers hard inside her, his thumb circling her clit. And at the same time he pinched the flesh on the inside of her thigh, just enough for the pain to drive her climax on.

She came, a thousand stars firing inside her head, hurtling her into space. She gasped for breath, a cry gathering in her throat.

"Oh . . . God, Alec!"

Her hips arched into his hand, pleasure still racing through her, dazzling her.

She fell back on the bed, blinded. Shivering. And he went with her, climbing onto the bed and pulling her into his lap. He turned her over, and even as the last waves of her climax shuddered through her body, he began to spank her.

His hand was like fire on her skin, smacking her over and over. But the pleasure was there, too, and she found herself rising up to meet him. She could hear the echo of flesh upon flesh from some distant place. She could hear the sound of his rasping breath. And it was as though that was all that existed, that and the hard ridge of his erect cock through his jeans pressing into her belly. The male scent of him.

He spanked her harder, faster. His other arm came around her waist, holding her firmly. Keeping her safe. The pain was pleasure itself; there was no longer any dividing line. She almost felt she could come again, just from this.

"Good girl. You can really take it."

She didn't know why it made her so happy to hear him say these things. She couldn't really think at all. She was out of her head.

She wanted him to fuck her. *Needed* him to.

She heard something else as desire rose, cresting, and realized it was her own ragged groans echoing in her ears. But she couldn't stop. She didn't want to.

"Dylan, you're going to come again."

"Oh . . . "

"For me."

"Yes. For you . . . "

He let go of her waist and slid his hand down her stomach and between her thighs, going right to work on her clit. She was sore from before, acutely sensitive, but he worked her hard, continuing to spank her. For several moments the pain was overwhelming, then the pleasure seeped into her body, her sex lighting up with need. And the pain was nothing but a higher level of sensation, driving her on. Every hard smack on her ass pressed her body into his hand, his clever fingers on her clitoris. And it was mere moments before she was coming again. Hard, clenching spasms of pleasure, surge after surge after surge.

Impossible. Powerful. Heat and need and *him*. She was crying out, drowning in pleasure.

"Alec!"

The force of it left her shaking. He pulled her upright so that she was sitting in his lap, holding her tight. And she let her head rest on his shoulder, felt the strength of his arms around her.

Inside, she was all lovely, lambent warmth: in her belly, her limbs, her head.

Her heart.

If she let herself think about it for even a moment, she would tell herself this could not be happening. She shut that voice out. She didn't want to hear it right now. Didn't want to think.

There would be plenty of time for that later. To look at this situation, take it apart, put it back together in a way that made sense. For now, none of that mattered. All that mattered was that she was here, with Alec.

Alec watched her as she caught her breath. Her cheeks were flushed a lovely shade of pink, like the delicate skin on her ass after he spanked her. A perfect ass, the curve of it sweet, cradled in his lap. Against his aching cock.

He reached between her thighs once more, felt her shiver as he slipped his fingers through the slick wetness there. She was soaked. Ready. And he couldn't hold back another moment.

He moved her, laid her back on the pillows long enough to grab a condom from the nightstand next to the bed and tear off his jeans. The air was cool against his naked skin, like a caress on his steel-hard cock.

Christ, he was going to explode, simply looking at her glazed gray eyes, like crystals and smoke. Her lush lips were pink, and as her gaze went to his erection, her tongue darted out to lick her lips.

Fuck.

He almost groaned aloud.

Her breasts were as flawless as the rest of her, her nipples a dark red against the pale flesh. His cock pulsed as he watched her.

"Alec . . . " Her voice was low, breathless.

"Yes?"

"Are you going to fuck me now? Because I need you to."

He smiled, his hand going to his cock and stroking, running the length of the shaft to the tip. "Yes, I'm going to fuck you. Good and hard. And I may spank you while I do it. And you'll come again for me, my girl."

She gave him a lazy smile, her eyes gleaming silver. No, not lazy. She was in subspace, floating. Yet she knew exactly what she wanted.

"Please" was all she said.

Can't wait one more moment.

He grabbed her, his arm snaking around her slim waist, and he pulled her down, placing her in the middle of the bed. He spread her thighs with his knees, looping her legs over his. Her skin was so damn soft he could barely stand it. And with her thighs open, he could see her pussy, that gorgeous pink flesh: wet, glistening, swollen. His cock jerked.

Need her. Now.

He used his other hand to grasp both her wrists, drawing her arms over her head, and she let him do it. There was no fight in her now, and knowing she had given herself over to him was something beyond the usual thrill of the power exchange. Something more, with this woman. But he couldn't think now. No, now he just needed to bury himself inside her. With one thrust of his hips, he did.

She gasped. He groaned. Pleasure was hot, pulsing in his cock. Inside, she was a sheath of heat and slick, clenching pleasure.

"Christ, Dylan. You're so damn tight. So damn wet. Just have to fuck you . . . "

"Yes . . . "

He began to move, his hips grinding. Her gaze was on his, locked there, her eyes half-lidded, her breath a panting sigh. The flush was on her once more, her nipples going darker, harder, and he leaned down and took one between his lips.

"Oh!"

He drew it deeper into his mouth, that sweet nub of flesh, and bit down.

"God, Alec!"

He drew back. "Does it hurt?"

"Yes," she hissed.

"And is it good?"

"Oh, yes."

He bent his head and sucked the other nipple into his mouth, used his teeth to grate against the flesh, then bit again.

"Ah . . . Alec."

Her hips bucked into his, her arms pushing against the tight grasp of his hand. But she wasn't really struggling against him. She was writhing in pleasure. The same pleasure roaring through his system as he drove into her. Her pussy grabbed his cock, a sleek glove, going tighter and tighter, and he knew she would come again soon.

He pulled back to look at her; he had to see her. Her brows were drawn together, her mouth loose with pleasure. Too fucking beautiful, this girl. He was shivering with pleasure himself, all over: his cock, his balls, his belly, arms and legs.

He let go of her waist and raised his hand to her mouth, touching her full lips with his fingertips.

"Suck," he commanded. She did it, sucking greedily, as though it were his cock he'd offered her.

He moaned, pulled his fingers from her lips with some effort, then slipped his hand under her ass, between her smooth cheeks. And keeping his gaze on hers, he pressed against that tight little hole with one fingertip. Her pupils widened, but she didn't protest. And when he slid the tip in, she sighed, and he felt her sex grab tighter around his aching cock.

He had to pause there, pleasure a thundering pulse-beat in his system.

Calm down.

He pulled in a breath, not wanting to come just yet.

Her ass was tight and hot, and he pushed a little deeper, past that first tight ring of muscle.

"Dylan, do you like this?"

She moaned.

"Say it," he demanded.

"Yes. I like it. I love it. I need more."

He pushed deeper, and she groaned, her hips pumping.

"More, Dylan?"

"Yes. Please."

"Take a deep breath."

He added a second finger a little at a time. She was breathing her way through it, her body relaxing around him. But he was so damn hard, barely hanging on to any control.

"Can you take it if I fuck your ass like this, with my hand?"

"Yes. I want it."

He pushed his fingers in, pulled out, pushed in again. She shivered beneath him. And he felt through the thin membrane the added texture of his own fingers against his cock, buried deep inside her.

Too much, too much.

"Ah, Christ, Dylan."

He released her arms, and they wrapped around him as he began to fuck her, a hard, driving rhythm, his fingers keeping pace in her ass. And she was pumping against him, fucking him as he was fucking her. Both of them gasping, panting.

Her body tensed, her sex spasming, tightening on his hard shaft. And she called out his name as she came, over and over.

"Alec! God, Alec . . . Alec . . . "

He held off, held back, wanting to just fuck her as long as he could. It was too good to stop. He thrust into her, his fingers still working her ass. She was trembling, her pussy still that hot, velvet fist. The heat and the wet were incredible. Pleasure was a hammer coming down on him, blinding him as he came, finally. And still he pounded into her.

"Just have to fuck you, girl. Just . . . ah . . . fucking you . . . yes . . . "

His head was spinning. They were all flesh and sweat and the scent of sex everywhere as he collapsed on top of her, his fingers slipping from her ass.

He was achingly aware of her body beneath him. Her breasts were soft, pressed against his chest, her stomach a smooth, concave surface against his. Skin like fucking porcelain; that was the only way he could think about it. But hot, alive. And her hair . . . wild red curls everywhere. He buried a hand in those silky spirals, pulled in the scent of it, of her.

His heartbeat was as wild in his chest as her hair was, laid out as it was on the pillows. But it was more than the hammering pulse of expended effort.

What the hell was going on with him?

He shifted off her, rolling onto his side.

"I still owe you a spanking," he told her.

A small laugh from her, then she turned over onto her stomach.

"I'll take it now," she said, her voice soft, her words coming out slowly, like they'd been coated in honey.

"Ah, getting smart with me, Dylan?"

"Just willing. Isn't that what you want from me? Demand from me?"

"Yes. Absolutely."

But was that entirely true? He wanted . . . more than that.

Fuck. Don't think about it.

He reached over and gave her ass a good, hard smack, smiled when she jumped.

Yes, that was more like it. In command. In control. It was his job to elicit a response from her. To be the one running the show.

He lifted his hand again, but paused.

He wasn't going to spank her to prove a point, damn it. He was too good at what he did for that. That was bullshit. And all about him, his own head trip.

Irresponsible.

Unforgivable.

Out of control, damn it.

He lowered his hand and said to her, "We'll leave that spanking for a while."

She remained quiet, on her stomach still. And looking at the smooth curves of her body, he didn't have the heart to make her move. Instead, he laid his hand over her ass, her cheeks small and warm beneath his palm. And thought, *Mine.*

Dangerous thought. He may be a dominant, and part of that was a sense of ownership, for those in a real relationship. But that was not what this arrangement was about. That was not what he did. Ever. And this time, this woman, was no different, God damn it.

He didn't want to think about why he had to mentally yell at himself to get his thoughts back in line.

He'd catch his breath, recover from the power of his orgasm, and think about it later. Or maybe he'd fuck her again and not think about it at all.

But he'd been thinking of nothing but Dylan Ivory since the moment he'd met her. He had no reason to think that was going to change any time soon.

Damn it.

nine

Dylan sat on her sofa, a soft blanket over her lap, listening to the fall of rain outside and sipping a cup of her favorite jasmine and green tea. She was tired, aching all over. She felt as though she'd been in a trance since the night before, ever since she'd arrived at Alec's house.

Simply going there at his instruction had been a mind-fuck. One she'd sunk into all too easily, especially once they'd gotten started. And what had happened between them after . . . That was nothing short of incredible. The sex. The sense of connection, which had made the sex different, somehow. Better. More intense. But this morning she was all doubt and nerves and her pulse was hammering with anxiety.

Had she really let herself do these things? Had she given up all control to a man? To make her lose her sense of control, of *self*. She still couldn't wrap her head around the idea.

He'd been right about her submissive side. There was no arguing that. But why was she so angry with *him* this morning about it? It wasn't his fault. Or was it?

She didn't want to be angry. She didn't want to feel scared. Right now, all she wanted was to sit where she was, sleepy and sore, comforted by her blanket and her tea and the sound of the rain. She wanted to revel in last night's experience. Because it had been good. Beyond good. Why did she have to screw it up with her endless questions today?

When her cell phone rang she thought about letting it go to voice mail. But then it occurred to her that it might be Alec. She grabbed the phone off the coffee table.

"Hello?"

"Hey, Dylan, it's Mischa."

"Oh. Hi."

"Well, I'm thrilled to talk to you, too."

"I'm sorry, Mischa. I thought you might be Alec."

"Ah."

"What do you mean, 'Ah'?"

"I mean, obviously something is going on, and why haven't you called to tell me?"

"I . . . " She bit her lip. "I don't know."

"I had a feeling we needed to talk."

"You and your 'feelings,' Mischa."

"You're avoiding the subject."

"Yes."

"Why?"

Dylan sipped her tea, inhaled the fragrant steam, letting it soothe her. "I just feel . . . like this is different for me. I don't even know how to talk about it yet."

"Why don't you tell me what's happened since I talked to you last week," Mischa prompted.

"Alec and I have talked. And I've seen him. He took me out to dinner, which seems . . . a bit bizarre under the circumstances. He's not what I expected when Jennifer told me about him, not at all. I thought he'd be some surly, snarling, silent type, and he's not. Now it seems ridiculous that I made that kind of assumption. But he's not even what I expected after the first time I met him. I had this impression of him initially . . . maybe it was that I wasn't comfortable with my own response to him, so I made up this story in my head about the kind of person he was. But the first time we met I knew he was smart. And not just book smart, but world smart. Savvy. And he's probably the most confident human being I've ever met. I thought he was cocky at first, and I focused a lot on that, but that's not it, because he has reason to be so utterly confident."

She paused, sipped her tea.

"There's a hardness about him that appeals to me, but every now and then I see a softness in him. And he's not afraid of that, either. To let it out. When he told me about losing his father . . . I could see how that had hurt him, how he still felt it. And usually men who are so . . . alpha, for want of a better term, are all about being macho hard-asses, but that's not him at all. He's more sophisticated about it. And he's not narcissistic at all, the way the more macho guys tend to be. Because that's usually a sign of insecurity, and believe me, this man has nothing to be insecure about."

She saw his face, his lush mouth, the startling blue of his eyes. Remembered the touch of his hand on her skin.

"Hello, Dylan."

"What?"

"You just spaced out on me."

"God, I'm sorry. I didn't get much sleep last night." She pushed a hand through her hair, sweeping her curls from her face.

"What happened last night?"

"I slept with him. But first I should tell you that he took me to the dungeon the other night—"

"What? Dylan, you've been holding out on me."

"I know, I know . . . "

Mischa's voice was suddenly sharp. "Are you okay?"

"Yes, I'm fine. I mean, physically I'm fine. It's been . . . amazing, when I let it be. My head is a little twisted up."

"No kidding."

Dylan sighed. "I can't seem to figure it all out. I feel like this process is tapping into something inside me. Opening me up. *He's* opening me up. And it's scary as hell, but I *have* to do it. But sometimes I just want to run, get the hell away from him. The way he makes me feel . . . weak."

"Yet you keep seeing him."

"Yes."

"Do you think there's something more going on than an infatuation with him? Something more than the excitement of him introducing you to something new? Something more than the sex?"

"Maybe."

"Wow."

"Yeah, wow. And the sex was incredible." There was a long pause on the other end of the phone. "Mischa? You're never this quiet. What are you thinking?"

"I'm . . . I'm thinking this is all pretty mind-blowing. Because it's *you* we're talking about, Dylan, and this girly stuff just does not happen to you. I'm surprised at how calm you sound about it. How accepting."

"Oh, I'm far from calm. I'm completely freaked out. But this morning I'm still sort of caught up in it. I'm still a bit dazed by it all."

"So, when will you see him again? How did you leave things?"

"We woke up late this morning and he had a conference call with his agent, so he put me in a cab. He said he'd contact me this week."

"Did he give you breakfast first?"

"Just coffee."

"Ah."

"Mischa, that's all I wanted. And he had to work. And *I* have to work. I have deadlines, which I've been ignoring too much lately. It was fine."

"Okay. If you say so. But I don't care how alpha he is, if he hurts you I am coming up there to kick his macho ass."

Dylan smiled. "Okay. That's a deal. But I won't let that happen. And I feel totally selfish for monopolizing the conversation. Tell me what's up with you."

"The usual. The tattoo shop is busy; I'm still booking four and five months in advance since I cut down to four days a week to keep up with my writing. I just turned in a novella a few days ago and will start another book, my first full-length novel, next weekend. I'm dating a few guys, but nothing serious. Certainly nothing as serious as you."

"This isn't serious. Not like that. And I don't expect it to be. Neither of us is interested in that."

But as Dylan hung up the phone, a small thought flashed through her head, a sliver of doubt that had her stomach clenching. Because she was no longer entirely sure that was true.

Alec found a seat at the bar, sat down and ordered a beer. He had no desire to get drunk but he definitely needed to take the edge off. The bartender put his glass in front of him and Alec took a long gulp, the rich, dark beer cooling him down.

It was still raining outside, had been all day. But he was as fired up as if he was in the middle of a desert. Heated through. He'd woken up that way and was annoyed as hell that he couldn't seem to get a handle on it. Which is why he'd lied to Dylan this morning and told her he'd had a meeting with his agent. Total bullshit. He'd simply had to be alone. To think it through.

He'd come up empty. Which was why he'd called Dante and asked him to meet him at their favorite bar tonight.

Alec glanced up and saw Dante walking through the door. His friend was tall and lanky, dark-haired and dark-eyed, and the women in the bar all turned to look him over. Half-Italian and half-Spanish, his looks usually got him any woman he wanted. But they were both more likely to hook up with women they met at the fetish clubs. Even though Dante wasn't as hardcore a player as Alec was, it was too difficult for either of them to relate to a woman who wasn't interested in kink on some level. And neither of them was the type to try to draft a "vanilla" woman into the lifestyle. Which didn't explain how he'd gotten wrapped up with Dylan Ivory.

Fuck.

He threw back most of his beer before Dante reached the bar.

"Hey, Alec."

"Hey."

Dante slid onto the stool next to him and Alec ordered a beer for him and another for himself.

"So what's on fire, Alec?"

"What do you mean?"

"It's not like you to ask for an impromptu date. Should I be flattered?" Dante joked, grinning at him.

"Yeah, about that . . . sorry to drag you out on a work night."

"No problem. I don't have to be in court tomorrow. What's up?"

Alec sat and sipped his beer, brooding. What the hell *was* up with him? "Maybe I need your help to figure it out."

Dante nodded, sipped his own beer, his eyes narrowing. "But something is up."

"Yeah."

"It's that woman you've been seeing, Dylan."

It wasn't a question. Like him, Dante was a practiced dominant, someone who took the time to read people. Alec wasn't surprised that he knew right away what the issue was.

"Yeah."

"Did you take her to the Pleasure Dome?"

Alec blew out a long breath. "Yeah, I did."

"How did it go?"

"It went great. She's every bit as submissive as I suspected. Goes down easy. Almost too easy. I expected a lot more fight from her." He rubbed a hand over his goatee. "She doesn't open up easily. In fact, there's something big she's keeping from me. That's okay; I can work around it."

"I'm sure you can. So what's the problem?"

"The problem is me."

He paused, drank some more of the beer down. Dante stayed quiet, giving him time to work it out in his head. One of the reasons they were friends was that sort of easy respect for each other, that immediate understanding.

Alec set his glass down on the bar a little too hard. "Okay. Okay. This is it. I like this woman. I like her a lot. And that is totally fucking with me."

"You like every woman you play, Alec. You keep it friendly, just like I do. Why would that mess with you?"

"Good question."

Dante was watching him, and Alec knew he was looking for more answers. Hell, so was he.

Dante leaned his elbows on the bar. "Come on, Alec. Let's get down to the root of this. You like this woman, you've played her, like you have dozens of others. What's different?"

"Everything." He blew out a long breath, kept his gaze on his beer, his fingers tapping the damp glass. "Every single thing. It's not just her body, which is fucking flawless. Or the sex, which is incredible. Or the way she submits to me, even. It's the whole package. It goes beyond the physical. I can't believe I'm saying that. But it's true.

"I feel like I'm losing it with this woman. I think about her too damned much. I want her with me all the time. And when she is, it's this ridiculous struggle to hang on to any sense of control, and then I need her to be gone so I can get myself back together. I don't like it. I'm pretty disgusted with myself. I feel like a god-damned teenager, if you want to know the truth."

When he looked up Dante was grinning at him.

"What?" He was annoyed now. He'd just poured his guts out, damn it.

"You really like this woman."

"I already said that."

"Yes, but it's more than that, isn't it?"

"Fuck," Alec muttered. "I just want to keep things status quo. I want to play her, then send her home and do my usual thing. Work. Whatever. I haven't been able to write the last few days. And this morning I sent her home after a night of play and I have no idea if she was ready to be on her own yet. She was a little glazed still, to be honest, and it was damn irresponsible of me to put her in a cab."

"Do you think she's okay?"

"Yes. She's probably fine. I told her to call me if she felt shaky. She's pretty self-reliant, though, and I don't know if she'd call even if she needed to. So that's really not good enough, is it?"

"Alec, you can stop kicking yourself. How often do you keep a woman with you all day, no matter how hard you play her? You always send them home eventually. So do I. Have you talked to her today? Checked in?"

"No. I told her I would."

Dante glanced at his watch, then back at Alec and shrugged.

"Yeah, I know. I'll call her. I am not the jerk dom. We don't operate like that, people like you and me, who play at this level. I've given lectures on how to be a responsible top, for God's sake. How *not* to be a jerk."

He was acting like a jerk with Dylan. He just had to figure out why. And meanwhile, he had to stop behaving this way. Being less than completely responsible for a woman he played.

"Are you going to keep seeing her?" Dante asked.

"Yes."

"All right. I know you'll do what you need to. What's right."

"I always do. I just need to . . . get this under control. Maybe I need to take a break from her."

"Maybe. Or maybe you need to keep seeing her until you figure things out. I can't decide that for you."

"I know. Thanks for coming, Dante."

"Anytime." Dante threw back the rest of his beer, set the empty glass on the bar. "You all right?"

"I'm fine. I'll be fine."

Dante clapped him on the back as he stood. "Give me a call, let me know how it goes."

"I will."

He finished his beer before heading outside, pulling the collar of his leather jacket up around his neck against the rain. He took in a deep lungful of the night air, the scents of damp pavement and exhaust from the traffic going by, and behind it, the salt scent of the ocean a few blocks away.

He meant to go to his car, to pull out his cell phone and call her. But he found himself walking. His hair was getting wet, the rain dripping into his collar, but he didn't care. Block after block, the buildings and the people going by in a blur. He didn't know what he was doing, exactly. He just needed to shut down his brain, to walk off the tension and the uncertainty and the anger at himself.

When he made his way back to his car it was after ten and he was soaked through, the legs of his jeans sopping wet. It would play hell on his leather seats, but he slid into the car anyway, starting the engine and slipping his jacket off.

He drove north, then west, heading toward the Space Needle, telling himself he wasn't going there because Dylan lived in Belltown, in the shadow of the Needle.

He passed by the old brick building where she had her loft and slowed to look up at the fourth floor. The lights were on, but he couldn't see anything else through the tall windows. What the hell had he wanted to see, anyway?

Her.

Fuck.

He hit the gas and drove on, his pulse hammering in his veins.

Somehow he ended up in front of the Pleasure Dome.

He parked, went inside. It was warmer in the club, the lights and the music a dim pulse-beat. Womblike.

He didn't bother to check his wet coat, just took it off and went immediately into the big main room, carrying it. There weren't a lot of people there; the beginning of the week was always quiet. He didn't mind. All he needed was to be there. To . . . what?

He walked across the half-dark room, nodding a greeting to several familiar faces, and headed for an empty couch across the room where he could sit and watch the action.

A dom he was acquainted with was setting up one of the large bondage frames, looping white rope through the eyebolts set into the wood. Alec rarely used white rope himself. He preferred the aesthetics of black or red. And bondage wasn't his biggest kink, anyway. He liked using sensation play. But he'd do whatever pulled the most response from a bottom. It was all about their needs, anyway, wasn't it?

Dylan's face, that lovely, delicate bone structure, those enormous, clear gray eyes, popped into his head, but he quickly shut it down.

Don't think about her.

He needed distraction. Wasn't that why he'd come here tonight? And he'd brought his toy bag in with him. If he didn't intend to play, why would he have bothered?

He got up and wandered upstairs, to the part of the club that held a dance floor. It was a raised platform with flashing lights and three stripper poles. And just as he'd expected, there were two women dancing on the poles, a tall blonde he'd seen at the club before, and a petite woman with golden skin and a long cascade of black hair. They were both dressed in the skintight outfits and soaring stiletto-heeled shoes that were common dress for the women at the club.

He glanced around to see if they were dancing for the entertainment of a particular dom, but he was the only man in the room paying attention; they were free.

He took a chair at the edge of the dance floor and settled in, keeping his gaze on the two girls. It didn't take them long to notice. He smiled, nodded his chin at them, giving them permission to approach him.

The blonde went down on her knees immediately; it took the brunette a moment longer. And a few minutes later he'd negotiated with them for an evening of play in one of the private rooms on the third floor.

He led them up the stairs, their heels clattering on the polished wood stairs, then muted by the carpeted hallway. He found an open curtain and led them through. Inside was a padded table with leather wrist and ankle restraints attached, a pair of chains suspended from the ceiling, a spanking bench.

"Down on your knees," he told them, and they both went down.

He took his time unpacking his toy bag, laying out the floggers on the table; the small, spiked neuro wheel; the vampire glove; the paddle; the cane. And all the time his heart was a dull thud in his chest.

Why did he feel like he could barely breathe?

He turned to look at them. Good submissives, both of them. They knelt on the floor, keeping their heads down, their palms turned upward on their parted thighs. Someone had done some training with them. They'd probably play well. They were gorgeous, especially together, the contrast of their coloring . . .

But he could not do it.

His hands tightened into fists.

What the hell was wrong with him?

He sighed, ran a hand through his damp hair.

This was fucking ridiculous.

He stood over the two of them, watching them breathe, felt the tension in the air, their anticipation, waited for the old thrill to kick in. But it never came. And the longer he stood there, the more anxious he felt. He had to stop this. Had to leave.

Go home.

No, go find her.

Dylan.

Fuck.

"I'm sorry." It came out in a gruff rumble.

"Sir?" It was the blonde, whispering as though she didn't dare disturb him.

"I'm sorry," he said more gently. "I find myself unable to . . . I'm not going to play tonight after all."

"Did we displease you, sir?"

"No, not at all. Go back downstairs. Some other lucky man will be happy to find you tonight."

They both rose to their feet, and the brunette flashed him a look of disappointment over her shoulder as they filed out through the curtained doorway. But he couldn't think about them now.

He packed up his equipment as quickly as he could, not as mindful as he should be of laying out the flogger tails evenly in the bottom of his black leather bag, avoiding damage. He simply needed to *go*.

He avoided all eye contact as he moved through the club and onto the streets once more. The rain had stopped, finally, but the sky was still dense with clouds, hiding the moon.

He wished he could hide away. But he had to face this. Had to face Dylan. Had to do something to get her out of his system, maybe.

He got in his car and wove his way through the dark streets, back to the old brick warehouse in Belltown. He cursed when he couldn't find parking right away, but finally someone pulled out half a block from her place and he took the spot. He turned the engine off. And sat there.

He didn't even know how late it was. Maybe he should call her first.

When was the last time he'd questioned his actions like this?

He swore under his breath as he got out, slamming the car door behind him, and stalked back down the street to her building. There was a locked gate, of course. He scanned the names on the call box next to it, found her number and hit the buzzer. Silence. He buzzed again. Ran a hand over his beard as he waited. He stepped back from the gate, into the street, looked up, and saw a light go on in her loft.

"Yes?" he heard from the intercom.

He bolted back to the gate.

"Dylan."

"Who's there?"

"It's Alec."

There was a long pause. Then, "It's almost midnight."

"I know. I'd like to come up."

He sounded a hell of a lot calmer than he felt. Actually, he felt like a damn stalker.

"I'm buzzing you in."

He grabbed the gate and let it clang shut behind him, got in the elevator and took it to the fourth floor. It seemed to take forever before the door swung open and he stepped into the wide hallway outside her apartment.

Her door opened and there she was, her red curls mussed, her face a little pale. But her full mouth was as lush and red as ever. She was dressed in a short, white nightgown made of old-fashioned white eyelet. Almost absurd how innocent it was on her, the shadows of her dark nipples showing through the thin fabric.

Pornographic. The nightgown and her bare feet, which looked oddly naked to him, the toenails painted a sweet baby pink.

"You were asleep," he said, only partially contrite. He'd *needed* to see her.

"I . . . yes. It's okay. Do you want to come in?"

She took a step back, and he moved forward. He had a vague impression of her apartment, lit by a single lamp somewhere, casting shadows on the smooth expanse of wood floors. The light shone through her nightgown, illuminating her slender body. He could just make out the shadow at the juncture of her thighs.

He hadn't meant to do it, exactly, but he was on her in a moment, his arms crushing her to him, his mouth coming down on hers. Her lips were so sweet, plush. And her breasts crushed up against him; the perfume of her hair was nearly unbearable.

She opened her lips to his, and his tongue slipped into her mouth. His hands moved down to her ass, cupping it, and she sighed when he pinched the flesh there through the fabric.

He was rock hard, but it was more than that. He felt a sense of desperation that he didn't want to question. He was all driving need. And she was responding, sighing into his mouth, her hips arcing into his thigh. And he swore he could feel the heat of her little mound through the denim of his jeans.

He pushed her back, into the apartment, until he found the sofa. He pushed her down on it, turning her around so that she was on her hands and knees on the cushions, pushed her pretty white nightgown up around her waist.

She was naked underneath.

He groaned at the sight of her taut ass, the lips of her sex peeking out from between her thighs, pink and beautiful.

He tore his jacket off. His shirt came next. Then he grabbed the fine flesh of her ass with both hands, his fingers biting, leaving marks. He wanted that—to mark her. *Needed* it.

Mine.

He pulled his hand away, paused, and she surged back, offering the sweet curve of her bottom to him. He let his palm come down hard, the sound echoing in the still air. He smacked her again, and her body moved with the force of it. Her skin was pinking, welting.

Too fast. Moving too fast.

He ran a hand through his hair, watching her. She was panting. So was he.

"Dylan."

"Alec?"

"Tell me."

"Tell you what?"

He went down on his knees next to the sofa, put a hand on the back of her neck, under her hair. Her skin was hot, burning up. He was hard as steel. He let his fingers go into her hair, tightening in the long curls until he was grasping the back of her scalp. He pulled her head up until her gaze met his.

"Do you want this? For me to be here. For me to touch you. Spank you. Fuck you."

"Yes. Yes . . . "

Her voice was a whisper, but that was all he needed. He let go the control, simply let it all go. He fell on her—that was the only way to think about it—planting his mouth on her throat, licking the tender flesh there. His hands went to her breasts, kneading, pinching her nipples through the fine fabric. And she was moaning softly, her nipples going hard.

He let her go long enough to kick off his shoes, his jeans. She stayed perfectly still while he did it, on her hands and knees, her nightgown in a bunch around her slender waist.

He could not wait.

He turned her over, pressing her down onto her back.

"Damn it. Condom."

He let her go so he could pull one from his pocket, and rolling it over his aching cock was pure torture. She watched him, her eyes gleaming silver in the light of the one lamp burning in the room. She was so damn beautiful it almost hurt to look at her.

He bent over her, drawing in a breath as she lifted her nightgown, revealing her breasts.

Perfect.

She was perfect.

Her legs opened for him, and he looked at her, her long, beautiful body, the slippery pink slit between her thighs. His cock throbbed.

Then he lowered his body over hers, and there was nothing in the power play but the force of his need, overwhelming hers. Overwhelming him. And when he slid into her, pleasure was an electric arc, burning him, shocking him.

He thrust into her, and she met his hips with hers. When she went to lace her arms around his neck, he took her wrists and held them over her head. He couldn't stand for her to hold him. He couldn't think about why. Now all he wanted was her body, the slick heat of her sex, burning him up. The sweet crush of her breasts against his bare chest. The scent of her skin. And he wanted her to come—wanted to make her come, over and over.

Make her.

Yes, that was it, what he needed.

Don't think. Just do it.

He pulled out of her then, still holding her arms over her head with one hand as he thrust the other between her thighs. He worked her clitoris mercilessly with his fingers, felt it swell beneath his touch.

He knew he was being rough with her. He knew she loved it as she writhed and panted beneath him. And as he pinched her clit, tugged on it, she came, her body arching up off the sofa.

"Ah, God, Alec . . . "

She shivered with her climax, her thighs tensing. And he kept working her, his cock still a hard, throbbing pulse between his thighs.

"Okay," she muttered, her eyes closed. "Okay."

"Again."

"I . . . just give me a minute."

"No."

He kept at her, his fingers pressing into her. She was burning hot, soaking wet. He pumped, angled his fingers, searching for her G-spot. He crooked his fingers until he felt that soft, spongy flesh, heard her whimper. And he pressed his thumb onto her clit at the same time.

"Alec . . . I'm . . . I'm going to come again."

"Yes. Do it, Dylan."

She started to shudder, inside and out, her breasts beautifully flushed. Her eyes were screwed tightly shut, and she bit into her lip as she came once more, her arms pulling against his tight grasp.

"Oh!"

His cock was a solid ridge of need, hard and aching. But he couldn't stop now.

"Again, Dylan."

"God, Alec," she panted, her eyes fluttering open.

Two dark crystals in her lovely face; they glowed in the light of the lamp, the cloud-dimmed moonlight coming through the window.

"I want you to look at me this time," he told her.

She simply nodded her head.

He began again, his fingers delving into her wet sex. It was streaming with her juices, so damn lush and hot. He could smell her, that sharp, sweet scent of arousal, of female come.

Her clitoris was swollen, and he was certain she was sore.

He could not stop.

Her gaze was on his, and she was biting her lip again. He wanted to taste that plump, red flesh. But not yet.

Pure torture, to watch her like this. To deny himself what he really needed—to bury himself in her body. To kiss her. He just wanted to fucking kiss her.

No.

He pushed his fingers deeper inside her, circled her hard little clit with his thumb.

"Alec . . . it feels so good . . . but I don't think I can do it again . . . "

"You can. You will."

He let go of her wrists and she left her arms where they were, stretched over her head. She was in a state of abandon now, her arms limp.

He loved seeing her like this. Overpowered. Overcome. Under his hands.

He slipped his hand under her, his fingers sliding in her juices. When they were well-lubricated, he moved between her ass cheeks, and pressed a finger into that tight hole, knowing—loving—that this did something to her, put her right into subspace, if she weren't there already. Taking her even deeper now.

"Ah . . . Alec."

He didn't have to ask if it was good. He could see it on her face. Her pupils were enormous, her cheeks flushed, her breath a panting rasp.

"Harder, Alec."

"Yes, that's what I need to hear. That's how I need to give it to you, Dylan."

He pushed his finger into her ass, began to pump, the other hand moving, fucking her pussy, rubbing her clit. And in moments she was coming again, her body clenching all over. She kept her crystal gaze on his, and it was like drowning in her pleasure.

Unbelievable.

Before she was done coming he was on her again, his still-hard cock pressing right into her. And this time when her arms went around him, he didn't try to hold her down. He couldn't even think about it. He just needed to be inside her, needed to *feel* her.

He plunged into her body, latching on to her mouth, finally. Her lips were as sweet as he knew they would be. His tongue went into her mouth, tasting, demanding. And pleasure was like some sweet-edged knife, lancing into him: cock, balls, belly.

He thrust harder, needing it to hurt. Her. Him. Their hip bones were slamming together. But he *needed* it, damn it. Needed to *feel*.

His climax came down on him like a brick wall: that hard, collapsing over him, into him. In his head were a million stars, going off like a solar flare. Fire and energy and a blazing brilliance.

He was shaking. Blinded. Covering her face with kisses.

He didn't know what the hell was happening to him.

All he knew was that there was some terrible, driving need inside him that had never been met before. Never recognized. And here it was, laid out before him. Before her.

For the first time in his life, he was scared.

ten

Dylan finally caught her breath. Alec's weight on her wasn't helping, but she didn't want him to move. She was sore all over. Exhausted. Exhilarated.

What had just happened between them? This was different.
There was power play, no doubt about it. She'd felt taken over by
him. Had sunk into it right away, her head emptying out the moment he'd pushed through the door. His hands on her had been
rough, but she'd loved it.

Don't think about it.

She didn't want to think about what admitting all of that
meant. No, when she thought too much about it, the fear came
back, swallowing the pleasure.

Stop.

Yes, stop thinking and simply be there. With him.

She could smell him all over her. That male scent of ocean and forest, sweat and sex.

He smelled *right*.

God, when had her thoughts taken this utterly girlish turn? It had been happening a little at a time, ever since she'd met him. But it was getting totally out of hand.

She was coming back to earth now. Becoming more aware of her body, the weight of Alec on top of her, the sound of his ragged breath. The texture of his skin beneath her hands. His goatee was a little rough against her cheek, his breath warm on her temple. And as the idea passed through her head that she *never* wanted him to move, it came with a small wave of panic.

She forced herself to hold still to swallow the panic down.

Alec lifted his head, looking at her. His eyes were the most brilliant shade of blue, making her breath catch in her throat. Or maybe that was the anxiety she was trying to hold back.

"Dylan? What is it?"

"What do you mean?"

"Your whole body just went rigid."

"I . . . I'm fine. You're a bit heavy . . . "

"Ah, sorry."

He pulled out of her, and she felt it like a keen loss. That, and the heat of his body as he sat up on his knees. He was still between her thighs, and she wanted to close them, to hold him there, to take him inside her once more.

Never enough.

She swallowed, emotion a hard lump in her throat.

What is wrong with you?

He was staring at her. But his usual piercing gaze was a little clouded over. The aftereffects of his orgasm, she supposed, but she was glad for it. He was too intuitive, and she didn't want to talk right now about what was going on with her. She didn't really understand it herself.

He reached out and stroked a finger over her cheek, her jaw, across her lower lip, smiling at her, and she melted. Just went soft all over, her limbs warm and liquid. She didn't know how to fight it.

She realized she didn't want to.

Why should she?

The idea came as a shock: sudden, but clear. Why not simply explore this, without questioning her every thought, every sensation, every act of intimacy between them? Neither of them was looking to ride off into the sunset together. That should be enough to keep her safe.

Oh yes, Alec was dangerous. He looked dangerous. He smelled dangerous. The way he kissed her was beyond dangerous. Never mind everything else: the sex, the BDSM play. Not that she considered herself a slut, but she'd been around, experimented. She could handle this man. And whatever her time with him would bring.

Her pulse calmed as she caught her breath.

She could do this. As long as he didn't back off from her again. That she wasn't sure she could take.

"Alec?"

"Hmm?"

"I need to ask you something."

"What is it?"

"I didn't expect to see you this soon. Or this late tonight."

"I didn't expect it, either."

He lifted his hand and stroked her hair. And there was a warm surge in her chest, an ache that had nothing to do with the sex. She closed her eyes a moment and allowed herself to feel it.

It doesn't have to mean anything.

But it does.

Don't think.

What did she want to ask him, anyway? Why he'd come over tonight? How he felt about her? That was ridiculous. She didn't need to know. She didn't know how she felt about *him*.

She opened her eyes and propped herself up on her elbows.

"Alec, have you eaten? I can make some tea, and I have some cookies you might like."

He grinned. "And you baked them yourself, I assume?"

She laughed. "I bought them at the gourmet grocery store down the street. Will that do?"

"From what you told me, it'll have to. Is that what you wanted to ask me?"

"Maybe."

He rolled his eyes. "Women."

She was relieved he was letting it go at that. She didn't know what she'd say to him now. She wished she could just turn her brain off. The way she did when Alec was kissing her. Spanking her . . .

He grabbed her hand and helped her to her feet, and standing next to him she was made aware once more of his great height, the breadth of his muscular body. He smelled of sex. She shivered.

"Are you cold? Do you have a robe?"

"In my bathroom."

"Go and get it."

She went to the bathroom, done in soft, soothing shades of gray and sage green, and pulled her pink satin robe from the hook behind the door, pausing to take in her reflection in the large, pewter-framed mirror over the sink.

Her hair was everywhere, the bright auburn curls wild. Her face was pale but her cheeks were flushed a dark pink. Her eyes were enormous. She leaned into the smooth maple cabinet, moving closer to the mirror. Her lips looked as though she'd been kissed as roughly as she had. They were red, swollen. She looked different. She *felt* different. But she would dissect it all later.

Right now, Alec was waiting for her.

She slipped her robe on, tied it around her waist, and went to find him.

He was standing next to the peridot green sofa, his jeans slung low on his hips. He wore nothing else. There was something incredibly sexy about a man in a pair of jeans, shirtless, his feet bare. The tattoos and the evil goatee only made it better. The sophisticated bad boy. And his body was heavily muscled. Gorgeous.

Perfect.

She shook her head at her girlish fantasies, those images that had developed in her mind, probably since childhood, about what a man was. What sexy was. Alec was her ultimate man, she realized: big and muscular, a little bad, but still kind. Educated, well-read, well-traveled, well-mannered. And, of course, kinky. And as comfortably removed from real intimacy as she was. Although that seemed to be changing for both of them . . .

She cleared her throat. "I'll make the tea," she told him, turning toward the kitchen.

He followed, seated himself on a tall stool at the bar that separated the small kitchen from the living area. He dwarfed it, as he
did everything else. He seemed almost too primal, in her stark,
modern kitchen, everything white tile and brushed steel, and
sleek, polished wood. He seemed too much alive in a place that
had seen so little use, that was so utterly *clean*. Alec was so . . .
purely animal. It made her feel oddly self-conscious at the ste-
rility of her kitchen. It made her think longingly of the earthy
comfort of his house, his kitchen.

She was being ridiculous. Maybe still flying on endorphins.
Yes, that must be it. That must explain the looseness in her muscles, the temptation to just relax with him.

She filled the kettle and put it on the stove, pulling tea and
mugs from the maple cabinets to distract herself.

"This is a great apartment," he said finally.

"Do you like it? It's so different from your house."

"Meaning my house is a little messy."

"No, not at all. It's comfortable. Welcoming."

"But it's not the designer showcase this place is. Did you do it
yourself?"

"Yes. It was just an open, empty space when I bought it, so I
got to design it all. The floors, the kitchen and bathroom. Actually, I refinished the floors myself, painted. It took months to get
it all put together. I loved every minute of it."

"You refinished the floors?"

She laughed. "Don't look so shocked. I'm not completely
incapable."

"I never thought you were. But that's pretty rough work."

"Man's work?" she challenged him, just to see the answering glow in his blue eyes.

He reached out and slid a hand over hers, up her arm, beneath the sleeve of her robe. "Maybe a little too rough for you."

"You're pretty rough on me," she said, surprised at the low, husky tone in her voice.

He smiled that wicked grin of his. "But you like it."

The kettle whistled, and she was saved from blurting out exactly how much she liked it. *Needed* it, lately.

She pulled her arm back and moved to the stove.

"You take sugar, don't you?"

"I like everything sweet. That's one of the reasons I like you."

She poured the boiling water into the mugs, and when she glanced up at him, found him watching her. "One of the reasons?"

God, she was taunting him, flirting like a teenage girl.

"One of many."

If she wasn't careful, she was going to ask him what the other reasons were.

She concentrated on spooning sugar into one mug and handing it to him.

"Thanks."

She sat next to him on the other stool, her palms cupped around the hot tea mug. It shouldn't feel so natural to have a man in her kitchen. It shouldn't feel so normal, with this man, to be doing anything other than having sex with him, being spanked by him.

"Alec . . . "

"Are you going to ask me now? Whatever it was you wanted to know earlier?"

"I . . . this is something else. Maybe . . . " She paused, looking at him. He was waiting for her. There was nothing mocking in his expression. "This is just so weird. That we can sit here so casually, after the things we do together, and just . . . talk. Like regular people. I . . . " She brushed her hair from her face. "I don't think I'm explaining myself well."

"You mean that because we're kinky together, we should simply be kinky, and nothing else?" He shrugged. "There's a lot more to kinky folk than the kink, Dylan. That's one part of who a person is. Sometimes it's a major part, but that doesn't have to define anyone."

"Okay. Okay. But . . . look, we're both writers. Being a writer *does* define me, to a large degree. I assume it does you, too?"

"Yes, sure. But I'm still not *only* a writer. I'm a lot of other things, too. Aren't you?"

She paused, thinking. What else was there to her life? Her talks with Mischa, which were often about writing. The occasional calls to her grandmother, the even less occasional calls to speak with her mother and her aunt. She wrote, worked out, did book signings. But otherwise, her life was fairly routine, and didn't include much personal contact of any kind. That was something she wasn't used to. Her childhood had trained her to be alone. She'd always thought of it as being self-reliant. Until recently.

"I suppose."

"Maybe that's something for you to look at."

"What do you mean?"

He was quiet a moment, sipping his tea. "You took a long time to answer that question. I took it to mean you had to think about whether or not you're more than a writer."

"Maybe sometimes I'm not certain that I am. That's what I've dedicated my life to."

"Don't you have other interests? People in your life?"

"Of course."

It felt like a lie. The answer had simply been automatic. But how to explain to him that putting her apartment together had been the only non-writing project she'd taken on in years? Even her travel was always writing related, either going to writers' conferences or to a city to do research for a book. And her only real friends were Mischa, and Jade and C.J., who she'd met through her writing. And Mischa was right; she should make more of an effort to foster her friendships with them.

God, she really knew nothing about having a personal life. A *real* life.

"Did I hit a sore spot?"

"What? No, I'm fine." She was thinking too much again. She didn't want to do that with Alec. Why was her mind all over the place tonight? It was going a thousand miles an hour. She needed to calm down.

She sipped her tea. It was too hot, scalding her tongue. "Oh!"

"Are you okay?"

"Burned my tongue."

"Poor baby. Come here."

Before she knew what was happening she was drawn into his arms and he was kissing her, his tongue sliding between her lips. She melted immediately, just went soft and hot all over, her mind mercifully slowing down.

He pulled back. "Is that better?"

"Much better."

Which didn't explain why her heart was beating like a jack-hammer in her chest.

This is just sex. Just sex.

Kinky sex. With the hottest man she had ever laid eyes on, never mind her hands. The best sex she'd ever had in her life, in fact. If that wasn't enough to distract her from these little epiphanies she was having, nothing would be.

"I can be even nicer," he said, his eyes glittering.

Desire there, in his brilliant blue gaze. Desire to match hers.

He set his mug down and got to his feet, and before she knew what was happening he'd picked her up, carried her around the bar and into the kitchen, and sat her down on the pale gray and white counter. It was cold and hard; she could feel it through the thin satin of her robe. And when he shifted her so that he could pull the fabric from beneath her, her naked sex resting on the cool granite, her body gave a hard squeeze all over.

"Alec, what are you doing?"

"Shh."

She knew better than to argue. And she hardly had time to question him, he was moving so fast. He pushed her back with one hand between her breasts until she had to support herself, her elbows braced on the counter behind her. With the other hand he untied her robe, and it fell open, baring the front of her body. Her nipples went hard immediately in the chilly air. Or maybe it was just him, being naked before him. The thrill of his command she could no longer deny.

He pulled her legs up until they rested on his broad shoulders, leaving her sex open to him, exposed, and moved between her thighs. He reached down and stroked her wet cleft.

"Ah, you're ready for me. I love that you're always ready for whatever I ask of you."

She licked her lips. She was shaking with need. She didn't know what to say.

He smiled that wicked grin again. He really had the most beautiful mouth she'd ever seen on a man.

He leaned in, laid a soft, tantalizing kiss on her lips. Then he bit her, just a small press of his teeth biting into the flesh of her lower lip. She moaned.

"You like my mouth on you?" he whispered against her lips.

"Yes . . . "

"Then you'll like it even better here."

He bent down, his dark head moving between her thighs. His shoulders were wide, the muscles of his back rippling. She caught a glimpse of the Tibetan script running down one shoulder and she wanted to touch it, to feel the ink beneath his skin. But the first whisper of his warm breath feathering over her mound distracted her. She spread her thighs wider, all conscious thought gone, nothing in her head but sheer, overpowering *want*.

"Yes, that's it," he murmured. "Open for me. Beautiful."

His tongue flicked at her swollen and needy clitoris, and her back arched, her breath coming out of her, leaving her gasping. It was so, so good. Another flick and she drew a breath in, sharply.

Pleasure like smoke coiling through her. It was even better when he used his hands to part the lips of her sex, holding on a little too firmly, hurting just enough. Then really pinching at the tender flesh there as he began to lick.

Long, lovely strokes of his tongue: over her slit, slipping into the entrance to her sex, then up to lap at her clitoris. And all the while the punishing pinch of his fingers on her pussy lips.

"God, Alec . . . "

He moved faster, his tongue hot and wet, licking and licking. Then sucking on her hard clit. Pleasure built, spiraled. Too fast. Too sharply. And as he plunged his fingers into her sex, still sucking, sucking, she came.

Her climax was a keen, pulsing ache, shimmering through her. The pulse beat harder, and another climax was right behind it, rolling together, blending. Her hips arched into his mouth, his hand, as he worked her with fingers and tongue and lips. Dizzying. Devastating.

She was panting when he pulled away.

"Was that good, Dylan?"

His face was damp with her juices, his lips plush and red. His dark goatee seemed more wicked to her than ever.

"Yes . . . so good."

"Then it's time to be bad."

He reached behind her and pulled a metal spatula from the white ceramic jar of cooking utensils she kept there. The handle was long and narrow, the spatula a flat expanse of shining chrome.

"Alec, you can't mean to use that on me."

"Oh, but I do."

His eyes held a dark, satisfied gleam, making her tremble. But it was far more desire than fear shivering through her veins, over her skin.

He set the instrument down, then he had both hands around her waist. He turned her and stood her on the floor, so that she was facing the cabinets. Then he bent her over the granite counter, warmed now from where her body had rested.

"Lean down," he told her. "I want your hands on the counter. And spread your lovely thighs. Good girl."

Some small part of her couldn't quite believe she was doing it. But she followed his instructions exactly. Another part of her was shivering at his words.

Good girl.

Lovely.

He pushed her robe up around her waist and came up behind her. He pressed against her, until she could feel the solid ridge of his erection against her hip.

"I'm so hard for you, Dylan. I want to fuck you so badly, it hurts. But first, I need to warm you up."

He smoothed a hand over her bare buttocks, his touch making her shudder. Then his hand slid down, into her wet slit.

"Ah, I love to feel your come on my hands, baby. So damn sweet in my mouth, I want to taste you again. I want to do everything to you."

"Yes, Alec. Do it, whatever it is."

His voice was a low, husky murmur. "Christ, what you do to me. That you are so in control in every way. Except like this, with me. That you give yourself over so completely. It wouldn't be so powerful if you were always the pliant little subbie girl. But you're not. You're strong. Strong enough that when you go down into subspace, when you hand yourself over, it almost brings me to my knees. No woman has done this to me before. You make me crazy, Dylan."

What was he saying? Her mind was numb. Desire was too keen in her body for her to really concentrate.

"Alec, please. Just touch me."

A small chuckle from him, but he sounded pleased; there was nothing mocking in it. And she was burning up with desire.

"Like this, baby?"

He stroked her swollen clitoris, a gentle touch. Too gentle. She moaned softly.

"Ah, you need more? Is that it?"

"Yes . . . "

He pushed two fingers inside her, and she surged back against him.

He pulled his fingers out and she groaned in disappointment.

"No, Dylan. I want you to hold perfectly still. I will do it all. Understood?"

"Yes, Alec."

"Say it."

"I understand. I won't move."

"Good girl."

Another long shiver at his words.

She held her breath, and waited.

His fingers brushed along the seam between her buttocks, still wet with her juices. Sliding down, down, until he was caressing the lips of her sex. She bit her lip, trying not to open for him, to push back until she impaled herself on his fingers, which was what she wanted to do. But he had told her to hold still, and she would. And he kept stroking, stroking. She could hardly bear it.

The snap of the metal spatula across one buttock took her by surprise; she'd forgotten all about it. But it made her tremble with desire, every bit as much as his stroking hand.

"Oh, Alec . . . "

"Yes, it's good, isn't it?"

He smacked her ass again, harder this time, and she jumped.

"Still, Dylan."

He pushed his fingers into her sex, and she panted, bit her lip. Held still.

"Excellent."

He spanked her once more, and she breathed into it, the pain searing, sharp. Lovely.

He began a hard rhythm, then, smacking her over and over: one cheek, then the other, down across the tops of her thighs. And his clever, probing fingers in her sex, moving in and out, pausing to stroke at her hard, needy clit, then back inside. She was soaking wet, her knees shaking. Her breasts were pressed into the hard countertop, the granite cold, her nipples aching.

His fingers thrust deeper, and he spanked her harder, until she could feel the welts rising on her skin. But it felt unbelievably good.

Alec's breathing grew harsh, and the spatula came down with a few loud cracks, making her cry out.

"Yes, you can take it, my beautiful girl."

"Alec, please . . . "

"Please what?"

"Please fuck me."

The spanking stopped. All she could hear was the rasping pant of her own breath and his. In moments she felt his strong, naked thighs pressed up against hers, his hand wrapped up in her hair, pulling tight. Then his sheathed cock was pressing at the entrance to her sex.

"Come on, baby. Open for me now."

She spread her legs, raised her ass higher, and he slid in. Pleasure surged in her body, warm and rippling and *right*, somehow.

"You feel so good, Dylan. Like heaven."

He moved deeper, thrusting hard and fast.

"Oh!"

"Yes, you can take it all. And you're so damn wet."

He leaned down, his muscular chest right up against her bowed back, one arm slipping around her waist, holding her firmly.

His face was next to her ear. "I am going to fuck you now, Dylan. I'm going to fuck you hard. I need to."

"Yes . . ."

She was out of her head. She was nothing more than this incredible, aching need. For him.

Alec.

He began to pump, his cock plunging into her over and over, so hard and fast she could barely breathe. Just as he'd promised.

"God, Alec," she gasped. "Harder . . . please."

He pounded into her, his hip bones crashing against her, hard, ramming thrusts of his hips. And desire was like a hammer in her veins: that solid and pummeling.

When she came, it thundered in her ears, like the roar of the ocean. And she was drowning in it: pure pleasure. Pain. Pain turned into pleasure.

He tensed behind her, his cock throbbing, and even through the condom she felt the hot pulse as he came.

"Dylan!"

A few more thrusts, and he slipped out of her. There was one brief moment when she felt the loss of his body, his heat. Then he was pulling her into him, setting her on the counter again. He moved between her thighs, and she wrapped them around him, needing nothing this time but his nearness.

He held her, his arms tight around her, his head resting on her shoulder. Her mind was a half-numb whirl.

How could she feel so connected to this man? A man she really hardly knew. Except that her body knew him, in a way it had never known another man. It was something about the pain play, the power play. The absolute trust she felt for him to take care of her.

Dangerous.

Yes. It was dangerous to rely on anyone to care for her. She'd always been the caretaker. That didn't have to change now.

But it was too lovely simply to be held by him. To hear his ragged breath in her ear. To feel the taut, muscled mass of his big body.

She let herself drift in that sense of safety, let her muscles go loose, relax all over.

What could it hurt, for now? As long as she kept her perspective, didn't come to expect too much. She could be reasonable when they weren't having sex, when they weren't engaged in power play. But he was right: She had to let it go when they were together or she wasn't going to truly experience this. And she wanted to. Not only for her research, but for *her*.

She felt as though she was about to discover something about herself. She was on the verge. It was frightening. And maybe wonderful.

Maybe.

Just don't get too caught up in it. Compartmentalize.

Yes, she could do that. She'd been doing it her whole life.

Alec had a lot to teach her. About sex. About how the human mind worked. Maybe about learning to trust another person, to some extent, at least. It didn't need to be anything more than that.

She ignored the small part of her brain whispering to her that it was more than that already.

eleven

Alec had carried her to bed. Too romantic, but she'd let him do it, too weak with orgasm and endorphins from the spanking to protest. He'd pulled back the bedspread, laid her down on the pristine white sheets, stretched out beside her.

She wanted to pillow her head on the high, hard curve of his shoulder, press her cheek to his chest to listen to the beat of his heart. But she didn't dare do it.

Ridiculous.

She'd never craved that post-sex closeness most women seemed to need. This must be that "bottoming out" they'd talked about, that crash after the flood of endorphins and other chemicals to the brain that came with the pain play. She felt open. Raw. Needy.

He turned to her then, as though he could read her mind. And he kissed her cheek softly, pulled her up against his side, his arm slipping beneath her shoulder.

Ah, so nice.

Don't get too used to it.

No, but for now, it was wonderful, to lie there with him. Cozy, with the sound of the rain hitting the windows, the soft light coming from the kitchen, like some pale and distant sun.

"Hey." His tone was a low, husky whisper.

"Hmm?"

"You okay?"

"Yes. I'm fine."

"Just 'fine'?"

She laughed. "Better than fine, if you must know."

"Good." He paused, his fingers rubbing absently over her collarbone. "Are you ready to tell me about your mother?"

Her stomach went tight, her jaw clenching. "Alec. No. I'm not."

"Dylan, you have to tell me sometime."

"Do I?"

"You can't expect to really let go until you can be open with me about everything. If there is any part of you that you keep shut down, it'll always be in the way."

"Is that absolutely necessary? Really letting go?"

"Isn't it? Isn't that what we're doing here?"

"I started out doing research for my book. I'm not sure what we're doing here anymore."

He was quiet a moment. "Neither am I."

It made her feel better, somehow, to hear him admit his uncertainty. As though she wasn't the only one. It made him seem more human to her. And perhaps less flawed, less weak, herself.

Her shoulders went loose, her jaw relaxing. She inhaled, pulling in the cool air, the scent of his skin. "Okay," she said quietly, as if she still wasn't quite sure.

"Okay, what?"

"I'll tell you."

"Okay. I'm listening."

"My mother is bipolar," she blurted, before she could edit herself. "It made for a . . . difficult childhood. Nearly impossible, really. I'm sure that's why my father left, although why he'd leave two small children behind . . . well, that's another story, I suppose."

Alec's hand slipped around hers, held on. "Tell me this one."

She paused, drew in a breath, then another. She wasn't accustomed to discussing her family with anyone other than Mischa, and even that was new for her, not something she was really used to, yet. But she *wanted* to tell him now.

"We were living in Portland. We had no other family there. So I had to take over from a pretty early age. We moved around a lot because Darcy forgot to pay the rent and the bills. By the time I was ten or so I'd figured it all out. I wrote the checks, signed her name. When there was money in the account, anyway, which didn't always happen."

"You called your mother Darcy?"

"She wasn't ever really a mother to us. Calling her 'Mom' never seemed like an option."

"Your brother was younger than you?"

"Yes, by three years. I took care of Quinn. Or I tried to, anyway."

"That's a lot for a kid to handle."

"Yes. But it was just . . . my life."

"Where is she now, your mother?"

"My aunt Deirdre took her in, finally. She moved Darcy to her place in Ashland, Oregon, not long after I left for college. Well, a few weeks after we lost Quinn." She stopped, breathed through that familiar sensation of being kicked in the chest. "Darcy was a mess after Quinn died. I was a mess. But I wasn't about to quit school and move back home. I didn't feel I had anything to move home for. And it was Deirdre's turn, frankly.

"I don't care for Deirdre much. She knew there was something wrong with my mother all those years, but never wanted to do anything about it until there were no other options. I *had* to get out of there, get back to school. I didn't go to college until I was almost twenty. I'd stayed to help my mother, to take care of my brother. I didn't do such a good job of that, apparently."

"I'm sure you were great. And you were *there*. That counts for something."

"Maybe. I was there until . . . until I left. And that's when Quinn died."

"How was that your fault?"

A hard knot pulled in her stomach. She'd asked herself that question a million times, and had never come up with any reasonable answer. The image of Quinn's bloody and mangled body, his pale, still face, always blanked out everything else. The very fact that he was gone was always the first and most powerful thought in her head.

"I don't know. But I've always felt it was, somehow. I can't seem to shake that idea."

"Dylan, it's not possible that it was your fault. It was an accident, from what little you've told me. It's not logical."

"Logic doesn't always play a part in this sort of situation, does it?"

"No. I guess not."

They were both quiet, thinking. Maybe he was absorbing what she'd told him. She didn't want to really know what he thought about it. She didn't want him to pity her.

"But there's more?" he asked.

She nodded. "Yes. A lot more. Someone who's bipolar has . . . episodes. Rages. She'd wander off sometimes and we'd be alone for days at a time. She managed to escape being hospitalized until I'd left and she was in Deirdre's care. I couldn't have done it, put her in the hospital, but my aunt has done it several times. If I had, we would have been put in foster care, probably, Quinn and I. And likely separated. I couldn't do that. I was all he had. And he was . . . all I had."

That old grief twisted in her stomach. But she'd gotten used to swallowing it down.

"You had no other family?"

"My grandmother Delilah. But she lived in West Virginia in those years. My grandfather had Parkinson's, so she already had her hands full. He was sick for as long as I can remember. After he died, she moved out to Ashland to be near my mother and help Deirdre. But it was too late for Quinn and me by then.

"I adore my grandmother. When we were kids, Quinn and I would spend summers with her. But after a while it made Darcy too anxious for us to leave for any length of time, and she'd be a wreck when we got back. So we stopped going. And to this day I don't know if my grandmother had any idea how bad my mother was. Not until she came to Oregon. I never told her, and I'm sure Quinn never said a word. It was our secret. It was how we protected her."

"She was your mother. She should have protected you. That's how it works."

"For most people, maybe. But she wasn't capable, Alec."

"I know. But it's pretty fucking awful, anyway."

"Yes. It was."

It felt better than she would have imagined hearing him say that. To be validated in that way. She squeezed his hand. She didn't know how else to express the strange gratitude she felt.

"So you spent your whole life being the one in charge of things," he said.

"Yes."

"And being alone."

Why did that make her want to cry, suddenly? She bit down against the tears pooling in her eyes.

"Damn it," she said quietly.

"Hey, it's okay."

"Is it?"

Alec held her more tightly, and she had to fight not to pull away. It comforted her. *He* comforted her. But she didn't want to let herself have that. She'd been handling life on her own for so long. If she allowed herself to get used to this, what would she do when he was gone, as he inevitably would be?

"You don't have to tell me anything more right now, Dylan. I have a feeling that was a lot for you."

"It was. And . . . "

"And what?"

"I guess I'm waiting for the questions. About my mother being bipolar. What it was like living with a . . . crazy person. About specific incidents. The details of losing my brother."

"You don't have to tell me those things now. Or maybe ever. But I do have one question."

She sighed. "What is it?"

"Do all the women in your family have names beginning with 'D'?"

She laughed, some of the tension draining from her body. How was it he brought out so much emotion in her, and could make her feel so good all at the same time?

"Yes. I forget that's weird to other people. My great-great-grandmother started it, apparently. It's silly."

"I think it's sort of sweet."

She tilted her head to look up at him. "You are a strange man, Alec Walker."

"Not the first time I've heard that. And it won't be the last. I don't mind. I'm a rebel at heart, you know."

The blue of his eyes gleamed from beneath his half-lowered lids, making her breath catch. He was too damn handsome

"I've known that since the first moment I saw you," she told him.

"I saw that in you, too. You aren't the usual woman."

"Gee, thanks."

"No, I like that about you. I like your creative mind. And your air of mystery."

"I don't mean to be mysterious. I'm just . . . private."

"So am I. There are certain things we keep to ourselves, people like you and me."

"I don't like to air my problems. I don't want anyone to feel sorry for me."

"Because it makes you vulnerable."

"Yes. Sitting here, telling you about these things, makes me feel more vulnerable than being tied up by you, spanked . . . more vulnerable than anything else possibly could."

"That's good. I want you to open to me. The more, the better."

"Because that's your job as a good dominant?"

"Yes. Maybe." He paused, ran a hand through his hair. "Maybe that's not the only reason."

"Does that make you feel vulnerable, Alec?" she asked quietly. "Telling me this?"

He nodded, pulled their clasped hands up to his chest and rubbed his fingers over hers. "Yes. I don't like to think about it that way, but yes."

"I'm not the expert, certainly, but I've read that this is supposed to be a reciprocal learning experience. The power play. It's an exchange of power, not a one-way thing. Is that right?"

"Yes, of course."

"So maybe this is what you learn with me. Because I don't see how it can be a reciprocal experience if you don't have something to learn, too. It's got to be about more than just you being in control, wielding the power. It has to work both ways, doesn't it? The bottom, the submissive, has some power in this whole thing. And I don't mean only the power in the submissive's ability to stop the scene by using their safe word. I've read about it, but I've never really understood it until now."

He was quiet a moment. Then he said, "I can tell you I'm not happy about admitting I am vulnerable in any way. But you're right. About it all. Maybe that's what's been holding me back. As a dominant. In life in general. I don't like to look at this too closely. It makes me damn uncomfortable."

"Isn't part of the BDSM scene about challenging your boundaries? Taking you out of your comfort zone?"

"Oh, I'm way beyond my comfort zone at the moment."

"So am I."

"Yet you're here with me. You're doing these things, talking with me. Telling me things you don't want to."

She nodded. "Yes. And I'm not even really sure why. Maybe the BDSM play has . . . opened me up."

"It does that."

"But not for you."

He smiled, but it was just a cynical lifting at the corners of his mouth. "I'm known for my absolute control."

"So am I, Alec."

He stared at her. She couldn't know what was going through his mind. His eyes were dark, thoughtful. There was an edge of danger about him. As though there was a slow anger simmering just below the surface. Maybe it was just his discomfort in realizing he had to open up, too.

"We are an odd pair," he said, his tone gentle. "But well-matched. We each have something holding us back from realizing our potential."

"God, you make it sound so . . . "

"Psychobabble?"

"Simple."

"Maybe it is. Maybe it's all a lot simpler than either of us make it."

"I'm used to everything being complicated. I don't know how to do simple."

"Maybe we'll learn that together."

She wanted that, suddenly. To be with him, learn with him. Grow with him. She didn't even know what that meant, exactly. She didn't want to admit to it, anyway.

You are falling for him.

No.

But it was true. She was falling, hard and fast, and when she finally hit bottom, it was going to be one ugly mess.

Don't do it.

But it was happening, whether she liked it or not. She couldn't stop herself. There was no way out of this but to move forward, wherever that would lead.

Alec sat at the enormous oak desk in his home office, staring past his computer monitor and out the window. He was supposed to be searching online for places to stay on his upcoming motorcycle road trip with Dante down to the Baja Peninsula. They'd been talking about it for months, and it was time to make solid plans. He had a break between book deadlines coming up, and Dante had already arranged for the time away from his office. Alec had been looking forward to it: a few weeks on the road on his favorite bike. That sense of utter freedom. They'd go diving down there. Parasailing. Lounge on the beach.

Why wasn't his heart in it today? Why was his mind wandering?

Outside, the sky was the usual Seattle gray, the dim sunlight filtering through the clouds, lighting them up in silver and white. He loved the Seattle sky, the moodiness of it. But today it was making him brood.

No, that wasn't it. It was Dylan.

He hadn't been able to think straight since he'd left her early Tuesday morning. Four days, he'd been like this. In his head too much. Sulky.

Except when he called her at night. Every night. They would talk for an hour. He'd never talked on the phone so much in his life.

He didn't dare see her yet. He was too raw from being with her the other night.

Maybe he should go to the club tonight. Dante would be there, some of his other acquaintances. But the truth was that he didn't want to go without Dylan. Couldn't bear to play with anyone else.

Dylan . . .

Don't think about it. Just do it.

He ran his fingers through his goatee, rubbed his chin. Then he picked up the phone, dialed, drummed a pen on the top of his desk while it rang.

"Hello?"

"Dylan. I'm taking you to the Pleasure Dome tonight. Don't say no."

"Alec. I . . . all right. I won't."

He got up, began to pace back and forth over the old Persian rug covering the dark hardwood floor. It was scratchy beneath his bare feet.

"Good. I'll be by to pick you up at nine."

"I'll be ready."

"Wear something that comes off easily."

His cock hardened at that thought: her pale skin being revealed inch by inch as he slipped the fabric from her delicate shoulders. That crazy hair of hers everywhere, like fire and silk in his hands . . .

"Anything else, Alec?"

"What?"

"Is there anything else you want me to do?"

Ah, he loved when her voice softened like that. When she began that slide into subspace. He loved that it happened just from him giving her simple instructions about what to wear.

"No. That's it." He paused, his gaze wandering to the misty skyline outside once more.

Pull it together.

"Dylan?"

"Yes?"

"I can't wait to see you."

A small pause on the other end of the line. Then he could practically hear the smile in her voice, the desire in her breathlessness. "I can't wait, either."

He hung up, sat down and stared at his monitor some more.

He had never said such a thing to a woman. Maybe that was some sort of character defect—he was pretty certain it was—but why was he deviating from his usual behavior now?

Everything was different with Dylan. He'd never been able to *talk* with a woman the way he did with Dylan. He'd tried to tell Dante about it the last time he'd seen him, but he hadn't said all there was to be said. He hadn't even admitted it all to himself.

The biggest thing was that he didn't like being apart from her. Crazy. He was the most independent person he knew, almost hermitlike at times, especially when he was in the middle of writing a book. If not for the lure of the Pleasure Dome, his love for travel, he'd probably hole up by himself and write his life away. Spend his life alone, as his father had. His father had been happy enough. Maybe. He'd begun to question that recently.

But now, he wanted to hole up with Dylan, and never let her leave.

Was there even any point in telling himself he could get a handle on this?

Maybe the Baja trip would be good for him. Give him some distance from Dylan, from the whole situation. Get something in his head besides the scent of her skin, the texture of her hair, the look in her eyes when she was going down into subspace. Her delicate body beneath his as he slipped his cock into her . . .

He was hard again. Or still. He didn't know anymore. He'd gotten himself off probably four or five times a day, like some hormonal teenager, ever since he'd last seen her. Hell, pretty much since he'd met her.

She was irresistible. Those perfect breasts, their tips growing darker as they hardened beneath his fingers . . . And Christ, when he slid into her, she was all soaking wet heat. Like burning silk, tight and sleek.

His cock pulsed, and he lowered a hand, pressed against the front of his jeans. It didn't help. Nothing was going to help. Not until he saw her again. Until he had her, naked, bound. Until he was inside her body again.

Fuck it.

He pushed back from his desk, unzipped his jeans and took his cock out, ran his hand over the rigid shaft. Pictured Dylan in his mind. She was all long, lean legs; taut stomach; smooth expanse of satin skin. And lower, she was mostly shaved, her pussy like some sort of flower, opening to him. He could see the pink lips, swollen with need, glistening with her desire.

He groaned, began to stroke. His cock was hard as steel, throbbing. He ran his fingertips over the head, imagining it was her mouth, those luscious red lips surrounding him, swallowing his flesh.

His hips arched into his fist, and he pumped, hard enough to hurt a little. Making him think of her, the way she loved to have him grasp her nipples and pinch. She always came like crazy when he pinched her, spanked her. She loved it.

He loved it.

He thrust into his palm, over and over.

Dylan . . .

Those big gray eyes, her hot little mouth. Her pussy, grasping him tight as she climaxed.

Two more rough strokes and he was coming.

Dylan!

All over his jeans, but he didn't care.

He was panting, his cock still pulsing with small waves of pleasure. He could see her if he closed his eyes. That beautiful face . . .

He didn't care about anything right now but her.

He would think about what the hell that meant later.

* * *

She was going to jump out of her skin when the damn doorbell finally rang. She'd been waiting for him all day, the tension and need building until she couldn't stand it anymore.

Dylan sipped at her glass of Perrier. She really could have used a glass of wine to soothe her nerves, but Alec was insistent that neither of them were intoxicated for a play session. And tonight would be more serious, she was certain. He wouldn't be taking her to the Pleasure Dome otherwise.

She wanted it. To be at the club, in that extreme environment with him.

To be with him.

She moved to the long mirror by the front door for probably the tenth time in the last twenty minutes. Her eyes looked enormous, outlined in black liner, the pupils wide and dark. Her lips looked full, almost as if they were waiting to be kissed, glossed in a sheer coating of red. Her dark red hair curled around her shoulders, bared by the strapless black dress she'd run out to buy that afternoon after Alec's call. It fit her like a glove, a simple satin sheath that came to mid-thigh. Shorter than anything she'd wear anywhere but to the club. She stepped back to look at her sleek, high black pumps, the thick black ankle straps accentuating her long legs.

She felt good. Well, she felt attractive, anyway. Inside she was all jittery need. Her tiny black silk thong was already damp, simply from anticipating the evening ahead.

Alec.

She was still amazed at her response to him. Her response to the pain, the way it translated to an intense pleasure she'd never felt in her life.

She'd never been able to admit to herself that she'd had fleeting fantasies about this sort of thing for years. Fantasies she'd repressed because she was too used to having to be the strong one, in charge, in control. Maybe he was right, and that was exactly why she needed so badly to let that control go once in a while.

She would let it go tonight. She already had. She could do it as long as she kept telling herself it was just sex. Pure sexual response, rather than something that defined her. Or something deeper. But that part was getting harder and harder to deny.

Her years with her out-of-control mother must have trained her well; she seemed to be awfully good at denial, which was counter to her usual, logical self. Or maybe not. Maybe when she'd thought she was being logical, reasonable, all these years, she'd been doing nothing more than hiding from her past, pretending to possess a strength she didn't truly have.

Scary thought.

Alec was bringing out a lot of scary ideas. Making her question everything she thought she knew about herself. Which brought her back to the denial.

She sighed. Her mind was going in circles. She needed to calm down and simply enjoy the evening ahead.

The buzzer went off and she started, pulled in a deep breath, and set her glass down on the console table beneath the mirror before hitting the intercom button.

"Alec?"

"Yes, it's me."

"Do you want to come up or shall I come down?"

"You'd better come down."

"I'll be right there."

She slipped into her leather trench coat, making sure her small wallet and her keys were in the pocket, then locked up and took the elevator down. Alec was waiting for her just outside the front door.

"Hi."

"You look . . . amazing, Dylan."

"Thank you."

Was she actually blushing?

He leaned over and brushed a kiss across her lips, and her sex pulsed, her body melting. He pulled back, his blue eyes searching hers for a moment, then he moved in and crushed her to him, his mouth coming down hard on hers. His lips opened, his tongue slipping between her lips. He was all sweet, minty tongue, wet and . . . lovely. Her knees were going to buckle. But he held her tight, his arms strong around her. She could feel every hard, muscular plane of his big body through his wool coat. She sighed into his mouth.

He pulled back. "Christ, Dylan." He let her go, ran a hand over his goatee. "I'm sorry I didn't come up. I didn't think we'd ever leave your place if I did."

He was smiling at her, that gorgeous, wicked smile of his. But she could see that he was perfectly serious.

She loved that she could affect him this way. That his desire seemed to be as overwhelming as her own. She'd always felt a certain feminine power in being able to bring a man to his knees—figuratively, anyway. But with Alec it was even more intense. Everything was.

"Shall we go before I rape you on your doorstep?"

He was grinning at her, but she saw the gleam of desire in his eyes, in the loose set of his mouth. Alec raping her on her doorstep didn't sound half bad.

She smiled to herself, nodded.

He took her hand and led her to his big, black truck, like some sleek monolith. The vehicle was pure Alec: huge, powerful. He opened the door for her, helped her in before going to the driver's side and getting in himself. Then they were off, the truck's engine a muted roar.

"How are you feeling about going to the Pleasure Dome?" he asked her.

"Excited. A little nervous. It's as though I'll have to perform, unless you're taking me to some dark corner again. But I have a feeling that's not what tonight is about. And I don't mind the idea of being in front of other people. The idea is a little thrilling. And a little frightening. But I don't really know what you have in mind."

He turned, grinned at her.

"And you don't plan to tell me," she said.

"Of course not."

She smiled, shook her head. "Part of the dominant mind-fuck."

"Yes. Absolutely. And the uncertainty is part of it for you. You have to simply trust me."

"I do."

"Good. Very good. Because tonight I'm going to explore some new ground with you. I think you're ready."

"Oh . . ."

He glanced at her, then back at the road. Her stomach had formed a small knot, but it was equal parts fear and an exquisite anticipation.

They arrived shortly at the club, and Alec parked the truck, came around to help her out. His hand on her arm was reassuring, yet her pulse was racing.

They passed through the high red door and into the interior of the club. Alec helped her out of her coat, then took her into the big main room. Dylan blinked, waiting for her eyes to adjust to the dim, colored lights.

The club was more crowded tonight than it had been the last time they'd come. There were people everywhere, it seemed: clad in dark leather, or naked. Or maybe she was simply more aware of it all tonight. Hyperaware of everything.

Music was a heavy pulse-beat in the pit of her stomach: something dreamy and trancelike, with a lot of bass. And beside her, Alec's body felt enormous, hulking, as he'd appeared to her the first time she'd seen him at the Asian Art Museum. That seemed a hundred years ago. Had it only been two weeks? How was that possible?

He pulled her closer into his side as he led her across the room. She couldn't quite take it all in, the activity around them. She was only dimly aware of the half-dressed and naked bodies bound to the crosses, the bondage frames, laid out over the laps of dominant men and women on the red leather sofas, or kneeling on the floor. There were corsets and collars and handcuffs. Ropes and harnesses and long, shining lengths of chain. And all of it lovely to her, titillating.

Wanting, like a hot tide in her veins. She wanted to be one of them. To be bound, tortured, stimulated. To be admired.

Her brain was shutting down, simply emptying out. And when Alec stopped in front of one of the enormous wooden Xs, a St. Andrew's Cross, her heart stuttered in her chest.

This was really about to happen.

twelve

Alec leaned in and whispered in her ear, "I am going to strip you now. And I am going to chain you to this cross. I love the chains. They're better for me than the ropes. More primal. I think you'll like them, too. I think the more extreme, the better, for you. It'll help you to reach that basic, primal part of yourself. To let go."

She could barely speak, wanted to groan. Her heart was hammering, her sex aching.

"Yes, Alec . . . "

He did it, just slipped her dress off, then her silky black thong, leaving her in nothing but her high shoes. Her nipples came up hard immediately.

She was keenly aware of being naked, with all of the other people in the club right there. It was thrilling as hell. It didn't even matter whether or not anyone was looking at her. Except Alec, of course. And she felt an odd sense of pride at being able to do this in front of all these people: to be naked, to have him play her. But all of these ideas were in some distant part of her brain. The rest of her was simply in the moment.

He kissed her shoulders as he turned her around to face the cross. She was shivering all over, a lovely thrum of desire shimmering over her skin, arrowing deep into her body.

"Just let me take care of everything, Dylan. Here, raise your arm up. Yes, that's it."

Before she knew what was happening, he'd fastened a thick leather cuff around one wrist, then, with one hand on the small of her back, he moved her in closer to the wooden X, until her breasts brushed the smooth wood. He took her other hand and fastened it even more quickly. She gave a small pull, felt how tautly she was held by the short lengths of chain running from the cuffs to the eyebolts embedded in the cross.

Her arms were spread wide. She felt vulnerable. Yet entirely safe at the same time, with Alec. And beautiful.

"I'm going to leave your pretty shoes on," he told her, bending to stroke her calf, then lower, to where her ankle was covered by the strap. "Such gorgeous legs."

He laid a soft kiss on the back of her knee, and the sensation shot straight to her sex. She moaned.

Then he was standing, his big body pressed against her back, his erection a heavy shaft of flesh against the top of her buttocks.

"I'm going to unpack my toy bag now. But I'm right here. I don't want you to move. Stay still, practice the breathing I've taught you. Do you understand me, Dylan?"

"Yes. I understand."

He moved away then, and she drew in a deep breath. In

through her nose, holding it in her lungs a few moments, then out through her mouth, willing herself to relax. Some small part of her mind was still engaged in nerves, a fear of the unknown. But mostly she was tuned into her body: her hardening nipples, her moistening sex, the tension in her muscles as she waited for things to really begin.

Alec was behind her once more, his hands on her waist. They were big and warm on her skin.

Touch me . . .

But she didn't dare say it out loud. She knew enough by now to understand that he would set the pace, and she would follow.

He began to stroke, his fingers feathering over her skin, bringing up goose bumps. He caressed her back, her sides, her buttocks, her thighs, and moving her hair to one side, the back of her neck. Desire rippled over her skin everywhere he touched.

"Ah, you like this, Dylan. I can feel it. I can hear it in your breath. Are you going under? Tell me."

"Yes . . . yes."

"Excellent. Good girl."

That now-familiar rush of pleasure at his approval.

Good girl.

Lovely.

"Are you ready?"

"Yes. I'm ready."

"And you remember your safe words?"

"*Yellow* for slow down, *red* for stop the scene."

"Very good. Now, then . . . "

He stepped back, and very quickly she felt the soft brush of leather on her skin. A heavy suede flogger, she could tell. But he was being gentle with it.

She let herself sink into the rhythm of it as he swung in a crisscross pattern over her upper back, warming her up. There was no pain, only a deepening pleasure. She tuned into the music, which he was working in time with. And the music became part of it, the thudding beat-beat of it almost a part of the touch of the heavy flogger.

Her limbs were melting all over, relaxing, blood flowing into her arms and legs, her belly. And her breasts and her sex were aching with it, but not urgently. Not yet.

She yelped when the flogger came down in one hard smack, thudding across her back. But before she could really absorb it, the gentle rhythm began again. And again, she let herself sink into it.

It seemed to go on forever, mesmerizing, until she was floating in some misty, beautiful dream place. She stayed there for an almost eternal period of time, waiting, drifting.

Another hard smack took her by surprise, woke her a little, yet her mind was still floating. And even though he was hitting her harder and harder, the flogger stinging, hurting, her mind was suspended in that lovely place, her body converting the pain to immediate pleasure. The pain *was* pleasure: desire, need, hot and aching.

He stopped, and ran his hand over her sore skin.

"Beautiful, the way you pink up. Gorgeous. Are you still with me, Dylan?"

"Hmm . . . "

"Dylan." His voice a bit sharper this time. "Answer me. Are you still with me?"

"Yes, Alec. I'm here."

The heat of his body vanished, and suddenly he was in front of her, lifting her chin with his hand, his gaze boring into hers.

"I want to see your eyes," he told her. "Oh yes, you're half gone, aren't you? That's good. That's exactly where I want you. But some part of you must stay present in your body. Do you understand me?"

"I . . . I don't know . . . "

"All right. I'll watch out for you. I'll check in. You must answer me when I speak to you, Dylan."

"Yes. I'll answer you."

He smiled. He had a beautiful smile, all white teeth and lush lips and that wicked goatee. She flooded with heat when he leaned in to kiss her.

His mouth was hard on hers, demanding, and she opened to him. And when he slipped a hand between her thighs, swiping at her wet sex, she moaned, her hips arching.

"Ah, not yet," he teased, giving her clitoris a small pinch.

"Oh!"

"You'll get to come, my girl. But not yet."

He kissed her again, briefly this time, then moved around behind her.

The flogging began again, but it was different this time. Sharper, keener-edged, and she knew in some distant way that he was using a different instrument. It came down on her back over and over, until her breath was a ragged pant in her ears. Stinging, stinging, her sex filling, hungry, wanting.

He stopped, his arm snaking around her waist, and he crushed her body to his.

His mouth was right next to her ear; she could feel the heat of his breath. "You are so goddamn beautiful, Dylan. I want you. And I will take you. But later. I want you to come for me now. In front of all these people, all of these sensualists who understand what we do here."

She became acutely aware then of the people around them. It still didn't matter if any were specifically paying attention. Knowing they were there was good enough. Better than good. Her sex clenched hard.

His hand moved down between her thighs, his fingers sliding in her juices, between the lips of her sex.

"Ah, Alec . . . "

"Does it feel good, my girl? Do you want to come?"

"Yes . . . yes, please . . . "

He pressed onto her tight clit with the heel of his hand, angled his fingers and slipped a few inside her.

God, she was going to come. Too soon, too fast. He began to pump, his breath hot in her hair, his body all solid planes, his hard cock crushed against her back. Burning hot, even through his jeans.

She was groaning aloud; she couldn't help it. He thrust deep inside her, his heel grinding onto her clitoris. And his other hand came up and pinched one of her nipples. A hard and punishing pinch that sent her over the edge, and into the abyss.

Pleasure, dark and swirling, screaming and hot in her veins, flowing like lava. Scorching her. Marking her.

She was coming so damn hard, she was crying out, shaking, shattering. Just coming apart. And Alec's arms held her safe.

Safe.

For the first time in her life.

She was trembling all over; he could feel the shiver of skin and muscle beneath his hands. Her breath was a soft pant. She smelled like leather and come and woman.

She was absolutely limp, held up only by the chains and his arms. He loved seeing her like this: full of endorphins. Spent.

His.

But she'd had enough. He had to take her down.

He shifted his hold on her, whispered, "I'm going to let you go long enough to take you out of the cuffs, Dylan."

He let her weight sag into the restraints, unfastened one cuff, then the other, caught her as she slipped into his arms. He lifted her, carried her to the small sofa at the edge of the play area and wrapped her in a blanket, sat down and laid her across his lap. Leaning down, he grabbed a bottle of water he'd set there earlier, held it to her soft, red mouth. "Drink, Dylan."

She did, opening her lips as he held the bottle for her. When she was done, he set it down on the floor once more.

Her eyes were clouded, gleaming sliver. Her cheeks were flushed. He checked her hands for circulation; she looked fine.

"Are you with me, Dylan?"

"Yes. I'm right here," she said, almost childlike, as if wondering that he couldn't see her, or feel her in his lap.

He laughed softly. "Oh, you're so far out there in subspace. But I love to see you like this. Are you ready for me to fuck you now, my girl? Because I can't wait. I'm so damn hard for you."

"Yes. Please . . . "

She was out of it, deep in subspace. But he could feel the need radiating off her skin in waves of pure heat. Molten. And when he slipped his hand beneath the soft blanket, he found her soaking wet. Still. Again.

"Oh, Alec, please . . . now," she groaned.

He stood up with her in his arms and moved to one of the curtained alcoves built into the outer walls of the club. There, he laid her on the high, padded table, unwrapped her, the blanket pooling beneath her, and simply stood, staring at the glory of her naked body. Aroused. Flushed. Well-used.

Not used enough. Not yet.

He kicked off his boots, then his jeans, yanked his T-shirt over his head, and sheathed his hard and aching cock. He climbed onto the table, kneeling between her open thighs.

Her sex was pink, glistening. He leaned in, tasting her. She was sweet and salty, the taste of her come rich on his tongue. He licked her, running his tongue the length of her slit, then slipping in between the plush lips and inside her.

"Oh . . . God, Alec."

His cock was throbbing, painful. Yet he couldn't stop teasing himself, teasing her.

He thrust his tongue deeper, and she panted, moaned. And when he used his fingers to part the lips of her sex, massaging them, she writhed, her hips arching off the table.

He pulled back. He had to see her face, the glow of her cheeks, her beautiful red lips, parted so that he could see the tip of her pink tongue resting against her teeth. So damn hot, for reasons he couldn't explain to himself.

His cock jumped, the condom tightening on his swollen shaft. He couldn't stand it.

He watched her face as he pushed two fingers inside her. Her long lashes fluttered, her cheeks darkening.

"Alec . . . Need to . . . come again."

"Yes. But this time my cock will make you come. You'll come with me inside you."

"Yes. Hurry, Alec."

Oh, he would hurry. He couldn't wait another moment.

Still kneeling, and holding her pussy lips wide, he drove his cock in, one sweet, sharp thrust.

"Oh!" Her eyes widened, like a pair of dark crystals, piercing him to the core.

The pleasure was sharp, excruciating. His knees were shaking. Drawing in a deep breath, he wrapped his hands around her slender waist and pulled her closer, her hips rising, until her little mound was pressed right up against him. He could see the tight nub of her clit. Remembered the texture of it on his tongue.

Another shot of pleasure, just thinking about the taste of her, seeing her body bowing in pleasure, arching in his hands. Her hair was like flames scattered everywhere. And her nipples were a dark red, as hard and swollen as her clit. Luscious.

He leaned over and took one nipple into his mouth, and she moved against him, pressing against his lips. He sucked, and began to push into her, his cock buried deep inside her, then pulling out, slowly, one agonizing inch at a time.

Her sex was like some sleek, wet glove around him. His body was tense with concentration, just fucking her in long, slow strokes, trying to keep from coming too soon, like some kid.

He felt like a kid, overwhelmed with pleasure. Lost in it. In her body.

She was too perfect. He felt overcome by it: her beauty, her willingness, her trust in him. Even more because he had some idea of how difficult it was for her.

Her gaze was on his, two points of crystal gray, glittering in the low light. He felt she was *right there* with him, in a way no other woman ever had been before. And as pleasure rose, higher and higher, pulsing through his veins like lightning, something in his chest surged.

His hands went into her hair, his fingers snagging in the wild curls. Her legs wound around his waist, her taut thighs pulling him in. He felt the tremors run through her, her sex tightening, gripping him.

"Alec!"

She came, shivering, grabbing his shoulders, her nails digging into his flesh. And that heat lightning flowed from his veins into his belly, lower, into his cock. He exploded, his orgasm searing, burning, blinding him.

He shook with it for an eternity. And when it was over, he was holding her tight in his arms, his face buried in her neck. She was clinging to him, her slender arms around his neck, her breasts crushed against his chest. Her perfume was all around him, in his head.

That surging in his chest hadn't gone away. It had grown, spread.

Stop it. You're fine. Fine.

But his pulse was hammering in a way that couldn't be explained by sheer exertion. It was different. Warmer. A gentle melting. He didn't know what the hell it was. He wasn't sure he liked it. Except that he did.

"Alec . . . "

"Are you all right, Dylan?"

"Yes. Yes."

"What is it, then?"

"I . . . I don't know."

Neither do I.

But he didn't say it out loud. He couldn't admit that something was wrong. Not to anyone else. He didn't want to admit it to himself. But something was going on with him. And maybe with her, too.

He didn't know what the hell this meant. All of this heart-pounding, bursting sensation, like he wanted to . . . what? He didn't know. He didn't fucking know.

He just pulled her in tighter, breathed her in, that dark, earthy vanilla scent, mixed with the salt of her skin.

Her arms twined tighter around his neck, her cheek still pressed to his chest. Her breath was warm and ragged. He waited to calm, for them both to calm: his racing pulse, her heartbeat fluttering beneath his lips on her neck. But he couldn't seem to quiet himself. That thundering in his chest wouldn't stop.

Her pulse wouldn't quiet, either, and in a few moments, he felt tears on his skin.

"Dylan, what is it. Can you tell me?"

Real concern in his own voice. Not simply the calm concern

of a good dom. He heard it as if it were coming from another person, it was so unfamiliar. So starkly personal.

"It's nothing," she said quietly.

"It's *something*. Are you panicking?"

"No. It's not panic."

"What is it, then?"

He *had* to know. And it was about more than doing his job, being responsible.

"Alec, I . . . I'm just feeling so much. I'm not used to this."

"Neither am I," he muttered.

"What?"

"Nothing. Nothing. What do you need from me?"

"Just . . . this. Just to sit here with you holding me. Or I need you to let me go and send me home right this minute."

"You know that's not happening, Dylan."

"Yes."

He held her tighter, nearly crushing her in his arms. But it seemed that was what she needed. What *he* needed, damn it.

"Alec?"

"What?"

"I'm glad you're not sending me home."

His breath hitched, like a kick in the gut. He was glad, too. But he couldn't say it. He'd never been rendered speechless in his life. Until now.

Until Dylan.

Just breathe.

He pulled in a long breath, blew it out, did it again. And eventually, as her tears dried, he was able to breathe normally again, without that strange pain in his stomach, his chest.

Dylan had relaxed a little. He reached up and untangled her arms from his neck.

"Alec?"

"Don't worry. I'm taking you home with me. Right now."

She nodded her head.

He helped her off the table, dressed himself, and walked her back to the play area they'd used. He helped her dress, and it was like dressing a doll, she was so silent, so helplessly limp.

He wanted to hold her again.

Just get her home, into bed. Lay down with her.

Somehow he packed up his toys and got them both into his truck, where he blasted the heater, turned on the seat warmers. She was languid, quiet. He popped in a CD of classical music, some light Chopin, keeping the volume low.

This late at night it didn't take long to get from downtown to his Beacon Hill neighborhood. He pulled up in front of his place and helped Dylan from the car. She was still half limp, silent, her face loose, dazed. He felt a little dazed himself.

He got her inside, up the stairs and into his bedroom, where he undressed her carefully and put her into his bed.

She looked fragile, lying there, her face pale against the white sheets, the down pillows.

"Alec, I'm cold."

"I'm coming."

He pulled his clothes off and slid, naked, into the bed beside her. She curled into him, in a way she never had before. Like a child, seeking the heat of his body. Hers was warm and soft and felt better than anything he'd ever felt before. Riding his motorcycle. BDSM play. Sex.

He was getting hard again, but it wasn't that stark, driving need he usually felt with her. It was simply an unavoidable response to her body, her presence.

She felt so damn good in his arms, in his bed. He didn't want to think about it. He wasn't going to like any of the answers. And he liked this too much.

Too much.

But he couldn't fight it, not tonight. Tonight, she was here with him. And that was enough. It was more than enough. It was exactly what he wanted.

thirteen

Dylan opened her eyes. Sunlight poured in through the slatted plantation shutters on the windows, the rays catching dust motes. She glanced at the clock and was surprised to see she'd slept until almost noon.

Alec was still asleep beside her, lying on his stomach, the wide muscles of his back revealed by the sheet bunched around his waist. Just the sight of that smooth skin made her want to touch him, made her body light up with desire. But she needed to take some time to get her head on straight. Because it sure as hell wasn't anywhere near straight this morning.

Funny that he used white sheets, just like her own. So many men she'd known preferred darker colors. But he was unusual, in so any ways. Maybe the purity of white linens appealed to him, as it did to her.

They had more in common than she would have thought

initially. They were both writers, but for some reason she hadn't expected anything more. She didn't know why, now. They were both sexually open people, liberal-minded. They seemed to agree on so many subjects. They seemed to be tuned to the same channel.

Or maybe she was simply being overly romantic again.

But something had definitely happened between them last night. Something intense. He'd felt it, too. Her memory of exact incidents was a bit vague, but the one thing she remembered clear as day was the look in his eyes. Connection. Wonder.

She'd felt it, too. That part—everything she'd *felt*, was still feeling—burned through the fog that was the subspace she'd been in last night. That she was still in a little this morning, maybe.

She was scared. Wanting to run again.

Calm down. Try to work through this in some rational way.

But she wasn't feeling rational at all. She wanted to cry. It was so unlike her, she was stunned by the urge. She wasn't a crier. Wasn't a sentimentalist. But as she'd said to Mischa, her experiences with Alec were opening her up. And maybe simply Alec himself.

Alec.

She turned to look at him. His face was buried in one of the big down pillows, but she could see the dark stubble coming up on his cheek and neck. His hair was mussed, the black curls tipped with blue where the light touched it. He looked so peaceful. She'd never seen him like this. But even now he radiated power, perhaps simply because of the sheer size of him. And she loved that about him—in some purely girlish way—that he dwarfed her, made her feel small and feminine. Fragile, as though he could crush her if he wanted to.

God, was she really thinking these things? What had happened to the independent woman she'd prided herself on being her entire adult life? Hell, since she was ten years old and her mother had really lost it, leaving Dylan to care for their small family. She'd always been the one in control, the one to run things. That was her life. Who she was. And now this man was making her question *everything*.

Her breath caught in her throat, a sob wanting to escape. She bit her lip, bit the sob back.

Calm down. Everything is fine.

She curled her fingers around the edge of the dark red quilt, forced herself to breathe evenly.

That was better.

She was being unreasonable. It was just the intensity of her night with him, that was all. They'd only known each other for two weeks. What did she really know about him?

She knew from looking at his bedroom that he was neat. That he loved heavy wood furniture, antiques, which seemed to imply an earthiness about him. That he was basically down-to-earth, despite his level of sexual sophistication, how well-traveled he was. From the books stacked on the shelf of the nightstand next to the bed she knew he liked to read the classics, science fiction, thrillers, like the ones he wrote himself. She'd known already that he loved to travel, but next to the books was a stack of travel magazines: *Travel + Leisure, Condé Nast Traveler.*

On top of the high wood dresser were framed photos: Alec

and several other men on top of a mountain. Alec and some of the same group again in diving gear on a boat floating on brilliant turquoise tropical water. Alec and one of the same men sitting on big, shining motorcycles on some curving mountain road, smiling broadly.

Interesting that there were no family photos. But maybe he had those downstairs.

He hadn't talked about his family, other than that one conversation. It seemed the only one he'd ever been close to was his father. But she understood that. The only one she was close with was her grandmother. She knew you couldn't choose your family, and being related to someone didn't mean you were automatically close. She knew that all too well.

She'd never had a choice. Not about her mother. Or about taking care of her brother. Or trying to, anyway. And she'd screwed that up. Horribly. And now Quinn was dead. Which was why she deserved to be alone.

She shook her head. She was being morbid this morning. And did she really think she deserved to be alone? She simply preferred it that way. Didn't she?

But at least she'd distracted herself enough that she no longer felt like she was about to jump out of her skin. As long as she didn't think too much about the part where she melted under Alec's touch like warm butter.

Alec shifted, sighed in his sleep, and she focused on him once more. His muscles really were massive, his body absolutely hulking, like a pro football player. He'd turned onto his side, and she could see his sleeping face. The black goatee always made him look a little evil, but his mouth was loose and lush, sort of the way it looked when they were having sex.

A wave of pleasure shimmered over her skin. She remembered clearly the way his cock felt pushing into her body. The way his eyes glowed with something purely animal as he raised himself over her.

God, she was crazy about him. About his body, what he could do to her. And maybe something more.

No.

But she couldn't deny it.

It was just sex, she reminded herself for the millionth time. Great sex. But just sex. She'd had great sex before. She understood how intense sexual chemistry could draw a person in.

You are so full of crap.

She sighed, ran a hand through her hair, her fingers tangling in the long curls.

Maybe she should go, before she had any more of these ridiculous ideas. Ideas like continuing to see him once she was done learning enough for her book.

She'd already learned plenty. If she was perfectly honest with herself, she was seeing him now, submitting to him, purely because she wanted to.

Damn it.

She threw back the covers and swung her legs over the side of the big bed.

"Oh no, you don't," Alec growled, his voice husky with sleep.

"Alec . . . "

"Where do you think you're going?"

His arm snaked around her waist, and he dragged her over the smooth sheets, until her bare flesh was pressed against his bare flesh. She could feel the heat of his body against her back, her buttocks. His silken skin.

"Alec, I have to get up. I have to go. Please."

"Not again. It's not happening, Dylan, so you might as well get used to it. You go when I say you can go."

"God damn it, Alec. How many times do I have to remind you I am not one of your subbie girls?"

"I'm not saying you are. But you could still be spacing and you're not going until I think it's safe."

"I can assure you, it's perfectly safe. I don't even have my car. I'd have to call a cab, so there's no danger of me driving. I want to go."

"No."

Oh, she was mad now. "Don't pull this power trip on me, Alec."

"You think that's what this is? A power trip?"

"You *are* physically restraining me."

"You were fine with that last night." His eyes were burning, dark. Angry.

"That was last night."

He released her, so quickly she would have fallen had she not already been lying down.

"Fine," he said through clenched teeth. "I don't do non-consensual."

"I didn't mean that."

He sat up. She felt the shift in his weight on the bed. But she couldn't look at him. If she saw him, she was afraid he'd have her.

"Dylan, what the hell are we doing here, huh? You're fighting this and fighting this."

"I never promised I could do this, Alec. That I could really submit."

"And yet you do, every time."

She was quiet a moment. She felt stunned.

"And," he went on, "you only panic the next day, when you have a chance to think about it. Stop thinking so much, Dylan."

"I can't." She turned to him then, fury burning through her. "That's the problem. I can't stop thinking. That's the way I operate. That's how I've gotten through life."

"Maybe it's time to learn another way."

"I don't think so."

He leaned toward her, the bulk of his big frame a little threatening. "It hasn't gotten you very far, has it? You have a career, and you managed to live through taking care of your family, but what's left for you, Dylan?"

"You're one to talk! Like you have any more personal connections than I do."

"It's different for me."

"Are you kidding me? Is that what you tell yourself? That's a flimsy excuse, Alec. At least I can be honest with myself. I have an empty life because I choose it. Because I'm not willing to deal with the emotional fallout of a relationship. Is that what you wanted me to say? Okay, I've said it. But you are no different from me. That's bullshit. You're the one trying to get me to stay here. And it may be presumptuous of me, but I don't think that's just you being the responsible dominant."

He sat, staring at her. *Through* her. His gaze was a burning, brilliant blue. And as she watched, the anger faded, his jaw and his shoulders loosening.

"You're right," he said.

She was ready to keep arguing. But his comment took all the wind out of her. Took her breath away.

"What?"

"I said that you're right. I want you here because I just . . . want you here."

"Damn it, Alec."

She did not want to hear this. And yet it was everything she wanted to hear.

Her head was spinning.

"Come here." He reached for her, grabbing her hand, and she tried to pull away.

"Alec, I have to think . . . "

"I said enough thinking. Christ, Dylan, stop fighting me and come here. I know you want to, so don't give me any non-consensual crap. Don't use my moral code against me, Dylan."

"Alec . . . "

But he had her, pulling her closer, until her breasts were pressed up against the hard planes of his chest, and suddenly she was half in his lap.

His cock was rigid beneath her, and he bent to kiss her, his lips crushing, bruising. Commanding her once more.

She wanted to fight him. To struggle. But he tasted right. Smelled right. *Felt* right.

He kept kissing her, until her blood sang with desire, her sex hot and needy. When he turned her body and grabbed her thighs, shifting her until she was straddling him, she didn't argue. She couldn't. She was a hot, melting pool of desire, helpless against it. Helpless against him.

He pulled his mouth from hers and fumbled in the nightstand with one hand, coming back with a condom. He tore the packet with his teeth, and she helped him roll it onto his hard cock.

Then he was kissing her again, hot, urgent kisses, his mouth devouring her. He lifted her and, arching his hips, impaled her.

She moaned into his mouth. He groaned into hers. Then he was pumping up into her, while pleasure shivered like an electric current through her body: her breasts, her sex.

His hand slipped between them, his fingers teasing her clitoris, and she was coming almost instantly, her climax hard and fast and brilliant. She let her head fall away from his mouth, let it fall back, keening his name.

"Alec, Alec, Alec . . . "

He was still thrusting, his cock driving into her, over and over, hot and thick and pulsing.

"Dylan," he gasped.

She opened her eyes, looked into his.

"Yes. I need you to look at me. You are so damn beautiful, my girl. *My* girl."

Their skin grew slick with sweat. She didn't care. She held on to his broad shoulders, pleasure rising once more, cresting impossibly.

"Dylan . . . baby . . . I'm coming."

A few more hard thrusts, and she felt the heat of it, his climax making him shudder all over. And feeling him come set her off again, another orgasm rippling through her in long, undulating waves.

"Ah, God, Alec . . . "

He bit into her neck, his tongue licking at her skin. And she was coming and coming.

His arms went tighter around her waist, held on to her so hard she could barely breathe as they both stopped moving.

"Fuck, Dylan."

"Yeah . . . "

They stayed that way for a long time. She thought they did, anyway. Time was suspended for her. All she knew was his body pressed against hers, the feel of his flesh, the scent of him.

"Dylan." His voice was muffled, his face still buried in her neck. His breath was warm on her skin.

"Hmm?"

"Don't think."

"I'm not. Not yet."

He lifted his face, but not enough that she could see him. "What's going to happen when you start thinking again?"

"I . . . I don't know."

"Then don't do it."

"I'll try," she told him, wanting it to be true, but still unsure as to what she was capable of.

"No, I mean it," he insisted. "Let's both just . . . not think. Let's do this. Be together. Without dissecting it."

"What does that mean, Alec?"

"I don't know. Does it have to mean something?"

"Maybe not . . . "

"You're thinking again, Dylan."

"Yes."

"Don't do it. Okay? Just don't do it. Let's see what happens."

She laughed quietly. "We're not really the 'go with the flow' kind of people, Alec."

"What do you mean? I'm totally laid-back."

She smiled against his shoulder. "Right. That's exactly the definition I would use for you."

She heard his quiet laughter as a deep rumble in his chest, taking some of the intensity out of the moment, making it simpler, lighter.

Maybe he was right. Maybe they could just let it *be* for now, whatever was happening between them. Maybe they didn't need to define anything, pull it apart and examine it.

She'd never lived her life that way. Neither had he. It felt easier, somehow, knowing this would be a challenge for him as well. That she wasn't alone in this.

He loosened his hold on her enough that he could lean back to look at her. Reaching up, he brushed her hair from her face. She was melting again. But she simply let it happen.

"Do we have a deal?" he asked her, his face perfectly serious.

"Yes. We have a deal."

"Good. Because I need to fuck you again. And that would be impossible if you get up and leave."

"You're insatiable."

"Yes. With you, I am."

He was hardening inside her again already, his cock beginning to pulse. And she was ready. Her body was always ready for him. Her mind, her heart, might be a different story. One in which she didn't know the ending.

If only she could create the ending herself. Choose it, as she did when she was writing. But she didn't even know where she wanted this to end.

She wasn't sure she wanted this to end at all.

Yes, she was going to have to stop thinking about everything or she was going to make herself crazy.

She was pretty sure she'd lost her mind already, the moment she'd met Alec.

She just had to be certain she didn't lose her heart.

Dylan kicked the front door of her flat shut behind her and dropped her purse on the floor, grabbing her ringing cell phone just in time.

"Hello?"

"Hey. I've been calling you all weekend."

"It's still the weekend, Mischa."

"It's nine o'clock on Sunday night." Her friend's voice was petulant.

"And?" Dylan asked, slipping out of her coat and hanging it in the tall, sleek lacquered armoire by the front door.

"And . . . I guess I'm not used to you being unavailable to me."

"I was with Alec."

"I figured."

Dylan leaned down, took her high heels off, leaving her feet bare. The wood floors were smooth and chilly. She flipped the heat on as she crossed the apartment, went into the kitchen and poured herself a glass of Cabernet. She felt good. Lazy. Sated.

Almost.

She couldn't seem to get enough of him.

Alec . . .

"Dylan?"

"What? Sorry, Mischa."

"I asked how your weekend was. God, you really are a mess over this guy, aren't you?"

"I'm . . . I don't know what I am."

"But things are going well? Are you any less confused than you were the last time we talked?"

"Things are going well. Because I've reformed." She grinned, sipped at her wine as she leaned against the counter.

"Reformed?"

"Yes. I've made an agreement to stop thinking. To stop dissecting every move he makes and everything I think, or have ever thought, about myself, relationships, sex, men . . . "

"You're kidding."

"Nope." She raised her glass in a small salute and took another sip. "I'm officially tired of fighting myself, Misch. It's ridiculous."

"I could have told you that," Mischa teased.

"Then why didn't you?" Dylan moved into the living area, set the glass down on the coffee table and settled onto the sofa, curling her bare legs beneath her and pulling a small, soft throw blanket over them. She said quietly, "I'm just seeing how . . . damaging this has been for me. Not letting anyone in by finding some flaw in everyone. Because if you dig deeply enough, everyone has one. And I go looking for it. I pick every man apart with a shovel."

"Dylan, don't be so hard on yourself."

"That's part of it, too. I tear myself apart every bit as much as I do other people."

"Yes, you do."

"Well, I want to stop. And Alec is helping me."

"What's really going on, Dylan?" Mischa asked, her tone gentle.

"I'm finally opening up. All of this power play stuff with Alec is opening me up. And I don't like everything I see, but I'm realizing I'm . . . human."

"I love you, anyway, you know. I always have."

"I know. I'm finally getting that."

Her buzzer rang and she got up and went to the intercom. "Hang on a second, Mischa. Who's there?"

"Dylan." Alec's voice was deep, soft with desire.

"Alec, you just dropped me off ten minutes ago."

"I know. I've changed my mind. I'm not ready to let you go yet."

"Oh . . . "

"Let me come up."

"Yes . . . come up."

It was several moments before she realized she still held her cell phone in her hand. "Mischa? I'm sorry, but Alec . . . he's here."

"So I heard. No problem. But call me soon."

"I will."

As they hung up she heard the grinding lurch of the building's industrial elevator, and in moments Alec was knocking on her door. She opened it.

She could smell his black leather jacket and his warm skin before she noticed anything else. Then she looked up and saw his crooked smile.

She smiled back. She couldn't help it. He was so damn handsome, so dark and wicked-looking, with his leather jacket and his dark goatee and that look in his eyes . . . as though he wanted to eat her up.

She went loose, hot all over, as he moved through the door and swept her into his arms. He bent to kiss her, his mouth hungry, sweet. Demanding.

He kissed her until she was shaking, her sex hot and needy. Soaking wet.

He pulled back, stripped his jacket off, letting it drop to the floor.

"I need you, Dylan. I couldn't even make it home. I had to turn around and come back."

She nodded, desire knotting her throat.

"I need to be inside you, now. Right this second."

"Yes . . . "

He turned her around, pushing her against the front door, so that she had to brace her hands against it, her face only inches from the smooth, painted wood. Then he unzipped her dress, the same one she'd worn to meet him at the Pleasure Dome Friday night, pulling it off her. She was naked underneath.

"Ah. Exactly the way I like you, my girl." He ran his hands down her sides, making goose bumps rise on her skin. Then lower, over her hips, her buttocks. "Spread for me, Dylan. I'm going to fuck you right here."

She felt herself going down, into that misty, lovely place, as she gave into him. Gave herself over.

She parted her thighs, heard him pop the buttons on his jeans, heard the tearing of a foil wrapper. Then one of his arms wrapped around her waist, and with the other he moved the hair away from her neck, sweeping it aside. He planted a tiny kiss there, making her tremble with need. Pure heat. A nearly unbearable urgency.

Using his hand, he guided his cock between her thighs, and she bent at the waist, spreading wider, letting him slip inside.

"Oh, that's good, Alec . . . So good."

Her sex was wet, clenching. And then he began to move. Deep, driving strokes, so hard and fast she could barely breathe. Her palms were splayed flat against the painted wood door, and she laid her cheek there, pressing into the hard surface. His hips arched, pumping, pumping, driving pleasure into her system, as deep as his thrusting cock.

His mouth was on the back of her neck, kissing, biting, then moving down her spine, over her shoulders. Then he slowed down, paused, and all she heard was their ragged breath. All she felt was his big body behind her, his lips resting against her shoulder, his swollen cock filling her. Pleasure was a held breath, suspended, edged with anticipation. And then his hand came down in a hard smack across one buttock, making her body surge toward the door, surge with desire.

"Yes, Alec . . . "

He slapped her again, the sound ringing in her ears, the pleasure like some deep echo in her body. Then he was smacking her, fucking her, everything at once, his breath harsh in her ear. Sensation poured like water through her system, pooling in her belly, her sex, her aching breasts. It spread, shimmered, dazzling her. And as she came, her eyesight dimmed, sound faded away. She was a being of pure sensation, pure pleasure, spiraling higher and higher. She was drowning in it.

He stopped.

She was panting. So was he.

"Alec?"

"Baby. I don't want it to be over so soon. Give me a minute . . . just hang on."

He pulled out of her, pulled her close against him. She could feel the rough fabric of his jeans against her thighs, the zipper biting into her skin. And the softness of the sweater he wore. Lovely on her bare flesh. That, and his hands smoothing over her stomach, teasing her nipples. Then slipping between her thighs, pressing into her.

"You're so damn wet. So ready."

"Yes."

"Even though I've been fucking you so hard . . . "

"Yes . . . "

"Do you need to come again, baby?" He plunged his fingers inside her.

"Yes!"

"Good. I want you to. Come on."

She knew by now not to ask any questions. And it was actually rather wonderful not to have to think.

She followed him as he led her into the bathroom. Stood quietly as he undressed, rid himself of the condom, and turned the water on before stepping into the white tiled shower with him.

He'd turned on the big overhead rain shower fixture, and the water cascaded down over them, exactly like a warm, falling rain. Soothing the sore skin on her bottom. Alec pulled her in, his arms closing around her, and she let herself fall into him, let him hold her up.

She was still full of need for him. So was he; she could tell by his cock, hard and ready and pressing against her belly. But it was nice to simply stand there together, skin to skin, the water falling warm all around them, the steam rising.

The high, arching window built into one wall of the shower let light in from the streets below, a wash of amber from the streetlights, along with a bit of pink and blue from the neon signs of the storefronts. It cast colored shadows onto the ceiling, the top of the shower walls. The light, the water, and Alec's huge body next to hers made her feel cocooned, as though the rest of the world no longer existed. As if it was just the two of them, in this moment.

He held her like that for a long while. And then he began to stroke her skin.

Long, gentle sweeps of his hands over her back, her sides, her buttocks. And eventually he began a series of small slaps. His hands were so much sharper on her wet skin, and the pain started immediately. So did the pleasure, her body readily converting the sensations. And lovely to have her hard nipples pressed against his chest, his cock nestled between her thighs now, growing harder by the second. She opened for him, and his cock slid in between her pussy lips, slipping in her juices without entering her.

"Ah, God, Alec. Please."

"Yes, you need to come, don't you, baby? Come on, then. Sit down here."

He shifted, setting her down on the edge of the tile bench built into the wall behind her.

"Spread for me. Ah, that's good. Beautiful."

She eased her thighs farther apart, watched as he took the

handheld shower massager from its hook on the tiled wall and aimed it at her open sex.

"Oh . . . "

He held it against her clitoris, moved it down over her cleft, then back again, teasing her. Soon she was panting, needing him.

"Is that good, my girl?"

"Yes . . . it's good."

"But you need more, don't you?"

She didn't answer him. She couldn't.

When he knelt between her thighs, she held her breath. And when he leaned in, his tongue licking at her aching slit, she moaned aloud. Pleasure surged through her, a tide of heat and need. And he was licking her, his tongue sliding up and down over her cleft, then pushing inside her. He aimed the water sprayer at her clitoris, the water pulsating against that needy nub of flesh.

"Alec . . . oh, God . . . it's too much . . . "

But it was enough. In moments she was coming once more. Coming apart.

For him.

With him.

"Alec!"

When she stopped shivering he pulled away, easing his body between her thighs, leaning in to kiss her. The water was streaming over them, but she could still taste her juices on his lips. Knew that he had made her come. *Made* her. And she loved it.

His cock was pressing against her again, a rigid shaft of flesh. She reached down and took it in her hand, felt it pulse, felt its strength. She wanted it. Wanted him. Wanted to please.

"Alec . . . let me . . . "

She sank to her knees, and he let her go, rising to his feet at the same time. Her hands wrapped around his thighs, his rigid cock before her. Beautiful.

She leaned in and slid her tongue across the rounded tip, smiling when he groaned.

"Christ, you're going to kill me, Dylan."

She licked again, pushing her tongue into the slitted hole at the tip, tasting him, the salt of his pre-come. She couldn't wait a moment longer.

Opening her mouth, she took him in, all at once, until his swollen flesh choked her, making tears rise in her eyes. But she wanted it, needed it, for some reason. She slid her mouth back, resting at the head of his cock, let her tongue slide around it, again and again.

Alec was writhing, his hips arching. When she glanced up, she saw that his head was thrown back, his hands braced against the walls of the shower on either side of him. His face was a study in ecstasy. Masculine. Sensual. Beautiful.

She swallowed him deeper, focusing on opening her throat, letting his cock slide all the way down. He began to pump into her mouth, and her fingers dug into his thighs, her nails biting deep, making him moan.

"Christ, Dylan. Dylan . . ."

His cock pulsed, hard and fast, and her mouth was flooded with scorching, liquid heat. He kept thrusting, his movements slowing. Finally, he brushed her wet hair from her face, helping her up. She leaned her head into the rain shower, letting the water wash away his seed.

"Dylan . . . that was incredible. You're incredible."

His hands were in her hair, gripping the wet strands, hanging on to her. She leaned into him, resting her head on his chest, heard the low and steady drumbeat of his heart.

He bent to kiss her face, long, slow, sweet kisses raining over her cheeks, her chin, her forehead, her eyelids. Kisses that left her shivering. Not with desire. But something more. What was it?

Don't think. Just stop. Just be.

But she knew. She felt the shiver in her belly, in her chest, in her racing pulse. It wasn't about the sex, although that was incredible, as Alec had said. It meant more. It was something deeper.

Something she had promised herself she would not think about.

She held on to him, her hands gripping his wide shoulders. He was so solid. She needed to focus on that, the sense of safety she felt in his arms. But it all seemed to circle back to the same thing: something else was happening here besides the sex and the opening up. And she didn't know how much longer she could pretend she wasn't falling for Alec. Falling hard.

She squeezed her eyelids, closing them tight, and bit her lip against a wave of dizziness. She'd never felt so out of control in her life, not even when Alec had her bound and physically helpless. That was nothing compared to this.

She was falling, despite every effort not to do exactly that. There wasn't a damn thing she could do about it. And when she hit the ground, it was going to be one hell of a mess.

fourteen

She'd been very good at not thinking for three weeks. After the
night with Alec in the shower, she had made a new deal with herself: since she was helpless over how she felt, she would just accept
it. It didn't have to change anything. The feelings were simply
there. She could choose what she would do about it—or not.

There had been other nights in the shower. And days. It had
become one of their favorite places to have sex. And she loved the
sharpness of the spankings on her wet flesh, the sound echoing
off the hard tiled walls of the shower, either hers or his.

Alec had made himself at home at her place, leaving a tooth-
brush there, an extra shirt. Not that it was a sign of anything. It
was simply convenient. Her place was so much closer to the Pleasure Dome than his; it was right down the street. And his laptop
sitting in one corner of her dining area was another convenience,
nothing more.

Anyway, she liked it when they wrote together in the afternoons, with Alec at her glass dining table, her sitting at her desk in the office area of her flat a few yards away. It was companionable. And if one of them needed to brainstorm a plot point, the other was right there. Of course, that often led to more sex. But since she was an erotica author she looked at it as inspiration. Her book was beginning to gel, the plot and the character dynamics all coming together, thanks in large part to Alec. It was always a good sign when her writing went well.

Mischa had called again, asked how things were going. Dylan hadn't mentioned most of these things to her. She wasn't sure why. Maybe she simply wanted to keep what was happening just for the two of them. Private. Or maybe she was afraid that talking about it would make it too real, would shatter her ability to deny what it might mean for them. For her. And she was better off if she let those thoughts get no closer than the edge of her consciousness. It was a weird sort of half-denial, but it made everything manageable. It kept that small bit of distance she required in order to maintain a sense of balance. Of control.

She hadn't left any of her own things at his place, no matter how much time she spent there.

This was one of the odd days when she was home alone for a while, sitting at the dining table, sipping a cup of her favorite jasmine and green tea, a plate of buttered toast at her elbow.

She was staring out the windows, as she so often did. The sun was trying to muscle its way through the Seattle morning fog, the light a sort of misty gold, making warm spots on the sleek wood floors, making them shine with a warm, golden glow. It reminded her of lying in bed the other morning with Alec, another sunny

day, like today. The sun had caught the soft hairs on his fore-
arm as he slept, tipping them in gold and amber. She'd reached
out and touched his arm with her fingertips. And he'd woken up,
smiling at her, his eyes that utterly impossible blue that seemed
to look right through her. *Inside* her.

It had still been half dark when Alec kissed her good-bye an
hour ago, leaving to go meet his friend Dante for a hike somewhere. They were to meet Dante later that evening for dinner.

She wrapped her hands around her cup of tea, lifted it and
sipped the hot liquid.

She wasn't sure how she felt about meeting his friends. It
seemed to be the natural course, she supposed. But the natural
course for a relationship. And that was not what was going on
here. Or was it?

Did this signal his desire for things to get more serious? He
was as anti-relationship as she was. That was what kept her safe.
No matter how close she felt to him.

They'd grown closer. They'd told each other nearly every
deep, dark secret. Certainly every sexual fantasy. He'd even
spanked her while wearing his leather jacket a few times after
she'd confided in him how much it turned her on: the scent of
the leather, the *badness* of it. Nothing she talked about sexually
shocked him. It was freeing. Exhilarating. She'd never met anyone like him. He was so open-minded. Intelligent, whether they
were discussing sex or anything else.

She loved that they could talk about art and literature, something that had always been lacking in the men she'd dated. She
suspected Alec was smarter than she was, but that was a good
thing. It made her respect him more. She realized there was a bit

of snobbery in her feeling that way, but she couldn't help it. And she felt a man deserved for the woman he was with, even if it was casual dating—or casual sex—to respect him.

Alec was kind, as well. Everywhere they went, people loved him immediately. It was only her own stubbornness, she could see now, that had made her so combative with him when they'd first met. He charmed everyone: waiters, bookstore clerks. And the charm wasn't simply some shallow façade, as it was with too many other men.

She realized she hadn't thought about another man, looked at another man, since she'd met Alec just over five weeks earlier. It seemed as though she'd known him for ages. Forever.

Forever . . . with him . . .

Her pulse fluttered, she smiled to herself. Then panic gripped her, and it was like being punched in the stomach.

What was she thinking?

There would be no forever. Not with Alec. Not with any man. Not for her.

Her cell phone jangled, and she pulled it across the table to read the caller I.D.

Alec.

Just breathe.

The panic downshifted, and her pulse flooded with familiar heat, simply seeing his name on the small screen.

She picked it up.

"Hi."

"Dylan. Hi."

His voice made her smile, that soft, deep whiskey and honey tone. The panic eased a little more.

"Alec. Are you done hiking already?"

"We haven't left yet. Dante had an emergency at his office, so I have a little time. Actually, I'm downstairs."

"What?"

"Are you going to let me in?"

She laughed. "Did you think I wouldn't?"

"Good girl."

She shivered as she went to press the door buzzer, her heart tumbling in her chest, her sex heating, knowing he was coming.

She opened the front door and waited for the elevator. It arrived, the doors swung aside, and there was Alec. He looked sleek and every inch the bad boy in his jeans and black T-shirt, carrying a dark leather jacket over his shoulder. He grinned when he saw her.

"You're not dressed," he growled, appreciation lighting his eyes.

"You hardly gave me time. You left an hour ago."

He dropped his jacket on the floor and slammed the door behind him. "I like to keep you on your toes. And on your back. Your knees."

A few strides and he was on her, backing her into the apartment, his jacket dropping onto the floor.

His hands were all over her in seconds, untying her robe and letting it fall to the floor, tweaking her nipples, making them hard, pleasure shimmering over her skin. Then he bent to kiss her, his mouth hard and bruising, his tongue wet and sweet. He tasted of mint. He tasted of Alec.

She moaned as he walked her backward, into the dining area,

then lifted her and sat her on the big glass table. It was cold on her bottom, the backs of her thighs.

He pulled his mouth from hers.

"These are pretty, but let's get rid of them for now."

He slid her panties off, one leg at a time, pausing to lay hot kisses on her knees, the tops of her thighs, making her tremble. Then he slipped his fingers right into her soaking wet slit.

"Oh, God, Alec. Just . . . give me a moment to think."

"There's nothing to think about. Christ, you feel good, baby."

He kept his eyes on hers as he raised his wet fingers to his lips, licked them. She shivered, desire shafting into her body.

"Alec . . . "

"What do you want, my girl?"

"You know what I want."

"Tell me."

"I want your mouth on me."

He smiled and pushed her back farther onto the table, laying her down. The cold glass against her back was a sensual counter-balance to the heat of her sex. Her body was growing hotter by the second. Alec pushed her thighs wider with his hands, and when he bent his head and tasted her, she gasped.

"Oh, yes . . . "

He dove in then, going to work with his tongue, his lips, his fingers. He licked her hard clitoris, sucked on it, harder and harder. With his fingers he massaged the lips of her sex, then dove inside, curving them to reach her G-spot.

"God, Alec. I'm going to come!"

He kept at it, pleasure like heat lightning in her body, the walls of her sex beginning to clench. And his silken head between her thighs, his dark, curling hair brushing against the skin there, adding to the sensations.

He sucked harder on her clit, pressed his fingers deeper. Lights flashed behind her closed eyes. Her body arched off the table, heat searing her, shivering through her in wave after wave.

She had barely quieted, her sex still clenching, when he unzipped his slacks, pulling a condom from his pocket and sheathing his erect cock. Her legs went around his waist and he raised her arms over her head, holding her wrists together in his big hand before he slipped inside her, just the swollen tip of his cock resting inside her entrance. Lovely. Excruciating.

"You're so wet, baby. So wet for me. I just need to fuck you. Just . . . fuck you, my girl."

His hips pistoned, his cock driving deep all at once, and she cried out. It was all pure animal fury then, their bodies joined in heat and need and urgency as he began to pump. And it was as though she were still coming in small flurries of sensation, her sex clenching at his rigid cock moving inside her.

He moved faster, deeper. Harder, his hips slamming into hers, the hard table beneath her bruising her spine. She didn't care. She loved it all: the pleasure, her wrists held tight in his, the sense of being taken over.

"Come on, Alec. Please."

"I'm coming . . . baby . . . "

His face torn in ecstasy, he came, shuddering, driving into her. Groaning, he thrust again, and again.

"Dylan . . . " He collapsed on top of her, breathing in hard, rasping pants. "Ah, that was good."

"Mmm."

He kissed her earlobe, gave it a small, nibbling bite. "I'm going to be late for my ride."

"Yes. What will you tell Dante?"

"Nothing. He'll know."

She only smiled at that. She felt too good to care.

Alec pushed off her, helping her to her feet.

He stood back, holding on to her hand. "I like this look on you." He reached between her thighs and pushed two fingers into her wet heat. She leaned into him, pleasure arcing through her system, sharp and electric.

"Jesus, Alec. You're never going to get out of here if you don't stop that."

"Don't tempt me, woman. I don't want to keep Dante waiting too long or I'd take you over my lap and spank your gorgeous ass until it was that beautiful shade of pink I love so much. I could almost get hard again already just thinking about it."

She shivered, picturing what he'd described.

"Are you sure we don't have time?"

He laughed. "We have plenty of time after dinner tonight. Too long to wait, maybe."

"Much too long."

"Come with me."

"What?"

"Come and ride with me today. Come hiking with us. Dante won't mind. Do you like to hike?"

"Yes. But, Alec, I'm not getting on your bike."

Her chest was going unpleasantly tight simply thinking about it.

"It's a short ride."

"That's not the point."

"I thought you trusted me."

"I do. And I will do almost anything, Alec, anything in bed, at the club. I'll submit to you in nearly every way, but I will not get on a motorcycle. With you, or anyone else. It's not personal."

"I just thought it'd be nice for you to come with us. To see that part of my life."

Was he hurt? But she was not going to do it.

"I'm sorry. I can't do that."

He shrugged. But she still didn't know if he was upset with her.

"It's okay." He stroked her hair, pushing it back from her face. "It really is, Dylan."

"Okay."

He leaned in, kissed her mouth, and she relaxed beneath his touch: his hand on her cheek, his lips on hers.

"I have to go. But you'll meet us tonight, Wild Ginger at eight?"

"Yes. Of course."

He grinned at her. "That wasn't an order, Dylan."

She blushed, thinking about Dante overhearing this conversation, then realized he would be used to such talk since Alec had mentioned that he was a dominant, as Alec was.

"All right. I can still be there at eight."

"Great." He zipped his jeans and she realized then that he'd never even undressed, just come at her, all pure, animal sex. And she was still naked. A trembling desire ran through her system. "Sorry to have to run," he told her, taking her hand and brushing his lips over her knuckles.

"It's fine."

"Okay. Have a good day. I'll see you tonight, baby."

A small shiver at the nickname.

Stop being such a girl.

"I'll be ready."

He slid an arm around her waist, pulling her close once more, murmured in her ear, "You're always ready. Have I told you how I love that, Dylan?"

She was wet again, her limbs going warm and loose.

"You'd better go or I'm really not going to let you out of here."

"Bossy girl." He laughed.

"I'm learning from the best. Go on. Have a good hike. I'll see you tonight."

She was smiling when she closed the door behind him, picked up her robe and slid it over her shoulders. God, she was turning into such a girl. She had to remind herself that it didn't make her any weaker. She *was* a girl. Alec was simply the first man who had ever really made her feel like one. Maybe because he was the first one who had broken through the tough façade she felt she had to show to the world. Not all the way through, but he had certainly cracked the armor and looked inside.

And he was still there. Still with her.

She didn't want to think too much about what that meant. Better to ease off and think about the girly stuff, let herself wallow in it a little.

The one thing she didn't want to wallow in was their conversation about the motorcycle. She still wasn't sure how he felt about her adamant refusal to ride with him, but the idea was unthinkable. Even imagining him hurtling down the highway on that thing scared her.

Don't think about that. Think about dinner tonight, being with him again.

She went into the bathroom to shower and dress for the day. Her eyes in the mirror were luminous, the pupils large. Her cheeks were flushed pink. And her lips looked as though they'd been bitten. She smiled at her reflection.

Everything was fine. Alec would be fine. She had to get some control over her fears. She'd been carrying them around for far too long.

Right now all she needed to worry about was what dress she'd wear tonight. Maybe she was more of a girl than she'd thought.

The day had passed quickly, and she'd gotten a dozen pages written, plus more edited. Even though she'd kept busy, Alec had been in the back of her mind all day long. She couldn't stop thinking about him.

Standing in front of the long mirror on her wardrobe door in her black underwear and bra trimmed in pretty purple lace, she wondered which outfit she should wear. She had to meet Alec and Dante in less than an hour and she should figure it out soon. Why was it so difficult to decide?

The soft, purple wraparound dress or the gray cashmere sweater and her black skirt? Both fit her well, showing off her figure. She held the dress up to her body. The neckline was low, the skirt flaring. She hung it on the door and held up the skirt. They were both sexy but sophisticated.

She always seemed to find her sexiest outfits to wear for him. She supposed that made sense, since they were sleeping together. But it had never mattered quite so much before.

She hung the skirt back up. Maybe she'd wear the purple dress . . . She liked the way the layers of fabric crossed over her breasts, leaving a deep V. She liked the softness of the fabric on her sensitized skin, the way it brushed against her legs.

She'd been hyperaware of everything for weeks, every nerve tuned in and on full volume. Sensations, tastes, scents, sounds, it all came to her amplified, as though Alec had woken her up in every way.

Alec.

She slipped the dress over her shoulders, tied it firmly at the waist. She skipped tights, even though it was chilly outside, and settled on knee-high black suede boots instead, with a high, stacked heel. She added a simple necklace of cascading silver rings and a pair of delicate hoop earrings.

She checked her reflection in the mirror, pleased with what she saw, knew Alec would be pleased. Warmth seeped through her system.

She smiled when her cell phone rang and she saw his name on the screen.

"Alec."

"Dylan, it's Dante. I'm using Alec's phone."

"Oh. Dante. Hi."

"Look, I don't want you to worry, and I'm only calling because we're going to be a little late for dinner."

Goose bumps crept up her spine.

"Worry about what?"

"Alec had an accident—a small one and he's fine—"

"An accident?"

"He really is fine, I promise."

"Where is he?"

"We're at Virginia Mason Hospital, in the ER."

"Oh my God. I'll be right there."

"There's no need to come. Really."

"I'm coming."

She snapped her phone shut, her pulse thrumming, hot and sharp with worry. Fear.

She grabbed her coat and her purse and slammed the front door behind her. The elevator seemed to take an eternity, but finally she was downstairs, in her car and racing across town.

Those damn motorcycles. Why must men be so obsessed with them? God, if anything had happened to Alec she'd never forgive him.

She reached the hospital quickly, parked and got out of her car. She headed for the ER and went inside.

That smell. She hated it—the scent of disinfectant and rubbing alcohol and worry. She hated the click of her heels on the pale linoleum floor. The stark coldness the pretty floral paintings on the wall could do nothing to soften. It all reminded her too much of losing Quinn. She could hardly stand it. But Alec was in here somewhere. She swallowed down the nausea and approached the desk. A nurse looked up.

"I'm looking for a . . . friend."

"Name?" the woman asked.

"Alec Walker."

"Dylan."

She turned and found Alec and a tall, lanky man who must be Dante just coming through the double doors. Alec's left arm was in a sling. Panic crept over her skin like a cold chill.

"Alec!"

"Dylan, you didn't have to come all the way down here."

"Are you kidding? Dante called and told me you'd been hurt."

"I'm fine. I jacked up my shoulder a little and Dante insisted I have it checked out."

"You are not fine. You went down on your bike? Is that what happened?"

"It was nothing. I took a turn too fast and there was a pile of leaves on the road. I should have handled it better."

She wanted to tell him he shouldn't have been on the damn bike at all. But she wouldn't embarrass him in front of his friend. And she knew she wasn't being entirely reasonable. But she couldn't help it. All she could think of was Quinn's still face. Quinn dead.

Her throat began to close up and she felt the hot, prickling tears at the back of her eyes.

Stop it. Calm down.

Alec moved closer, took her hand in his. It was warm. Reassuring. If only they could get out of there, get away from that smell.

"I swear I am perfectly fine, Dylan. A little sore, nothing broken."

"Okay. Okay." She pulled in a deep breath, then another, trying not to let him see.

"I'm sorry if I alarmed you," Dante said. His eyes were a light golden brown, their expression kind. "Alec said I should call you."

"No, I . . . thank you. I know you were just being considerate. I was just . . . worried."

"Nothing to worry about," Alec insisted. "I've done worse in my own kitchen. Lots worse on the basketball court."

"That's because you're too bulky to play ball," Dante teased him.

"I killed you in football, my friend," Alec said, his mouth quirking in a grin.

"Only because you're a freaking giant," Dante answered.

Dylan watched their easy exchange, still trying to get her heartbeat to normalize. "Can we . . . are you able to leave yet?"

"Yes, sure. We were on our way out when you arrived. We were going by Dante's place to change." Alec was watching her, his blue gaze hard on hers. "Are you all right? You're not going to pass out on us, are you?"

"What? Of course I'm all right. I just don't like hospitals very much."

He put his hand on her back, rubbing in small circles. It made her want to cry all over again. She didn't understand it.

"Let's get out of here, then."

"You can't ride your bike like that."

"We went by my place and traded our bikes for my car," Dante told her.

"We can meet you at the restaurant in half an hour," Alec said. "You should go ahead, get yourself a drink."

She nodded. A drink sounded perfect. "Okay."

He drew her in, close to his side, brushed a kiss over her hair. She still wanted to cry, but the hard knot of fear in her throat was untying itself, bit by bit.

They all walked out to the parking lot together, and Alec brushed another kiss over her hair before putting her in her car. She put on a classical CD and the music and the drive soothed her, helped to calm her frayed nerves. She parked across the street from Wild Ginger.

It was the same restaurant where they'd had their first dinner date. Is that what they were doing? Dating?

She supposed she was dating this man.

Just dating.

Just sex.

She pulled in a breath. And now he wanted her to meet his best friend, to get to know him. Did that mean something, or was she reading too much into it?

She'd asked him the other night what Dante was like, and Alec had told her he was great, smart, funny. That she'd like him, that he would love her. And when she'd asked him why he assumed that, he'd answered with "What man wouldn't?"

Her chest knotted.

What man wouldn't.

Maybe Alec?

Don't be silly. That's not what you want.

What did she want? She wasn't certain anymore.

She sighed as she got out of the car and went inside, heading for the bar. She ordered a vodka tonic, needing the burn of the vodka tonight, trying not to think while she waited for the two men to arrive.

She hadn't been there more than twenty minutes when they walked in, both dressed in dark slacks and shirts, Alec all broad, hulking shoulders, Dante all long legs, his dark hair short and spiky.

She saw as they moved closer that he was nearly as great-looking as Alec, with a dazzling white smile, dimples flashing in both cheeks.

Alec leaned in and kissed her cheek, warming her. "Hey. I forgot to tell you how gorgeous you look," he whispered into her hair.

"I'm sorry we got off to such a bad start," Dante told her, taking her hand. "I'm usually a lot smoother." He smiled at her, and she couldn't help but be a bit charmed by him.

"It's fine, really."

"Our table should be ready soon. Can I get you another drink?"

"All charming manners, Dante?" Alec asked, a teasing note in his voice.

"As always, Alec."

"This one is mine, my friend."

"Ah, don't think I'm not fully aware of that."

His?

She looked at Alec, but he was grinning at Dante, apparently unaware of what he'd just said about her. What did he mean? Or was it only a turn of speech, some ribbing between friends that didn't mean anything?

"I think I would like another drink, thanks," she said.

"A glass of wine?" Alec asked.

"Another vodka tonic, please."

Alec raised a brow at her, but ordered the drink, and one for himself. She knew he was aware that she didn't often drink hard alcohol. Let him think she was simply nervous about meeting Dante.

Alec slid onto a stool beside her, keeping a hand at the small of her back. She loved the heat of his hand on her, but she was jumpy. She was trying hard to ignore the white sling on his left arm, the reason he wore it. The urge to think was nearly overwhelming.

"So," Dante said to her as he sat down on her other side, "Alec tells me you write erotica?"

"Yes."

"And you two met so you can research our . . . extreme practices."

"Yes, that's right." The bartender delivered her drink and she took a long sip, swallowing hard against the burn in her throat, Alec's presence and the vodka doing their work, relaxing her. "I thought most of the people involved in BDSM called it a lifestyle?"

Dante shrugged. "I don't see it as a lifestyle. It doesn't define my life. Just my sexual—and sensual—practices. And I practice as often as possible."

He grinned. He was charming. Warm. She did like him, as Alec had said she would.

"You're an attorney Alec tells me?"

"Yes, a divorce attorney. I've been working at a large firm for a few years, but I just got news that I landed a job at a smaller firm here in town, a job I've been after for months, so I'm pretty happy about it."

"Congratulations on the job."

"Thanks."

"But divorce law—that must be intense."

"It is. I like intense."

He grinned again, his golden-brown eyes glittering.

"You enjoying these little innuendos, Dante?" Alec asked from behind her.

Was that a hint of real jealousy in his voice, or was he simply teasing his friend?

"I enjoy everything, Alec. But you already know that about me. Ah, looks like the hostess has our table. Shall we?"

Dante offered his arm to Dylan and she thought it would seem rude to refuse. She smiled a little when she caught Alec's faint glare.

They were given a booth: Dante sat on one side, she and Alec sat on the other. She studied the menu, but knew Alec would order for her. A small part of her wanted to argue the point, but she'd gotten over most of that weeks ago. Instead, she sat back and placed her menu on the table.

Dante glanced at her, then at Alec. He didn't say anything. But she could feel him assessing the situation. As a dom, she realized he was trained to observe people in the same way Alec was. That it came almost automatically for them. And somehow, she didn't mind it, even though some section of her psyche was still convinced she should.

The waiter arrived and the men gave their orders, Alec ordering for her, as expected. It made her a little warm all over, something she hated to admit, even to herself. But it was happening, all the same.

"Tell me how you two met," she said, looking from Alec to Dante. She couldn't help but notice what a gorgeous pair they made. The two of them must turn every woman's head everywhere they went, especially together.

"We met at the Pleasure Dome. It's been, what, three years?" Dante asked Alec.

"About that, yes."

"We found out pretty quickly that we have a lot in common," Dante said, "aside from the things that happen at the club. We both love to travel, although Alec has been a lot more places than I have. Between law school and starting my career, I haven't had much free time. But it was the motorcycles that really connected us. Except his taste in bikes is atrocious."

"Ducatis are classics. Mechanical perfection," Alec said.

"I keep telling you, nothing drives like a BMW," Dante insisted. "They're the best cruising bikes in the world. You can't beat German engineering."

"I can tell you two have had this argument before," Dylan said, pretending the mere mention of the motorcycles wasn't making her chest pull into a tight knot, the fear kicking her like a punch to the stomach.

Alec laughed. "Maybe a time or two."

He turned to her and smiled, his hand squeezing her thigh. And despite the dizzying mix of emotions she was feeling, a small thrill went through her. It happened every time he touched her. And even though Dante was amazing-looking, and every bit as smart and charming as Alec said he would be, he didn't have the slightest effect on her. Not even a spark. It was as though she saw other men from a distance now, always comparing them to Alec. And they always came up short.

She'd always had a healthy libido and a great appreciation for a good-looking man. Why was it that suddenly she only had eyes for this one?

She glanced back at Alec, and his gaze was on her, that brilliant blue, looking right through her, inside her, making her pulse hot and thready.

Oh, you are in trouble.

Dinner came, and she ate her way through miso soup, the sharp curry flavor of Singapore street noodles, gorgeously prepared sushi, trying to ignore the thoughts cycling through her brain at a thousand miles an hour.

Why was it she was more aware than ever before of Alec's effect on her? Maybe because her response to him was in such sharp contrast to her lack of response to the handsome Dante. Or maybe her body was still buzzing from the sex on her dining room table this morning. Or maybe it was the attraction and connection mixed with the worry of his accident. But what really made her head spin, if she let herself linger on the thought, was the fact that she so clearly had eyes only for Alec.

Lust had never made her look to one man, and one man only. Nothing ever had. But the fact was, she didn't want anyone else. She only wanted Alec.

She wanted to be *his.*

God . . .

She set her chopsticks down, the food suddenly like lead in her stomach. They had switched from their cocktails to some good, cold sake during the meal, and she picked up her cup and drank. What she really needed was more vodka. Or maybe she shouldn't be drinking at all. It would only dull her senses. She'd spent enough time being dulled, not thinking. Things were getting scary now as a result. She'd allowed too much to happen. Had let things go too far.

She turned to watch Alec as he talked to his friend, his hand gestures animated as they argued something about basketball. He paused and looked at her, his smile disarming, sincere, beautiful. And reflecting . . . what? Pride?

She was feeling shaky. Too shaky. She had to calm down.

"Will you two excuse me for a minute?"

"Of course," Alec stood, his hand on her waist as she got to her feet.

She moved as quickly as she could toward the ladies' room. There was an attendant standing by the sink, nodding and smiling. Dylan rushed into a stall, slamming the door behind her.

She pushed her hair from her face with shaking hands, then, her legs weak, braced herself with one palm flat on the door.

She had to calm down. This didn't have to mean anything.

Except that it did.

It was too late. Too damn late.

How could she have let this happen?

She pulled her cell phone from her purse and dialed Mischa's number.

"Hi, this is Mischa. Leave me a message and I'll call you back as soon as I can. If you'd like to make a tattoo appointment, please call my shop, Thirteen Roses. Thanks!"

"Mischa, it's me, Dylan. I really need to talk to you. I'm sort of losing my mind. I'm calling you from a bathroom stall, for God's sake. I'm standing here like some lunatic, wringing my hands. Or I was, until I had to use one to hold the damn phone.

"The thing is, Mischa, I've fallen for Alec. More than fallen.

I'm . . . falling in love with him. Oh, God. Did I just say that? I can't believe I said that. I can't believe this is happening to me. *Me*, of all people! I can't love him. I don't know how to do this. I need your help. I need to calm down. I need to—"

Click.

"Your message has been completed. If you would like to erase it and record it again, please press one."

"Damn it."

She hit the OFF button, not knowing if the message would even go through. Why had she babbled on so long?

She was going to have to pull it together, to go back out there and pretend like nothing had changed.

But everything had changed, in that one brief moment when she'd realized the truth.

She was in love with Alec Walker.

Even letting the words roll through her mind was frightening. Overwhelming. Impossible.

But it was true.

Her fingers tightened around her cell phone, her knuckles going white.

Goddamn her traitorous heart. She was in love with him. And there wasn't a damn thing she could do about it.

fifteen

She'd taken several minutes to breathe, to reapply her lip gloss, to wash her hands, letting the cool water run over her wrists. Her cheeks were still flushed when she'd left the ladies' room, but she didn't want to leave the men waiting for too long. She didn't want anyone asking questions. Luckily, they were deep in conversation when she returned to the table.

Alec stood to let her into the booth, barely looking at her, although he slid an arm over her shoulders once they were both seated. He leaned forward, talking to Dante.

"I've found some great places for us to stay once we're there. A real mix. There's this amazing place a friend told me about, right on the beach. Just grass shacks on the sand, really primitive, but I figured you wouldn't mind."

"No, of course not. You know me. I can sleep on a bed of nails if I have to."

"The food there is supposed to be incredible, and it's got one of the best beaches. And on the way down I though we'd stop in San Francisco the first day, then maybe Santa Barbara."

"I like Santa Barbara," Dante said, sipping his sake. "There's this small gallery there that has a collection of antique erotic carvings in ivory and bone from Japan. Wait until you see them. You'll go crazy over this stuff. Where do you want to stop in San Francisco?"

"You two are going to San Francisco?" Dylan asked, pushing her food around with her chopsticks, trying to act normal. Trying to keep her head from spinning. Trying not to surge into Alec's big body beside her, just give up all the fight and melt into him.

"Nope. We're heading to Baja in a few weeks. San Francisco will just be an overnight stop."

"Baja? Mexico?"

"Yeah," Dante answered. "A motorcycle trip. We've been planning it forever. I finally got some time off work, cleared my court calendar. Have you ever been there?"

"I . . . no." Her stomach twisted into a knot, the knot pulling tighter and tighter.

Alec. On his motorcycle. Riding halfway across the country. Or at least, down to the southern tip and into Mexico. How many days on the road, on the motorcycle? How many chances for him to go down on his bike again? Challenging the odds. He'd come out of it okay this time. But next time . . .

Images of Quinn, his twisted body. Her baby brother. She'd been the one to go to the hospital. Her mother couldn't have handled it. And she'd had to identify his body. His poor, beautiful body, damaged beyond repair. She would never get that sight out of her head. Out of her heart.

Her heart had been damaged beyond repair, as well.

Not again.

How could he do this? Not now. Not when she loved him. It was too damn dangerous. She could lose him.

You were going to, anyway. You weren't really going to stay with him. Not now that you love him. Because you can't love anyone.

She put a hand to her suddenly aching head.

"Dylan?" There was concern in Alec's voice. She couldn't even look at him. "Are you okay? Is the food not agreeing with you?"

"I'm . . . no, I'm fine. Fine."

"You don't look fine. You look like you've just seen a ghost."

That's because I have.

She waved his hand away when he tried to get her to drink some water.

"Why don't I take you home? Dante, we'll catch up next week and finalize our plans."

"Yes, that's fine. Dylan, I'm sorry you're not feeling well. It's been a pleasure. We'll meet again, I'm sure."

"Yes. I'm sorry."

She shook her head. She didn't know what to say.

She followed Alec mutely as he guided her through the restaurant, got her coat, slid it over her shoulders. She didn't say a word as they crossed the street, as he handed her into the passenger seat of her car. He was as gentlemanly as ever, concerned, which made her heart ache even more.

The rain started as they pulled into the street. It beat in a soft staccato against the windows.

"Are you going to be okay?" he asked her.

She nodded. "Yes. Sure."

She could not look at him. She couldn't stand that surge of emotion whenever she saw him. She didn't want to breathe so that she wouldn't draw in his scent. But she had to breathe, of course. The car was inundated with that scent of forest and ocean. Clean and masculine and earthy and Alec.

Oh, God.

She really did not want to lose it until she was home alone. She couldn't do this in front of him. Because if she did, she'd have to admit to him why.

Impossible.

She bit her lip, clenched her fingers until the nails bit into her palms, hard and hurting enough to distract her.

She kept her gaze straight ahead, letting her vision blur, until the rain and the lights from the streets all blended together in some watercolor smear. Alec reached over and tried to take her hand, but she avoided him, pretending she needed to pull a tissue from her purse, cleared her throat.

Surprisingly, he didn't try to talk to her anymore, didn't ask her any more questions. Finally, he pulled up a few buildings down from her place and parked. She started to open the door, but he grabbed her arm.

"Okay, Dylan. You're going to tell me what's going on now." His voice was firm, demanding. He obviously knew something was wrong, that she wasn't really sick.

"Alec—"

"No, Dylan. Tell me."

"I can't."

"Can you at least look at me?"

She shook her head, staring straight ahead. "No."

"Is this going to be another scene like the one where you refused to tell me about your mother?"

"This isn't going to be a scene at all. And please don't mention my mother right now. That's not fair."

"Why not? I won't know why unless you tell me, Dylan. What the hell is this about? Did I say something to offend you? Did Dante?"

She laughed, a short, sharp bark that hurt her throat on the way out. "No. You haven't offended me, Alec. Can I go now?"

"Hardly. Not unless I'm going up with you. And I have a feeling that's not happening."

"No, it's not," she said quietly. "I'll have to ask you to take a cab home. May I have my keys?"

"Fuck, Dylan." He handed them over, and she shivered at the heat of his fingers as he pressed the keys into her palm.

He was quiet a moment, but she could hear his breath through the patter of the rain on the roof of the car. She wanted to get out, to run, but she couldn't gather enough breath, enough strength, to move.

Maybe because you know this is it. The last time you'll see him.

A sob burst out: that suddenly, that unexpectedly. She didn't even have a moment to bite it back.

"Jesus, Dylan."

He yanked her into his arms—his good arm, anyway—but she fought him off, pushing him away as hard as she could.

"Stop it, Alec. Just stop it. This is not your job right now. This is no BDSM scene. You are not the dom."

"What? I didn't think I was at the moment. This is just *us*."

She looked at him then, saw the shock on his face. And an edge of pure fury.

"No it's not, Alec. There is no 'us.' I have to go. Please just let me go."

"And you're not going to tell me why?"

"Why? Because you are not a relationship type of guy, Alec. And I am not a relationship kind of girl. Which makes this all impossible from the start. But now . . . it's more impossible than ever. And I cannot do this."

Tears were pouring down her face. She didn't bother to wipe them away. It was too late for that. Too late for everything.

"Dylan, is that what this is about, the state of our relationship? Look, we need to talk about this."

"I'm done talking," she said, her voice low, her throat tight. Strangling her.

His eyes were blazing. He looked stunned. He looked very much the way she felt. Painful, to see him like that.

She turned away. And opened the door. He paused just long enough for her to jump out, her feet hitting the wet sidewalk with a thud.

She moved down the street toward her building as fast as she could in her high-heeled boots. The rain soaked her hair in seconds, dripped down the collar of her coat.

He wasn't coming after her; she would have heard him open the door of the car, would have heard his footsteps. And with his long legs, he would have caught up to her easily.

Come after me, damn it.
Don't come after me.
Damn it.

It had been three or four days. She'd lost track, somehow. She'd been sleeping, mostly, waking to make a cup of tea, a piece of toast, then back to bed, retreating under the covers, under the extra quilts piled on. She couldn't seem to get warm, though, no matter what she did.

She hadn't read a book, watched television, spoken with anyone on the phone. And she certainly hadn't worked, hadn't written a word. She couldn't bear to be in her own head, but she couldn't bear to be out of it, either. And talking to anyone about this, even Mischa . . . impossible to say the words out loud.

She sat in her bed, curled beneath the white comforter, her pillows piled around her like a gentle fortress. There was a cup of tea on the nightstand, a box of tissues. A small pile of them crumpled and scattered on the floor like snowflakes.

She'd opened the curtains that first night, and hadn't bothered to close them. She'd been watching the sky, as it went from the deep black of midnight to the iridescent fog of morning to the paler gray of midday. But always, the sky was shades of dark, just as she felt on the inside. Dark and partially numb, when she wasn't sleeping or crying like a baby.

The worst times were those moments when the sobs came spewing out of her, wrenching her, hurting her throat, until she had to wrap her arms around her body, physically holding herself together. She never let that go on for too long. She was too shamed by it. Disgusted by her own weakness. It was too . . . obvious. Too literal. Too ugly. But it kept happening, again and again, as though it was never enough. She couldn't seem to empty herself of grief.

She thought of him constantly. His strong hands, his beautiful, masculine face. His impossibly broad shoulders. The contrast of his roughness and his gentleness with her. His laughter, always tinged with a wicked edge. His scent.

She swore she could still smell him all over her apartment. On her skin. Like something that had become so deeply ingrained in her bed, her walls, her body, it would never go away. Maybe she believed that was true.

Perhaps she really was losing her mind.

She almost wished she would. Maybe then she wouldn't be wracked with pain every waking moment, her chest twisting with a hard, cold lump that seemed to never go away.

Sleep wasn't much better. She dreamed of him constantly. Erotic dreams of Alec touching her, kissing her, spanking her. Terrible dreams where they were arguing, or he was holding her down and yelling at her that she was a fool and he was leaving her. Or the most horrible, the dreams where some faceless person came to her to tell her he was dead, where she saw his pale, still body, just as she'd seen her brother's.

She didn't know which was worse: waking up wanting him, or crying because he was gone. Either way, she felt absolutely adrift. Lost. Abandoned, even though she'd been the one to walk away.

It would have happened sooner or later. He would have left her somehow. And she could not take it. Better to get it over with.

To grieve for him and be done with it, because the longer she was with him, the more she loved him, and the more this would hurt.

She'd picked up the phone a dozen times to call him, and put it right down again. What was there to say? Neither of them was any different just because she loved him. No, that was a lie. *She* was different. She was a mess. Out of control. Weepy. Immobilized in a way she hadn't been since she'd lost Quinn. And even then she'd functioned in at least some minimal way because she'd had to, for her mother's sake. Someone had had to keep it together.

Not this time. This time there was no one to care but her.

She'd never felt so lonely in her life.

He hadn't called her. Not that she would have picked up the phone. But the fact remained, he hadn't tried to talk to her, to stop her, to see her. Which only deepened her conviction that she'd done the right thing, that she'd done what was necessary.

It didn't make her feel any better. Nothing did.

She picked up her tea and sipped, but it had grown too cool. She set the cup down. She was too lethargic to get up and brew more.

They drank tea the first time they'd met, at the café at the Asian Art Museum. It was amazing, how much he'd revealed about himself in that first interview. How unself-conscious he'd been. He always was, on a mental or psychological level. The only thing he'd ever refused to discuss with her was emotion.

Not that she was great at that herself. Emotions were something she normally avoided like the plague. A character defect, she knew. But it had kept her safe. Until now.

Her eyes pooled once more, and she sniffled, wiped her face

with a clean tissue. Her eyes, her nose, were raw. And she was an idiot to have let this happen.

She lay back on the pillows, let her body sink in, remembered how fluffy and white the down pillows at Alec's house were. How safe, how cocooned, she felt there. With him.

The tears spilled over, ran down her cheeks, and she let them fall while she watched the afternoon sky darken, watched the rain start. Watched as the drops built on the windows, slid down the glass in long liquid rivulets. Let her sobs blend with the sound of the rain hitting the glass, a hard, rhythmic pelting. Nearly painful to hear: the rain, the sounds she was making.

The rain fell harder, turning into a heavy downpour, and she cried harder, in deep, hurting surges.

She felt hopeless. Helpless. Empty. And she felt at that moment she might never recover. Never feel any better. She felt doomed to the very grief she'd been avoiding her entire life. And that she had now caused herself.

Alec paced his office, back and forth, full of impatience, fury, like a caged animal. His computer was on, the cursor waiting in his open document like some blinking, nagging voice. But he couldn't sit down, couldn't write. He felt like he was going to crawl out of his skin.

He hadn't written since Dylan had left him sitting in her car on Sunday night. It was Thursday evening now, but he'd done no work at all, despite a pressing deadline.

He'd gone for long rides on his bike, worked out like crazy at the gym. He'd driven out to Granite Mountain and done eight miles of strenuous hiking, but he still couldn't seem to get his head on straight. Tomorrow he'd drive up to Camp Muir on Mount Rainier; he'd heard that was a rough nine miles or more. A hike like that should wear him to the bone, exhaust him. Maybe that's what he needed . . .

What he needed was Dylan.

God damn it.

He sat down in his chair, stared at the screen, pulled up his e-mail, found her address. He started to type. But what would he say? That he missed her? He did. He missed her so badly it was like a wound in his chest that never closed, never stopped aching. That he wanted to see her? Not likely. She'd made that very clear. And he didn't do non-consensual. If she didn't want him there, he wasn't going to force himself on her.

Chicken.

He sighed, ran a hand over his goatee.

He was a goddamn chicken. The non-consensual crap was just that: crap. It was a great excuse for not allowing himself to get in over his head.

That was crap, too. He was already in over his head. Way over. As in fucking drowning.

He loved the woman.

"Ah, Christ."

He stood up, paced some more.

Had he actually just admitted that to himself?

Did it count if he never told anyone?

But he wanted to tell someone. He wanted to tell *her.* If only he hadn't screwed this up already with his Mr. Non-relationship Guy line. He'd always thought he was simply being honest with the women he saw. He liked to get that out in the open right away. But it was nothing more than a self-protective device. It kept him at a distance from everyone. And now he'd finally found someone he actually wanted to get close to . . . But how would she be able to trust his feelings for her after the things he'd said to her?

He barely trusted his feelings for her, and he felt it like a knife in the chest: that cutting, that deep, that intense.

He loved her.

Dylan.

He pictured her face, her high, rounded cheekbones, that lush mouth, her huge gray eyes, as clear as if they were cut from pure quartz. That hair of hers, like flames around her face, wild and smelling so damn good he wanted to taste it, to touch those silken curls with his tongue. And a body that was smooth, lithe sin.

She responded like a natural submissive. But underneath it was raw fire, enough intelligence, with a touch of stubborn anger, to challenge him in a way he'd never been challenged before.

He didn't want to feel that ever again. Not with anyone else. It was only her.

Dylan.

He wanted to get on his bike and ride it off, this realization. This truth. He felt dazed by it. Stunned. But the rain was coming down too hard outside. And his bike wouldn't work this off, no matter how long the ride.

He loved her.

His heart hammered. With love. With a strange, biting fear. And he realized suddenly that he'd been afraid, and running, his whole life. That in order to love, he had to shift his ideas about love, the ideas he'd learned from the father he'd worshipped. Maybe too much, he realized now. He had to take his father off the pedestal he'd had him on since he was a kid. A pedestal that had grown even higher after Dad had died, until it was some sort of towering, unrealistic monument.

After his parents divorced, his father had lived alone for the remainder of his life. He was absorbed in his work to the exclusion of everything else, other than his time with Alec. And Alec realized now it was this behavior that had most likely been the cause of the breakup of his parents' marriage.

He'd been a good father. He'd taken Alec on some of his first travels, on amateur archeological digs in Mexico, a junior science outing to study the volcanoes in Hawaii. But other than Alec, the man had never really loved anyone. Had loved nothing but pure science. He'd told Alec often enough that all he needed was his son and his science, that nothing else mattered to him. It had taken Alec thirty-six years to realize there was something wrong in that.

Just because his father had lived without love didn't mean it was ideal, or even desirable. He had to admit, for the first time, that maybe his father, brilliant as he was, didn't know everything.

That idea was like a kick to the gut. Hard and painful. But it was the truth, finally.

His father hadn't known that love was important, too. And Alec, for all his spiritual quests, had never gotten past questioning the randomness of the universe his father had preached to him. Alec's travels, his quests to Nepal, Thailand, all over Europe, had ultimately taught him nothing. Not what was really important. He'd been full of false pride, thinking he'd done all of these amazing, eye-opening things. His trips to Tibet, to India, to Israel, to the spiritual centers of the world. He'd sought out those incandescent, intense experiences: backpacking the Himalayas or reef diving with sharks, facing death in some weird sort of urge to prove that the random universe would not take him, too, as it had his father. But he'd never gotten to the real root of any sort of self-awareness. He realized now with sudden, aching clarity that the real root was love.

He loved Dylan Ivory.

He had to tell her.

His head was still spinning with epiphanies when he grabbed his keys and ran out into the rain.

Dylan's cell phone rang. She looked at it, watched it light up. With one breath-catching beat of her heart she wanted—*wanted*—it to be him.

But it was Mischa's name on the caller ID. Suddenly, she couldn't remember why she'd avoided calling Mischa. She realized she had to talk to her best friend. *Had* to.

She punched the button with her thumb, picking up the call. "Mischa, thank God it's you. I didn't know I needed to . . . needed you, until you called just now. I mean, I left that ridiculous message the other night . . . "

"Message? I haven't gotten any messages from you, Dylan. I haven't heard from you in days. Are you okay? What's up? You sound awful."

Dylan swallowed a sob. "I am awful."

"Tell me what's happened."

"I left him. Not that there was really anything to leave. We never talked about it. We never called it anything. But I . . . I got out of the car the other night and just . . . left."

"You're not seeing Alec anymore? Is that what you're saying?"

A sharp pang, hearing his name. "Yes. No, I'm not seeing him anymore. Never again."

Her friend paused on the other end of the line. "Are you sure, honey? Because you don't sound convinced."

"I'm sure. It's for the best . . . " The tears were coursing down her cheeks, choking her so hard she could barely talk. "It is."

"I'm sorry, Dylan."

She blew her nose, wiped her eyes, but the tears came as quickly as she could wipe them away. "I'm sorry I'm such a mess. I can't believe I'm doing this. Crying like a little girl."

"It's normal after a breakup. Not to suggest you weren't normal before."

"Oh, I wasn't. I know that. But this is just so different for me. This is not *me*."

"Maybe it is now. And that's not a bad thing. It's okay to feel, honey. You can't keep everything locked down tight inside your entire life."

"That's worked really well until now."

Mischa paused, then asked quietly, "Has it? Has it really?"

Dylan sniffed. "Maybe. I don't know. God, maybe not. Because until I met you a couple of years ago, I haven't even had any real friends. Not even as a kid. I was too busy taking care of my mother and my brother. And too embarrassed by Darcy. My situation. Then I met you and . . . how sad is it that I had to wait so long to even have a friend? And now, I still only have you. And that's never been an issue until right now. I've never realized that I needed . . . anyone."

"You have other writer friends. You met C.J. and Jade at the same conference where you met me."

"I'm not as close with them."

"I think they'd like to be, if you'd let them in. I *know* they would. And, Dylan, the fact that you have people in your life now *is* different, just as you said. The fact that you want that. It shows change. Growth. Don't linger on the past. Focus on what's happening right now. On who you've become."

"I don't know who I am, anymore. I am not this weak person . . . "

"Why do you think you're weak?"

"Because . . . because I let myself love him."

The tears turned into harsh sobs, and it was a few moments before she could swallow them down.

Mischa said gently, "Dylan, I don't know how you've gotten this far in your writing career, writing about relationships as much as you do sex, and still believe that loving someone is a sign of weakness. It's just something we do. Part of the human condition. Love is not something you have any control over. You should know that by now."

"I do. Which is why this is so awful for me."

"Welcome to the human race, honey," Mischa said, but there was no sarcasm in her voice, only concern.

"God, I'm so pathetic."

"You're not. You're just in love."

Dylan shook her head. It was entirely different hearing some-one else say it. It made it more true.

"I'm also . . . drowning in fear. Mischa, he had an accident on his bike. Not a big one, but he went to the emergency room and that just threw me. I mean it really messed with my head. And that same night he tells me he's going on some long motorcycle trip down to Baja . . . I can't deal with it. I cannot deal with being so damn afraid."

"God, honey, I'm sorry. That must have been awful for you."

"It was beyond awful. Mischa, what am I going to do now?"

"You're certain you two can't work this out?"

"Yes. I'm certain. If he wanted to, he would have been in touch, but he hasn't been. And I didn't expect him to be."

"Men are stubborn sometimes. All that male ego."

"But . . . if he felt the same way I do, wouldn't he put that aside and . . . God, that's so stupid. I'm so stupid. I love him, and still I walked away. Without really giving him a chance. Because I'm too scared."

"Fear can be a very powerful thing. But you don't have to let it control you, Dylan."

She nodded, sniffling. "And it has. It has my entire life. The need for control, it's all about fear. If I don't take care of every-thing, who will?"

"Maybe you need to give him the opportunity to do that. And because of that male ego thing I mentioned, maybe you need to be the one to take that first step, to tell him how you feel. If you love him, it's worth the risk, isn't it?"

She had to take several moments to absorb what Mischa was saying. But she felt the truth of it down deep.

"You're right. I've been so stubborn. Hanging on to these old ideas just because they're familiar. Unwilling to grasp the way my life has changed. How I've changed. How he's changed me." She ran a hand through her hair, her fingers tangling in the curls. "I need to talk to him. I need to show him. I need to take the chance that he'll totally shoot me down. That he'll walk away. And he might, especially after the way I walked away from him the other night. But I have to do it. It's better than sitting here feeling sorry for myself. I've done enough of that in the last few days to last the rest of my life. And it's time for me to stop letting the fear control everything."

"Good for you, Dylan. You can do it. And I'm here, no matter what happens. If you need me to get on a plane and come up there, I will. Whether it's to celebrate or to help you get over him. Either way. You just let me know."

"Thank you, Mischa. You're a very wise woman."

"Probably not. But I'm a romance author. I'm supposed to know about love. And so are you. It's about time you experienced it for yourself. You deserve it, you know."

"I'm going to get up and pull myself together and go see him. I know what I have to do."

"Good. Call me and tell me how it goes. And, Dylan? You'll be fine either way."

"Maybe. I honestly don't feel like I can be fine without Alec. But I have to try, to see what happens. Thank you, Mischa."

They hung up, and Dylan jumped up and went into the bathroom, turned on the shower, blasting the hot water. She got in and out as quickly as she could.

She looked at her reflection in the mirror while she dried

herself with one of her fluffy white towels. She looked pale, and there were dark circles beneath her eyes. They were rimmed in red from crying. She looked awful. But there wasn't time to do much about that. She was afraid if she waited too long, even long enough to put on some makeup, she'd lose her nerve. And if Alec still wanted her, he'd have to take her as she was.

There was some fight in her again. But she was done resisting the inevitable. The fight was being channeled into making something happen, rather than stubbornly running away. And it felt good. She felt stronger than she had in a long time. Maybe ever.

She combed her hair out, leaving it to air dry, and went into the bedroom to dress in a pair of jeans, boots and a soft black cashmere sweater, throwing a scarf around her neck against the cold and the damp.

She grabbed her wool coat, her wallet and her keys. Her pulse was racing. With nervous anticipation. With fear. With the absolute driving need to tell Alec she loved him.

He would love her, or not. And there wasn't a damn thing she could do about it.

She still had to do this.

She took the big warehouse elevator down and it seemed to take forever, the gears grinding, the squeaking of old metal on metal. She could smell the damp sidewalks already, the musty scents of old concrete and old wood from the building itself. The scents of years gone past, history.

She'd let too much of her life go past without really appreciating everything. She went speeding through life, ignoring history, people, *life*.

Not anymore. Her life started now. Good or bad.

The elevator reached the ground floor and she waited with her heart hammering in her throat for the doors to open. They did, finally, and she moved to the large door leading to the street, swung it open and stepped outside. Into whatever life had in store for her. She wasn't running away anymore. No, she was walking straight into it.

sixteen

The rain was coming down so hard she could barely see when she got to Alec's house. She'd left her umbrella at home. It didn't matter. She was exactly where she needed to be. She grabbed the motorcycle helmet she'd stopped to buy on the way over, tucked it under her arm and, ducking her head, made a dash onto the sidewalk—and hit something with a hard thump. She stumbled, nearly fell. Then a hand on her arm, a grip strong and sure, and Alec's voice.

"Dylan. Are you okay? What are you doing out here?"

"Alec? I was coming to find you. What are you doing out here?"

"Coming to see you. I have something important to tell you."

Even in the downpour she could see his serious, brilliant blue gaze, his dark brows drawn together. He was without an umbrella, too, his hair tipped in raindrops, his face dripping. A shiver went through her. Partly from his presence, his broad hands on her shoulders. Partly because she didn't know what it was he wanted to tell her, if it was good or bad.

"Alec, I have to tell you something, too."

"Dylan, let me say this."

His grip on her tightened, but there was no command in it, only urgency. Her breath stuttered in her lungs, her body tensing, waiting for it to come, whatever it was.

"Dylan." He gave her a small shake, and her gaze locked to his, her heart kicking up a notch. "Christ, don't look at me like that. Like you're going to cry. Fuck, I'm sorry."

She shook her head mutely. What could she say? She *was* going to cry again, damn it.

"Dylan . . . "

The sky rocked with a shuddering rumble of thunder. She felt it as though it had come from inside her own body. She began to shake.

"Alec, please just tell me." She closed her eyes, squeezing them tight.

"Dylan . . . I'm falling in love with you."

"What?"

Her eyes opened. She wasn't sure she'd heard him right over the pouring rain, the splashing tires from the traffic going by.

"I love you." He gave her another small shake. "Please say something."

His face looked tortured, his eyes shadowed, worried.

"I love you, too, Alec."

"You do?"

"I was coming here to tell you." The tears were coming, her

heart opening up, flooding with warmth and relief and a little panic that she still hadn't really heard him say it.

"Are you sure?"

"Of course I'm sure. I don't do anything unless I'm sure."

He pulled her to him, squeezing her so hard she could barely breathe. But she was breathless, anyway, trying to absorb what he'd just said to her. He *had* said it.

He loved her!

She buried her face in his leather jacket, breathed him in, that dark, clean scent, the earthy tang of old leather, along with the falling rain. She was getting soaked to the skin. She didn't care.

"Dylan? What the hell is this?" He pulled the motorcycle helmet from her hand.

"I was going to ask you to take me for a ride."

"What? Jesus. I need you to explain this to me. But let's get out of this rain."

He looped an arm around her waist and propelled her toward his house, onto the porch. She followed him numbly, her heart racing. He set the helmet down on a small wrought-iron table, then settled his hands on her shoulders, his blue gaze piercing her. "Okay. Tell me what this is about. You said you'd never get on my bike in a million years."

"Alec, the whole thing with you and your motorcycle, it scares the hell out of me. And when you had your accident, when you talked about going to Baja with Dante . . . I couldn't handle it. I couldn't handle loving you and risking losing you the same way I did my brother. That's why I ran from you. I've been afraid, on one level or another, since I met you. But I love you. I've had to face that. That I need to be with you, whether I'm afraid of you dying in an accident on your bike, or that I'm . . . that I can't love anyone. I was scared to death and trying to pretend I wasn't. Now I just need to work through the fear and be with you."

"You've tried, at least. Which is more than I can say for me."

"What do you mean?"

"I've spent my entire adult life on the run, telling myself I was searching rather than running. But then I met you. I found what I was really searching for. And I couldn't recognize it at first. Because I had deluded myself all those years into thinking the only option for me was not to get attached to anyone. Because anything we can't control is random. Love is random. And I'd spent my life fighting that universal rule. I'd spent my life trying to be my father. I thought that was ideal. I thought *he* was. But he was a loner. And probably lonely. By his own choosing. But I can choose differently. I had to love you before I understood that. I've been so damn stubborn, hanging on to those ideas even after I began to suspect they were wrong."

"I've been just as stubborn," she told him, swallowing her tears. "I've prided myself on being so independent. So brave, able to handle anything. But the one thing I couldn't handle was loving anyone. I ran away from you because I was afraid of losing you."

"I'm not going anywhere."

"But you are. You're going to ride your motorcycle to Baja with Dante. And after that, you'll ride somewhere else. And do your crazy backpacking trips, and diving, and God knows what else. And I could lose you. I could lose you in some horrible and tragic way."

The last words came out on a sob, and he hugged her close, kissing her wet hair.

"You won't lose me. You won't. I've done all those crazy things and I'm still here, aren't I?"

"So far."

He held her, and they were both quiet a few moments. The rain was coming down harder, but it didn't matter.

Finally, she said, "Alec, some part of me wants desperately for you to tell me you'll quit all of that, get rid of your bike, stop doing those wild trips. But I know that's not fair."

"I can't promise you that. I love you, but I can't do that. It would be a lie. I'd get restless. Resentful. One of the things I love about you is your fierce independence. I know if I travel somewhere without you, you won't sit home alone, wilting, like some women would. You're not helpless without a man."

"No. But I'll still be scared."

"I understand why. I get it. And, baby, I wish you'd never had to go through that kind of loss. But I have to be realistic with you. I have to be *real*." He kissed the top of her head again, his grip on her crushing. "So, what the hell do we do? Without either of us changing who we are?"

"Alec, I'm the one who has to learn to adapt here. I can't make you pay for me having lost my brother. I've already paid for far too long. I won't do that to you. That's why I bought the helmet."

"You don't have to prove yourself to me."

She shook her head. "I needed to. For myself, maybe, as much as for you."

"Not for me, Dylan. I love you just as you are." He paused,

held her hand to his lips, kissed it, making her heart surge. "But I need you to ask yourself if you can really be with me." He pushed away from her, held her at arms' length, looked into her eyes. "Tell me Dylan. Tell me the truth. I don't want you to live in fear."

"I don't want to, either. But you are the man I love. I love your fearlessness." She stopped to sniff, and he reached up, brushing at her tears with his thumb. "It's a big part of who you are. If I'm going to love you, I have to accept it all. I love who you are." The tears welled in her eyes once more. She wiped them away with a wet, impatient hand. "And Alec . . . "

"What is it?" he asked quietly.

"Why the hell haven't you kissed me yet?"

He smiled then, pulled her close and crushed his lips to hers.

It was a hard kiss, full of intensity, emotion. His arms had never felt so strong around her, so solid. His tongue was sweet as it slipped between her lips, opening her up. As he always did. And as always, she melted all over. With desire. With love blossoming in her chest, opening her up even more. And it felt good.

He pulled back, murmured against her mouth, "I love you, Dylan."

"I love you. But, Alec, I'm still going to be scared for a while. This love stuff will take some getting used to. And learning to trust that you won't be taken away from me . . . I may never get over that completely. I just don't know. But I'm willing to try. I love you too much not to."

"Good girl."

At his words a shiver of desire ran up her spine.

"Alec . . . "

He stroked her hair from her face. His was beautiful, the shadows gone from his blue eyes.

"Shh . . . let's not talk anymore right now. We're going to be together. We have time to figure things out. Let me take you upstairs and show you how I love you."

She nodded. He looped his arm around her waist and together they went inside. He kissed her all the way up the stairs, his kisses growing more heated until they had to stop at the landing so he could pick her up and carry her the rest of the way to his bedroom. She was panting, needy, her body aching for him when he kicked the door open.

He set her down, and with his mouth still on hers, they pulled off their wet coats, dropping them on the floor. His sweater came next, then hers, then their boots, their jeans, until they stood, naked, at the foot of his bed.

He never stopped kissing her. His hands were on her now, stroking, caressing, his fingertips, his palms, like little kisses everywhere they touched, warming her cold skin.

He was hard and gentle all at once: his mouth, his hands, his panting breath. And everything felt different to her. More tender. More urgent. It didn't make sense. But then, love didn't make sense, did it?

He slid slowly down her body to his knees, his lips brushing over her neck, her stomach, then lower. His breath was hot at the apex of her thighs. His hands were stroking the small of her back, her buttocks, the curve of her hips. She was trembling all over, desire moving through her in one warm surge after another. And when he bent and laid a soft kiss on her cleft, she sighed, the surge spiraling, her hands going into his wet hair.

"Ah, Alec . . . "

He kissed her again, just that brief press of his lips, and she was aching, soaking wet, pulsing.

He brought his hands around her body, still that gentle stroking that was making her crazy, used his thumbs to part the lips of her sex. And leaning in, he ran his tongue across the tip of her clitoris.

"Oh . . . "

He did it again, pleasure seeping through her like a warm flood: her sex, her breasts, her thighs.

He began in earnest, then, licking, licking, the gentlest of touches with his warm, wet tongue. And she slipped over that edge and into orgasm, her body shivering with pure pleasure.

She cried out, her legs shaking. But he held her up with his strong hands. And he didn't stop until the last quivering sigh had left her.

He stood, then, lifting her in his arms, and laid her on the bed. He stayed where he was for several moments, simply watching her. And what she saw in his face was breathtaking: desire and admiration and love shining through it all.

She reached for him and he came to her, covering her body with his. And even with his enormous strength, he was still gentle with her. Tender. There was no power play between them now, yet every touch, every whisper, every sensation, was purely sensual, the most erotic experience of her life.

She ran her hands down his back, loving the size of him, the hard muscles like steel curving beneath the smooth skin. And when she moved her hand between them to curl her fingers around his hardening cock, he pulled in a breath, sighed it out on her name.

"Ah, Dylan . . . what you do to me. I need to be inside you."

"Yes."

He reached over her and pulled a condom from the nightstand drawer, quickly sheathed himself.

"Alec, hurry. I need you. Need you . . . "

"Baby . . . "

Holding himself over her, he ran a hand over her cheek, down the side of her neck, across her collarbone, until finally, he cupped her breast in his warm palm. Desire ran through her in long, sweet shivers, her nipples going hard, her sex filling, swelling once more.

As she watched his face, he pushed into her. One long, lovely stroke, and he was buried deep. His eyes were blazing, that glittering blue, as he looked at her, looked *inside* her in a way no one else ever had.

She knew he could see her, saw all of her. And loved her, anyway. Some part of her still couldn't believe it. But he was there with her, in a way he never had been before. Maybe because she was allowing it, finally. Maybe because they had said the words to each other. The first time for them both. There was magic in that. And, practical girl that she was, even she could believe in that kind of magic.

He pressed deeper, making her moan, and her hands clutched at his broad shoulders.

"Alec, kiss me."

He smiled, that dazzling smile of his, and bent his head to

hers. She leaned up, taking his mouth, opening his lips with her tongue, slipping inside. It was all sweet heat and slippery tongues. Passion as hot as their bodies moving in rhythm. His hands went under her, around her waist, holding her close. Her hands went into his hair, still wet with rain. She breathed him in: rain and earth and that elemental thing that was uniquely him.

Alec.

Hers.

"Baby," he breathed, his voice filled with smoke. "I love you."

"I love you, Alec. So much."

He thrust, pleasure shimmering over her skin, through every nerve in her body.

"Tell me, Dylan. Tell me you're mine."

"Yes. I'm yours."

She was. They belonged to each other. And she would face down whatever she had to, her fears and his, not to lose him.

He had taught her to be brave, to be *truly* brave, not to simply put on a façade and run in the other direction. Love had taught her.

It was a lesson long overdue. But it didn't matter now.

He tightened his grip on her body, his tensing. And as he pumped into her, she held his face, watched him come, his features loose in ecstasy. Her own body trembled with dizzying pleasure, and when she came, he was still shivering, holding her close.

They stayed that way for a long time, their breathing in sync, bodies pressed together, flesh to flesh. Heart to heart.

And she knew, for the first time, that this was what was important. This was what she'd been missing. They'd both lived their lives on the edge, in different ways. They'd both been running so hard. But somehow they had ended up together, had crashed into each other, full of fear and fury. And despite that, had ended up with love.

"Dylan . . . " His voice was still rough with passion.

"What is it?"

"I can't stand that you're afraid, baby. How can I help? How can I make you not so scared?"

Her heart melted at his concern. No one had ever cared the way he did.

"I have to find my way. But I will. Just . . . love me, Alec. That's how I can do this. That's what will pull me through. Make me as brave as I've pretended to be all these years."

"You're braver than you think, Dylan. You're brave and beautiful and amazing."

How was it possible that this man thought these things about her? Was it possible it was because they were true?

The idea hit her like a soft blow. And for the first time, she was able to trust it, to know there was truth in what he said.

"I've learned so much from you, Alec."

His hand went into her hair, stroking, then to her cheek, and he held her cheek in his big palm. "You've taught me just as much. Maybe that's why we're here, together."

"Mischa said something like that to me once, when I was talking to her about you. I didn't believe it then."

"Do you now?"

"Yes. I can believe it because I love you. And maybe even more because you love me."

He kissed her, his lips a soft stroking against hers. When she pulled back to look at him, she saw everything he felt in his eyes. It was amazing. Beautiful. True.

Love was the key. Love was the strength she'd always been afraid she was lacking.

She didn't have to be afraid anymore. Love would keep her as safe as anyone could be in this world. Alec would keep her safe.

She breathed out on a long sigh, a breath she'd been holding her entire life.

Safe.

Loved.

Finally.